DE PROFUNDIS

THE BALLAD OF READING GAOL

and other writings

DE PROFUNDIS

THE BALLAD
OF READING GAOL

and other writings

Oscar Wilde

WORDSWORTH CLASSICS

First published, in 1999, by Wordsworth Editions Limited
Cumberland House, Crib Street, Ware, Hertfordshire SG12 9ET

ISBN 1 84022 401 0

Typeset by Antony Gray
Printed and bound in Great Britain by
Mackays of Chatham plc, Chatham, Kent

CONTENTS

DE PROFUNDIS

. . . Suffering is one very long moment. We cannot divide it by seasons. We can only record its moods and chronicle their return. With us time itself does not progress. It revolves. It seems to circle round one centre of pain. The paralysing immobility of a life every circumstance of which is regulated after an unchangeable pattern, so that we eat and drink and lie down and pray, or kneel at least for prayer, according to the inflexible laws of an iron formula: this immobile quality, that makes each dreadful day in the very minutest detail like its brother, seems to communicate itself to those external forces the very essence of whose existence is ceaseless change. Of seed-time or harvest, of the reapers bending over the corn or the grape gatherers threading through the vines, of the grass in the orchard made white with broken blossoms or strewn with fallen fruit: of these we know nothing and can know nothing.

For us there is only one season, the season of sorrow. The very sun and moon seem taken from us. Outside, the day may be blue and gold, but the light that creeps down through the thickly muffled glass of the small iron-barred window beneath which one sits is grey and niggard. It is always twilight in one's cell, as it is always twilight in one's heart. And in the sphere of thought, no less than in the sphere of time, motion is no more. The thing that you personally have long ago forgotten, or can easily forget, is happening to me now, and will happen to me again tomorrow. Remember this, and you will be able to understand a little of why I am writing, and in this manner writing . . .

A week later, I am transferred here. Three more months go over and my mother dies. No one knew how deeply I loved and honoured her. Her death was terrible to me; but I, once a lord of language, have no words in which to express my anguish and my shame. She and my father had bequeathed me a name they had made noble and honoured, not merely in literature, art, archaeology and science, but in the public history of my own country, in its evolution as a nation. I had disgraced that name eternally. I had made it a low byword among low people. I had dragged it through the very mire. I had given it to brutes that they might make it brutal, and to fools that they might turn it into a synonym for folly. What I suffered then, and still suffer, is not for pen to write or paper to record. My wife, always kind and gentle to me, rather than that I should hear the news from indifferent lips, travelled, ill as she was, all the way from Genoa to England to break to me herself the tidings of so irreparable, so irremediable, a loss. Messages of sympathy reached me from all who had still affection for me. Even people who had not known me personally, hearing that a new sorrow had broken into my life, wrote to ask that some expression of their condolence should be conveyed to me . . .

Three months go over. The calendar of my daily conduct and labour that hangs on the outside of my cell door, with my name and sentence written upon it, tells me that it is May . . .

Prosperity, pleasure and success may be rough of grain and common in fibre, but sorrow is the most sensitive of all created things. There is nothing that stirs in the whole world of thought to which sorrow does not vibrate in terrible and exquisite pulsation. The thin beaten-out leaf of tremulous gold that chronicles the direction of forces the eye cannot see is in comparison coarse. It is a wound that bleeds when any hand but that of love touches it, and even then must bleed again, though not in pain.

Where there is sorrow there is holy ground. Someday people will realise what that means. They will know nothing of life till they do. — and natures like his can realise it. When I was brought down from my prison to the Court of Bankruptcy, between two policemen, — waited in the long dreary corridor that, before the whole crowd, whom an action so sweet and simple hushed into silence, he might gravely raise his hat to me as, handcuffed and with bowed head, I passed him by. Men have gone to heaven for smaller things than that. It was in this spirit, and with this mode of love, that the saints knelt down to wash the feet of the poor, or stooped to kiss the leper on the cheek. I have never said one single word to him about what he did. I do not know to the present moment whether he is aware that I was even conscious of his action. It is not a thing for which one can render formal thanks in formal words. I store it in the treasure-house of my heart. I keep it there as a secret debt that I am glad to think I can never possibly repay. It is embalmed and kept sweet by the myrrh and cassia of many tears. When wisdom has been profitless to me, philosophy barren, and the proverbs and phrases of those who have sought to give me consolation as dust and ashes in my mouth, the memory of that little, lovely, silent act of love has unsealed for me all the wells of pity: made the desert blossom like a rose, and brought me out of the bitterness of lonely exile into harmony with the wounded, broken and great heart of the world. When people are able to understand, not merely how beautiful —'s action was, but why it meant so much to me, and always will mean so much, then, perhaps, they will realise how and in what spirit they should approach me . . .

The poor are wise, more charitable, more kind, more sensitive than we are. In their eyes prison is a tragedy in a man's life, a misfortune, a casuality, something that calls for sympathy in others. They speak of one who is in prison as of one who is 'in trouble' simply. It is the phrase they always use, and the expression has the perfect wisdom of love in it. With people of our own rank it is different. With us, prison makes a man a pariah. I, and such as I am, have hardly any right to air and sun. Our presence taints the pleasures of others. We are unwelcome when we reappear. To revisit the glimpses of the moon is not for us. Our very children are taken away. Those lovely links with humanity are broken. We are doomed to be solitary, while our sons still live. We are denied the one thing that might heal us and keep us, that might bring balm to the bruised heart, and peace to the soul in pain.

I must say to myself that I ruined myself, and that nobody great or small can be ruined except by his own hand. I am quite ready to say so. I am trying to say so, though they may not think it at the present moment. This pitiless indictment I bring without pity against myself. Terrible as was what the world did to me, what I did to myself was far more terrible still.

I was a man who stood in symbolic relations to the art and culture of my age. I had realised this for myself at the very dawn of my manhood, and had forced my age to realise it afterwards. Few men hold such a position in their own lifetime, and have it so acknowledged. It is usually discerned, if discerned at all, by the historian, or the critic, long after both the man and his age have passed away. With me it was different. I felt it myself, and made others feel it. Byron was a symbolic figure, but his relations were to the passion of his age and its weariness of passion. Mine were to something more noble, more permanent, of more vital issue, of larger scope.

The gods had given me almost everything. But I let myself be lured into long spells of senseless and sensual ease. I amused myself with being a *flâneur*, a dandy, a man of fashion. I surrounded myself with the smaller natures and the meaner minds. I became the spendthrift of my own genius, and to waste an eternal youth gave me a curious joy. Tired of being on the heights, I deliberately went to the depths in the search for new sensation. What the paradox was to me in the sphere of thought, perversity became to me in the sphere of passion. Desire, at the end, was a malady, or a madness, or both. I grew careless of the lives of others. I took pleasure where it pleased me, and passed on. I forgot that every little action of the common day makes or unmakes character, and that therefore what one has done in the secret chamber one has some day to cry aloud on the housetop. I ceased to be lord over myself. I was no longer the captain of my soul, and did not know it. I allowed pleasure to dominate me. I ended in horrible disgrace. There is only one thing for me now, absolute humility.

I have lain in prison for nearly two years. Out of my nature has come wild despair; an abandonment to grief that was piteous even to look at; terrible and impotent rage; bitterness and scorn, anguish that wept aloud; misery that could find no voice; sorrow that was dumb. I have passed through every possible mood of suffering. Better than Wordsworth himself I know what Wordsworth meant when he said –

> Suffering is permanent, obscure, and dark,
> And has the nature of infinity.

But while there were times when I rejoiced in the idea that my sufferings were to be endless, I could not bear them to be without meaning. Now I find hidden somewhere away in my nature something that tells me that nothing in the whole world is meaningless, and suffering least of all. That something hidden away in my nature, like a treasure in a field, is Humility.

It is the last thing left in me, and the best: the ultimate discovery at which I have arrived, the starting-point for a fresh development. It has come to me right out of myself, so I know that it has come at the proper time. It could not have come before, nor later. Had anyone told me of it, I would have rejected it. Had it been brought to me, I would have refused it. As I found it, I want to keep it. I must do so. It is the one thing that has in it the elements of life, of a new life, a *Vita Nuova* for me. Of all things it is the strangest. One cannot acquire it, except by surrendering everything that one has. It is only when one has lost all things, that one knows that one possesses it.

Now I have realised that it is in me, I see quite clearly what I ought to do; in fact, must do. And when I use such a phrase as that, I need not say that I am not alluding to any external sanction or command. I admit none. I am far more of an individualist than I ever was. Nothing seems to me of the smallest value except what one gets out of oneself. My nature is seeking a fresh mode of self-realisation. That is all I am concerned with. And the first thing that I have got to do is to free myself from any possible bitterness of feeling against the world.

I am completely penniless, and absolutely homeless. Yet there are worse things in the world than that. I am quite candid when I say that rather than go out from this prison with bitterness in my heart against the world, I would gladly and readily beg my bread from door to door. If I got nothing from the house of the rich I would get something at the house of the poor. Those who have much are often greedy; those who have little always share. I would not a bit mind sleeping in the cool grass in summer, and when winter came, sheltering myself by the warm close-thatched rick, or under the penthouse of a great barn, provided I had love in my heart. The external things of life seem to me now of no importance at all. You can see to what intensity of individualism I have arrived – or am arriving rather, for the journey is long, and 'where I walk there are thorns'.

Of course I know that to ask alms on the highway is not to be my lot, and that if ever I lie in the cool grass at night-time it will be to write sonnets to the moon. When I go out of prison, R— will be waiting for me on the other side of the big iron-studded gate and he is the symbol, not merely of his own affection, but of the affection of many others besides. I believe I am to have enough to live on for about eighteen months at any rate, so that if I may not write beautiful books, I may at least read beautiful books; and what joy can be greater? After that, I hope to be able to recreate my creative faculty.

But were things different: had I not a friend left in the world; were there not a single house open to me in pity; had I to accept the wallet and ragged cloak of sheer penury: as long as I am free from all resentment, hardness and scorn, I would be able to face the life with much more calm and confidence than I would were my body in purple and fine linen, and the soul within me sick with hate.

And I really shall have no difficulty. When you really want love you will find it waiting for you.

I need not say that my task does not end there. It would be comparatively easy if it did. There is much more before me. I have hills far steeper to climb, valleys much darker to pass through. And I have to get it all out of myself. Neither religion, morality, nor reason can help me at all.

Morality does not help me. I am a born antinomian. I am one of those who are made for exceptions, not for laws. But while I see that there is nothing wrong in what one does, I see that there is something wrong in what one becomes. It is well to have learned that.

Religion does not help me. The faith that others give to what is unseen, I give to what one can touch, and look at. My gods dwell in temples made with hands; and within the circle of actual experience is my creed made perfect and complete: too complete, it may be, for like many or all of those who have placed their heaven in this earth, I have found in it not merely the beauty of heaven, but the horror of hell also. When I think about religion at all, I feel as if I would like to found an order for those who *cannot* believe: the Confraternity of the Faithless, one might call it, where on an altar, on which no taper burned, a priest, in whose heart peace had no dwelling, might celebrate with unblessed bread and a chalice empty of wine. Everything to be true must become a religion. And agnosticism should have its ritual no less than faith. It has sown its martyrs, it should reap its saints, and praise God daily for having hidden Himself from man. But whether it be faith or agnosticism, it must be nothing external to me. Its symbols must be of my own creating. Only that is spiritual which makes its own form. If I may not find its secret within myself, I shall never find it; if I have not got it already, it will never come to me.

Reason does not help me. It tells me that the laws under which I am convicted are wrong and unjust laws, and the system under which I have suffered a wrong and unjust system. But, somehow, I have got to make both of these things just and right to me. And exactly as in art one is only concerned with what a particular thing is at a particular moment to oneself, so it is also in the ethical evolution of one's character. I have got to make everything that has happened to me good for me. The plank bed, the loathsome food, the hard ropes shredded into oakum till one's finger-tips grow dull with pain, the menial offices with which each day begins and finishes, the harsh orders the routine seems to necessitate, the dreadful dress that makes sorrow grotesque to look at, the silence, the solitude, the shame – each and all of these things I have to transform into a spiritual experience. There is not a single degradation of the body which I must not try and make into a spiritualising of the soul.

I want to get to the point when I shall be able to say quite simply, and without affectation, that the two great turning-points in my life were when my father sent me to Oxford, and when society sent me to prison. I will not say that prison is the best thing that could have happened to me: for that phrase would savour of too great bitterness towards myself. I would sooner say, or hear it said of me, that I was so typical a child of my age, that in my perversity, and for that perversity's sake, I turned the good things of my life to evil, and the evil things of my life to good.

What is said, however, by myself or by others matters little. The important thing, the thing that lies before me, the thing that I have to do, if the brief remainder of my days is not to be maimed, marred and incomplete, is to absorb into my nature all that has been done to me, to make it part of me, to accept it without complaint, fear or reluctance. The supreme vice is shallowness. Whatever is realised is right.

When first I was put into prison some people advised me to try and forget who I was. It was ruinous advice. It is only by realising what I am that I have found comfort of any kind. Now I am advised by others to try on my release to forget that I have ever been in a prison at all. I know that would be equally fatal. It would mean that I would always be haunted by an intolerable sense of disgrace, and that those things that are meant for me as much as for anybody else – the beauty of the sun and moon, the pageant of the seasons, the music of daybreak and the silence of great nights, the rain falling through the leaves, or the dew creeping over the grass and making it silver – would all be tainted for me, and lose their healing power, and their power of communicating joy. To regret one's own experiences is to arrest one's own development. To deny one's own experiences is to put a lie into the lips of one's own life. It is no less than a denial of the soul.

For just as the body absorbs things of all kinds, things common and unclean no less than those that the priest or a vision has cleansed, and converts them into swiftness or strength, into the play of beautiful muscles and the moulding of fair flesh, into the curves and colours of the hair, the lips, the eye; so the soul in its turn has its nutritive functions also, and can transform into noble moods of thought and passions of high import what in itself is base, cruel and degrading; nay, more, may find in these its most august modes of assertion, and can often reveal itself most perfectly through what was intended to desecrate or destroy.

The fact of my having been the common prisoner of a common gaol I must frankly accept, and, curious as it may seem, one of the things I shall have to teach myself is not to be ashamed of it. I must accept it as a punishment, and if one is ashamed of having been punished, one might just as well never have been punished at all. Of course there are many things of which I was convicted that I had not done, but then there are many things of which I was convicted that I had done, and a still greater number of things in my life for which I was never indicted at all. And as the gods are strange, and punish us for what is good and humane in us as much as for what is evil and perverse, I must accept the fact that one is punished for the good as well as for the evil that one does. I have no doubt that it is quite right one should be. It helps one, or should help one, to realise both, and not to be too conceited about either. And if I then am not ashamed of my punishment, as I hope not to be, I shall be able to think, and walk, and live with freedom.

Many men on their release carry their prison about with them into the air, and hide it as a secret disgrace in their hearts, and at length, like poor poisoned things, creep into some hole and die. It is wretched that they should have to do so, and it is wrong, terribly wrong, of society that it should force them to do so. Society takes upon itself the right to inflict appalling punishment on the individual but it also has the supreme vice of shallowness, and fails to realise what it has done. When the man's punishment is over, it leaves him to himself; that is to say, it abandons him at the very moment when its highest duty towards him begins. It is really ashamed of its own actions, and shuns those whom it has punished, as people shun a creditor whose debt they cannot pay, or one on whom they have inflicted an irreparable, an irremediable wrong. I can claim on my side that if I realise what I have suffered, society should realise what it has inflicted on me; and that there should be no bitterness or hate on either side.

Of course I know that from one point of view things will be made different for me than for others; must indeed, by the very nature of the case, be made so. The poor thieves and outcasts who are imprisoned here with me are in many respects more fortunate than I am. The little way in grey city or green field that saw their sin is small; to find those who know nothing of what they have done they need go no further than a bird might fly between the twilight and the dawn; but for me the world is shrivelled to a hand's-breadth, and everywhere I turn my name is written on the rocks in lead. For I have come, not from obscurity into the momentary notoriety of crime, but from a sort of eternity of fame to a sort of eternity of infamy, and sometimes seem to myself to have shown, if indeed it required showing, that between the famous and the infamous there is but one step, if as much as one.

Still, in the very fact that people will recognise me wherever I go, and know all about my life, as far as its follies go, I can discern something good for me. It will force on me the necessity of again asserting myself as an artist, and as soon as I possibly can. If I can produce only one beautiful work of art I shall be able to rob malice of its venom, and cowardice of its sneer, and to pluck out the tongue of scorn by the roots.

And if life be, as it surely is, a problem to me, I am no less a problem to life. People must adopt some attitude towards me, and so pass judgement both on themselves and me. I need not say I am not talking of particular individuals. The only people I would care to be with now are artists and people who have suffered: those who know what beauty is and those who know what sorrow is; nobody else interests me. Nor am I making any demands on life. In all that I have said I am simply concerned with my own mental attitude towards life as a whole; and I feel that not to be ashamed of having been punished is one of the first points I must attain to, for the sake of my own perfection, and because I am so imperfect.

Then I must learn how to be happy. Once I knew it, or thought I knew it, by instinct. It was always springtime once in my heart. My temperament was akin to joy. I filled my life to the very brim with pleasure, as one might fill a cup to the very brim with wine. Now I am approaching life from a completely new standpoint, and even to conceive happiness is often extremely difficult for me. I remember during my first term at Oxford reading in Pater's *Renaissance* – that book which has had such strange influence over my life – how Dante places low in the Inferno those who wilfully live in sadness; and going to the college library and turning to the passage in the *Divine Comedy* where beneath the dreary marsh lie those who were 'sullen in the sweet air', saying for ever and ever through their sighs:

> 'Tristi fummo
> Nell aer dolce che dal sol s'allegra.'

I knew the church condemned *accidia*, but the whole idea seemed to me quite fantastic, just the sort of sin, I fancied, a priest who knew nothing about real life would invent. Nor could I understand how Dante, who says that 'sorrow remarries us to God', could have been so harsh to those who were enamoured of melancholy, if any such there really were. I had no idea that some day this would become to me one of the greatest temptations of my life.

While I was in Wandsworth prison I longed to die. It was my one desire. When after two months in the infirmary I was transferred here, and found myself growing gradually better in physical health, I was filled with rage. I determined to commit suicide on the very day on which I left prison. After a time that evil mood passed away, and I made up my mind to live, but to wear gloom as a king wears purple: never to smile again: to turn whatever house I entered into a house of mourning: to make my friends walk slowly in sadness with me: to teach them that melancholy is the true secret of life: to maim them with an alien sorrow: to mar them with my own pain. Now I feel quite differently. I see it would be both ungrateful and unkind of me to pull so long a face that when my friends came to see me they would have to make their faces still longer in order to show their sympathy; or, if I desired to entertain them, to invite them to sit down silently to bitter herbs and funeral baked meats. I must learn how to be cheerful and happy.

The last two occasions on which I was allowed to see my friends here, I tried to be as cheerful as possible, and to show my cheerfulness, in order to make them some slight return for their trouble in coming all the way from town to see me. It is only a slight return, I know, but it is the one, I feel certain, that pleases them most. I saw R— for an hour on Saturday week, and I tried to give the fullest possible expression of the delight I really felt at our meeting. And that, in the views and ideas I am here shaping for myself, I am quite right is shown to me by the fact that now for the first time since my imprisonment I have a real desire for life.

There is before me so much to do that I would regard it as a terrible tragedy if I died before I was allowed to complete at any rate a little of it. I see new developments in art and life, each one of which is a fresh mode of perfection. I long to live so that I can explore what is no less than a new world to me. Do you want to know what this new world is? I think you can guess what it is. It is the world in which I have been living. Sorrow, then, and all that it teaches one, is my new world.

I used to live entirely for pleasure. I shunned suffering and sorrow of every kind. I hated both. I resolved to ignore them as far as possible: to treat them, that is to say, as modes of imperfection. They were not part of my scheme of life. They had no place in my philosophy. My mother, who knew life as a whole, used often to quote to me Goethe's lines – written by Carlyle in a book he had given her years ago, and translated by him, I fancy, also:

> Who never ate his bread in sorrow,
> Who never spent the midnight hours
> Weeping and waiting for the morrow –
> He knows you not, ye heavenly powers.

They were the lines which that noble Queen of Prussia, whom Napoleon treated with such coarse brutality, used to quote in her humiliation and exile; they were the lines my mother often quoted in the troubles of her later life. I absolutely declined to accept or admit the enormous truth hidden in them. I could not understand it. I remember quite well how I used to tell her that I did not want to eat my bread in sorrow, or to pass any night weeping and watching for a more bitter dawn.

I had no idea that it was one of the special things that the Fates had in store for me: that for a whole year of my life, indeed, I was to do little else. But so had my portion been meted out to me; and during the last few months I have, after terrible difficulties and struggles, been able to comprehend some of the lessons hidden in the heart of pain. Clergymen and people who use phrases without wisdom sometimes talk of suffering as a mystery. It is really a revelation. One discerns things one never discerned before. One approaches the whole of history from a different standpoint. What one had felt dimly, through instinct, about art, is intellectually and emotionally realised with perfect clearness of vision and absolute intensity of apprehension.

I now see that sorrow, being the supreme emotion of which man is capable, is at once the type and test of all great art. What the artist is always looking for is the mode of existence in which soul and body are one and indivisible: in which the outward is expressive of the inward: in which form reveals. Of such modes of existence there are not a few: youth and the arts preoccupied with youth may serve as a model for us at one moment: at another we may like to think that, in its subtlety and sensitiveness of impression, its suggestion of a spirit dwelling in external things and making its raiment of earth and air, of mist and city alike, and in its morbid sympathy of its moods, and tones, and colours, modern landscape art is realising for us pictorially what was realised in such plastic perfection by the Greeks. Music, in which all subject is absorbed in expression and cannot be separated from it, is a complex example, and a flower or a child a simple example, of what I mean; but sorrow is the ultimate type both in life and art.

Behind joy and laughter there may be a temperament, coarse, hard and callous. But behind sorrow there is always sorrow. Pain, unlike pleasure, wears no mask. Truth in art is not any correspondence between the essential idea and the accidental existence; it is not the resemblance of shape to shadow, or of the form mirrored in the crystal to the form itself; it is no echo coming from a hollow hill, any more than it is a silver well of water in the valley that shows the moon to the moon and Narcissus to Narcissus. Truth in art is the unity of a thing with itself: the outward rendered expressive of the inward: the soul made incarnate: the body instinct with spirit. For this reason there is no truth comparable to sorrow. There are times when sorrow seems to me to be the only truth. Other things may be illusions of the eye or the appetite, made to blind the one and cloy the other, but out of sorrow have the worlds been built and at the birth of a child or a star there is pain.

More than this, there is about sorrow an intense, an extraordinary reality. I have said of myself that I was one who stood in symbolic relations to the art and culture of my age. There is not a single wretched man in this wretched place along with me who does not stand in symbolic relation to the very secret of life. For the secret of life is suffering. It is what is hidden behind everything. When we begin to live, what is sweet is so sweet to us, and what is bitter so bitter, that we inevitably direct all our desires towards pleasures, and seek not merely for a 'month or twain to feed on honeycomb', but for all our years to taste no other food, ignorant all the while that we may really be starving the soul.

I remember talking once on this subject to one of the most beautiful personalities I have ever known: a woman, whose sympathy and noble kindness to me, both before and since the tragedy of my imprisonment, have been beyond power and description; one who has really assisted me, though she does not know it, to bear the burden of my troubles more than anyone else in the whole world has, and all through the mere fact of her existence, through her being what she is – partly an ideal and partly an influence: a suggestion of what one might become as well as a real help towards becoming it; a soul that renders the common air sweet, and makes what is spiritual seem as simple and natural as sunlight or the sea; one for whom beauty and sorrow walk hand in hand, and have the same message. On the occasion of which I am thinking, I recall distinctly how I said to her that there was enough suffering in one narrow London lane to show that God did not love man, and that wherever there was any sorrow, though but that of a child in some little garden weeping over a fault that it had or had not committed, the whole face of creation was completely marred. I was entirely wrong. She told me so, but I could not believe her. I was not in the sphere in which such belief was to be attained to. Now it seems to me that love of some kind is the only possible explanation of the extraordinary amount of suffering that there is in the world. I cannot conceive of any other explanation. I am convinced that there is no other, and that if the world has indeed, as I have said, been built of sorrow, it has been built by the hands of love, because in no other way could the soul of man, for whom the world was made, reach the full stature of its perfection. Pleasure for the beautiful body, but pain for the beautiful soul.

When I say that I am convinced of these things I speak with too much pride. Far off, like a perfect pearl, one can see the City of God. It is so wonderful that it seems as if a child could reach it in a summer's day. And so a child could. But with me and such as me it is different. One can realise a thing in a single moment, but one loses it in the long hours that follow with leaden feet. It is so difficult to keep 'heights that the soul is competent to gain'. We think in eternity, but we move slowly through time; and how slowly time goes with us who lie in prison I need not tell again, nor of the weariness and despair that creep back into one's cell, and into the cell of one's heart, with such strange insistence that one has, as it were, to garnish and sweep one's house for their coming, as for an unwelcome guest, or a bitter master, or a slave whose slave it is one's chance or choice to be.

And, though at present my friends may find it a hard thing to believe, it is true none the less, that for them living in freedom and idleness and comfort it is more easy to learn the lessons of humility than it is for me, who begin the day by going down on my knees and washing the floor of my cell. For prison life with its endless privations and restrictions makes one rebellious. The most terrible thing about it is not that it breaks one's heart – hearts are made to be broken – but that it turns one's heart to stone. One sometimes feels that it is only with a front of brass and a lip of scorn that one can get through the day at all. And he who is in a state of rebellion cannot receive grace, to use the phrase of which the church is so fond – so rightly fond, I dare say – for in life as in art the mood of rebellion closes up the channels of the soul, and shuts out the airs of heaven. Yet I must learn these lessons here, if I am to learn them anywhere, and must be filled with joy if my feet are on the right road and my face set towards 'the gate which is called beautiful', though I may fall many times in the mire and often in the mist go astray.

This New Life, as through my love of Dante I like sometimes to call it, is of course no new life at all, but simply the continuance, by means of development and evolution, of my former life. I remember when I was at Oxford saying to one of my friends as we were strolling round Magdalen's narrow bird-haunted walks one morning in the year before I took my degree, that I wanted to eat of the fruit of all the trees in the garden of the world, and that I was going out into the world with that passion in my soul. And so, indeed, I went out, and so I lived. My only mistake was that I confined myself so exclusively to the trees of what seemed to me the sunlit side of the garden, and shunned the other side for its shadow and its gloom. Failure, disgrace, poverty, sorrow, despair, suffering, tears even, the broken words that come from lips in pain, remorse that makes one walk on thorns, conscience that condemns, self-abasement that punishes, the misery that puts ashes on its head, the anguish that chooses sackcloth for its raiment and into its own drink puts gall – all these were things of which I was afraid. And as I had determined to know nothing of them, I was forced to taste each of them in turn, to feed on them, to have for a season, indeed, no other food at all.

I don't regret for a single moment having lived for pleasure. I did it to the full, as one should do everything that one does. There was no pleasure I did not experience. I threw the pearl of my soul into a cup of wine. I went down the primrose path to the sound of flutes. I lived on honeycomb. But to have continued the same life would have been wrong, because it would have been limiting. I had to pass on. The other half of the garden had its secrets for me also. Of course all this is foreshadowed and prefigured in my books. Some of it is in 'The Happy Prince', some of it in 'The Young King', notably in the passage where the bishop says to the kneeling boy, 'Is not He, who made misery, wiser than thou art?' a phrase which when I wrote it seemed to me little more than a phrase; a great deal of it is hidden away in the note of doom that like a purple thread runs through the texture of *Dorian Gray*; in *The Critic as Artist* it is set forth in many colours; in *The Soul of Man* it is written down, and in letters too easy to read; it is one of the refrains whose recurring *motifs* make *Salomé* so like a piece of music and bind it together as a ballad; in the prose poem of the man who from the bronze of the image of the 'Pleasure that liveth for a moment' has to make the image of the 'Sorrow that abideth for ever' it is incarnate. It could not have been otherwise. At every single moment of one's life one is what one is going to be no less than what one has been. Art is a symbol, because man is a symbol.

It is, if I can fully attain to it, the ultimate realisation of the artistic life. For the artistic life is simply self-development. Humility in the artist is his frank acceptance of all experiences, just as love in the artist is simply the sense of beauty that reveals to the world its body and its soul. In *Marius the Epicurean*, Pater seeks to reconcile the artistic life with the life of religion, in the deep, sweet and austere sense of the word. But Marius is little more than a spectator: an ideal spectator indeed, and one to whom it is given 'to contemplate the spectacle of life with appropriate emotions', which Wordsworth defines as the poet's true aim; yet a spectator merely, and perhaps a little too much occupied with the comeliness of the benches of the sanctuary to notice that it is the sanctuary of sorrow that he is gazing at.

I see a far more intimate and immediate connection between the true life of Christ and the true life of the artist; and I take a keen pleasure in the reflection that long before sorrow had made my days her own and bound me to her wheel I had written in *The Soul of Man* that he who would lead a Christ-like life must be entirely and absolutely himself, and had taken as my types not merely the shepherd on the hillside and the prisoner in his cell, but also the painter to whom the world is a pageant and the poet for whom the world is a song. I remember saying once to André Gide, as we sat together in some Paris café, that while metaphysics had but little real interest for me, and morality absolutely none, there was nothing that either Plato or Christ had said that could not be transferred immediately into the sphere of art and there find its complete fulfilment.

Nor is it merely that we can discern in Christ that close union of personality with perfection which forms the real distinction between the classical and romantic movement in life, but the very basis of his nature was the same as that of the nature of the artist – an intense and flamelike imagination. He realised in the entire sphere of human relations that imaginative sympathy which in the sphere of art is the sole secret of creation. He understood the leprosy of the leper, the darkness of the blind, the fierce misery of those who live for pleasure, the strange poverty of the rich. Someone wrote to me in trouble, 'When you are not on your pedestal, you are not interesting.' How remote was the writer from what Matthew Arnold calls 'the Secret of Jesus'. Either would have taught him that whatever happens to another happens to oneself, and if you want an inscription to read at dawn and at night-time, and for pleasure or for pain, write up on the walls of your house in letters for the sun to gild and the moon to silver, 'Whatever happens to oneself happens to another.'

Christ's place indeed is with the poets. His whole conception of Humanity sprang right out of the imagination and can only be

realised by it. What God was to the pantheist, man was to Him.
He was the first to conceive the divided races as a unity. Before his
time there had been gods and men, and, feeling through the
mysticism of sympathy that in himself each had been made
incarnate, he calls himself the Son of the one or the Son of the
other, according to his mood. More than anyone else in history he
wakes in us that temper of wonder to which romance always
appeals. There is still something to me almost incredible in the
idea of a young Galilean peasant imagining that he could bear on
his own shoulders the burden of the entire world; all that had
already been done and suffered, and all that was yet to be done
and suffered: the sins of Nero, of Caesar Borgia, of Alexander VI,
and of him who was Emperor of Rome and Priest of the Sun: the
sufferings of those whose names are legion and whose dwelling is
among the tombs: oppressed nationalities, factory children,
thieves, people in prison, outcasts, those who are dumb under
oppression and whose silence is heard only of God; and not
merely imagining this but actually achieving it, so that at the
present moment all who come in contact with his personality,
even though they may neither bow to his altar nor kneel before his
priest, in some way find that the ugliness of their sin is taken away
and the beauty of their sorrow revealed to them.

I had said of Christ that he ranks with the poets. That is true.
Shelley and Sophocles are of his company. But his entire life also
is the most wonderful of poems. For 'pity and terror' there is
nothing in the entire cycle of Greek tragedy to touch it. The
absolute purity of the protagonist raises the entire scheme to a
height of romantic art from which the sufferings of Thebes and
Pelops' line are by their very horror excluded, and shows how
wrong Aristotle was when he said in his treatise on the drama that
it would be impossible to bear the spectacle of one blameless in
pain. Nor in Aeschylus nor Dante, those stern masters of
tenderness, in Shakespeare, the most purely human of all the
great artists, in the whole of Celtic myth and legend, where the
loveliness of the world is shown through a mist of tears, and the
life of a man is no more than the life of a flower, is there anything
that, for sheer simplicity of pathos wedded and made one with
sublimity of tragic effect, can be said to equal or even approach

the last act of Christ's passion. The little supper with his companions, one of whom has already sold him for a price; the anguish in the quiet moonlit garden; the false friend coming close to him so as to betray him with a kiss; the friend who still believed in him, and on whom as on a rock he had hoped to build a house of refuge for Man, denying him as the bird cried to the dawn; his own utter loneliness, his submission, his acceptance of everything; and along with it all such scenes as the high priest of orthodoxy rending his raiment in wrath, and the magistrate of civil justice calling for water in the vain hope of cleansing himself of that stain of innocent blood that makes him the scarlet figure of history; the coronation ceremony of sorrow, one of the most wonderful things in the whole of recorded time; the crucifixion of the Innocent One before the eyes of his mother and of the disciple whom he loved; the soldiers gambling and throwing dice for his clothes; the terrible death by which he gave the world its most eternal symbol; and his final burial in the tomb of the rich man, his body swathed in Egyptian linen with costly spices and perfumes as though he had been a king's son. When one contemplates all this from the point of view of art alone one cannot but be grateful that the supreme office of the church should be the playing of the tragedy without the shedding of blood: the mystical presentation by means of dialogue and costume and gesture even of the Passion of her Lord; and it is always a source of pleasure and awe to me to remember that the ultimate survival of the Greek chorus, lost elsewhere to art, is to be found in the servitor answering the priest at Mass.

Yet the whole life of Christ – so entirely may sorrow and beauty be made one in their meaning and manifestation – is really an idyll, though it ends with the veil of the temple being rent, and the darkness coming over the face of the earth, and the stone rolled to the door of the sepulchre. One always thinks of him as a young bridegroom with his companions, as indeed he somewhere describes himself; as a shepherd straying through a valley with his sheep in search of green meadow or cool stream; as a singer trying to build out of the music the walls of the City of God; or as a lover for whose love the whole world was too small. His miracles seem to me to be as exquisite as the coming of spring and quite as natural. I see no difficulty at all in believing that such was the charm of his personality that his mere presence could bring peace to souls in anguish, and that those who touched his garments or his hands forgot their pain; or that as he passed by on the highway of life people who had seen nothing of life's mystery, saw it clearly, and others who had been deaf to every voice but that of pleasure heard for the first time the voice of love and found it as 'musical as Apollo's lute'; or that evil passions fled at his approach, and men whose dull unimaginative lives had been but a mode of death rose as it were from the grave when he called them; or that when he taught on the hillside the multitude forgot their hunger and thirst and the cares of this world, and that to his friends who listened to him as he sat at meat the coarse food seemed delicate, and the water had the taste of good wine, and the whole house became full of the odour and sweetness of nard.

Renan in his *Vie de Jesus* – that gracious fifth gospel, the gospel according to St Thomas, one might call it – says somewhere that Christ's great achievement was that he made himself as much loved after his death as he had been during his lifetime. And certainly, if his place is among the poets, he is the leader of all the lovers. He saw that love was the first secret of the world for which the wise men had been looking, and that it was only through love that one could approach either the heart of the leper or the feet of God.

And, above all, Christ is the most supreme of individualists. Humility, like the artistic acceptance of all experiences, is merely a mode of manifestation. It is man's soul that Christ is always looking for. He calls it 'God's Kingdom', and finds it in everyone. He compares it to little things, to a tiny seed, to a handful of leaven, to a pearl. That is because one realises one's soul only by getting rid of all alien passions, all acquired culture, and all external possessions, be they good or evil.

I bore up against everything with some stubbornness of will and much rebellion of nature, till I had absolutely nothing left in the world but one thing. I had lost my name, my position, my happiness, my freedom, my wealth. I was a prisoner and a pauper. But I still had my children left. Suddenly they were taken away from me by the law. It was a blow so appalling that I did not know what to do, so I flung myself on my knees, and bowed my head, and wept, and said, 'The body of a child is as the body of the Lord: I am not worthy of either.' That moment seemed to save me. I saw then that the only thing for me was to accept everything. Since then – curious as it will no doubt sound – I have been happier. It was of course my soul in its ultimate essence that I had reached. In many ways I had been its enemy, but I found it waiting for me as a friend. When one comes in contact with the soul it makes one simple as a child, as Christ said one should be.

It is tragic how few people ever 'possess their souls' before they die. 'Nothing is more rare in any man,' says Emerson, 'than an act of his own.' It is quite true. Most people are other people. Their thoughts are someone else's opinions, their lives a mimicry, their passions a quotation. Christ was not merely the supreme individualist, but he was the first individualist in history. People have tried to make him out an ordinary philanthropist, or ranked him as an altruist with the unscientific and sentimental. But he was really neither one nor the other. Pity he has, of course, for the poor, for those who are shut up in prisons, for the lowly, for the wretched; but he has far more pity for the rich, for the hard hedonists, for those who waste their freedom in becoming slaves to things, for those who wear soft raiment and live in kings' houses. Riches and pleasure seemed to him to be really greater tragedies than poverty or sorrow. And as for altruism, who knew better than he that it is vocation not volition that determines us, and that one cannot gather grapes of thorns or figs from thistles?

To live for others as a definite self-conscious aim was not his creed. It was not the basis of his creed. When he says, 'Forgive your enemies,' it is not for the sake of the enemy, but for one's own sake that he says so, and because love is more beautiful than hate. In his own entreaty to the young man, 'Sell all that thou hast and give to the poor,' it is not of the state of the poor that he is thinking, but of the soul of the young man, the soul that wealth was marring. In his view of life he is one with the artist who knows that by the inevitable law of self-perfection, the poet must sing, and the sculptor think in bronze, and the painter make the world a mirror for his moods, as surely and as certainly as the hawthorn must blossom in spring, and the corn turn to gold at harvest-time, and the moon in her ordered wanderings change from shield to sickle, and from sickle to shield.

But while Christ did not say to men, 'Live for others,' he pointed out that there was no difference at all between the lives of others and one's own life. By this means he gave to man an extended, a Titan personality. Since his coming the history of each separate individual is, or can be made, the history of the world. Of course, culture has intensified the personality of man. Art has made us myriad-minded. Those who have the artistic temperament go into exile with Dante and learn how salt is the bread of others, and how steep their stairs; they catch for a moment the serenity and calm of Goethe, and yet know but too well that Baudelaire cried to God:

'O Seigneur, donnez moi la force et le courage
De contempler mon corps et mon coeur sans dégoût.'

Out of Shakespeare's sonnets they draw, to their own hurt it may be, the secret of his love and make it their own; they look with new eyes on modern life because they have listened to one of Chopin's nocturnes, or handled Greek things, or read the story of the passion of some dead man for some dead woman whose hair was like threads of fine gold, and whose mouth was as a pomegranate. But the sympathy of the artistic temperament is necessarily with what has found expression. In words or in colours, in music or in marble, behind the painted masks of an Aeschylean play, or through some Sicilian shepherd's pierced and jointed reeds, the man and his message must have been revealed.

To the artist, expression is the only mode under which he can conceive life at all. To him what is dumb is dead. But to Christ it was not so. With a width and wonder of imagination that fills one almost with awe, he took the entire world of the inarticulate, the voiceless world of pain, as his kingdom, and made of himself its eternal mouthpiece. Those of whom I have spoken, who are dumb under oppression, and 'whose silence is heard only of God', he chose as his brothers. He sought to become eyes to the blind, ears to the deaf, and a cry in the lips of those whose tongues had been tied. His desire was to be to the myriads who had found no utterance a very trumpet through which they might call to heaven. And feeling, with the artistic nature of one to whom suffering and sorrow were modes through which he could realise his conception of the beautiful, that an idea is of no value till it becomes incarnate and is made an image, he made of himself the image of the Man of Sorrows, and as such has fascinated and dominated art as no Greek god ever succeeded in doing.

For the Greek gods, in spite of the white and red of their fair fleet limbs, were not really what they appeared to be. The curved brow of Apollo was like the sun's disc crescent over a hill at dawn, and his feet were as the wings of the morning, but he himself had been cruel to Marsyas and had made Niobe childless. In the steel shields of Athena's eyes there had been no pity for Arachne; the pomp and peacocks of Hera were all that was really noble about her; and the Father of the Gods himself had been too fond of the daughters of men. The two most deeply suggestive figures of Greek mythology were, for religion, Demeter an Earth Goddess, not one of the Olympians, and for art, Dionysus, the son of a mortal woman to whom the moment of his birth had proved also the moment of her death.

But life itself from its lowliest and most humble sphere produced one far more marvellous than the mother of Proserpina or the son of Semele. Out of the carpenter's shop at Nazareth had come a personality infinitely greater than any made by myth and legend, and one, strangely enough, destined to reveal to the world the mystical meaning of wine and the real beauties of the liles of the field as none, either on Cithaeron or at Enna, had ever done.

The song of Isaiah, 'He is despised and rejected of men, a man of sorrows and acquainted with grief: and we hid as it were our faces from him,' had seemed to him to prefigure himself, and in him the prophecy was fulfilled. We must not be afraid of such a phrase. Every single work of art is the fulfilment of a prophecy: for every work of art is the conversion of an idea into an image. Every single human being should be the fulfilment of a prophecy: for every human being should be the realisation of some ideal, either in the mind of God or in the mind of man. Christ found the type and fixed it, and the dream of a Virgilian poet, either at Jerusalem or at Babylon, became in the long progress of the centuries incarnate in him for whom the world was waiting.

To me one of the things in history the most to be regretted is that the Christ's own renaissance, which has produced the cathedral at Chartres, the Arthurian cycle of legends, the life of St Francis of Assisi, the art of Giotto, and Dante's *Divine Comedy*, was not allowed to develop on its own lines, but was interrupted and spoiled by the dreary classical Renaissance that gave us Petrarch, and Raphael's frescoes, and Palladian architecture, and formal French tragedy, and St Paul's Cathedral, and Pope's poetry, and everything that is made from without and by dead rules, and does not spring from within through some spirit informing it. But wherever there is a romantic movement in art there somehow, and under some form, is Christ, or the soul of Christ. He is in *Romeo and Juliet*, in *The Winter's Tale*, in Provençal poetry, in *The Ancient Mariner*, in *La Belle Dame sans merci* and in Chatterton's *Ballad of Charity*.

We owe to him the most diverse things and people. Hugo's *Les Misérables*, Baudelaire's *Fleurs du Mal*, the note of pity in Russian novels, Verlaine and Verlaine's poems, the stained glass and tapestries and the quattrocento work of Burne-Jones and Morris, belong to him no less than the tower of Giotto, Lancelot and Guinevere, *Tannhäuser*, the troubled romantic marbles of Michelangelo, pointed architecture, and the love of children and flowers – for both of which, indeed, in classical art there was but little place, hardly enough for them to grow or play in, but which, from the twelfth century down to our own day, have been continually making their appearances in art, under various modes and at various times, coming fitfully and wilfully, as children, as flowers, are apt to do: spring always seeming to one as if the flowers had been in hiding, and only came out into the sun because they were afraid that grown-up people would grow tired of looking for them and give up the search; and the life of a child being no more than an April day on which there is both rain and sun for the narcissus.

It is the imaginative quality of Christ's own nature that makes him this palpitating centre of romance. The strange figures of poetic drama and ballad are made by the imagination of others, but out of his own imagination entirely did Jesus of Nazareth create himself. The cry of Isaiah had really no more to do with his coming than the song of the nightingale has to do with the rising of the moon – no more, though perhaps no less. He was the denial as well as the affirmation of prophecy. For every expectation that he fulfilled there was another that he destroyed. 'In all beauty,' says Bacon, 'there is some strangeness of proportion,' and of those who are born of the spirit – of those, that is to say, who like himself are dynamic forces – Christ says that they are like the wind that 'bloweth where it listeth, and no man can tell whence it cometh and whither it goeth'. That is why he is so fascinating to artists. He has all the colour elements of life: mystery, strangeness, pathos, suggestion, ecstasy, love. He appeals to the temper of wonder, and creates that mood in which alone he can be understood.

And to me it is a joy to remember that if he is 'of imagination all compact', the world itself is of the same substance. I said in *Dorian Gray* that the great sins of the world take place in the brain; but it is in the brain that everything takes place. We know now that we do not see with the eyes or hear with the ears. They are really channels for the transmission, adequate or inadequate, of sense impressions. It is in the brain that the poppy is red, that the apple is odorous, that the skylark sings.

Of late I have been studying with diligence the four prose poems about Christ. At Christmas I managed to get hold of a Greek Testament, and every morning, after I had cleaned my cell and polished my tins, I read a little of the Gospels, a dozen verses taken by chance anywhere. It is a delightful way of opening the day. Everyone, even in a turbulent, ill-disciplined life, should do the same. Endless repetition, in and out of season, has spoiled for us the freshness, the *naïveté*, the simple romantic charm of the Gospels. We hear them read far too often and far too badly, and all repetition is anti-spiritual. When one returns to the Greek, it is like going into a garden of lilies out of some narrow and dark house.

And to me, the pleasure is doubled by the reflection that it is extremely probable that we have the actual terms, the *ipsissima verba*, used by Christ. It was always supposed that Christ talked in Aramaic. Even Renan thought so. But now we know that the Galilean peasants, like the Irish peasants of our own day, were

bilingual, and that Greek was the ordinary language of inter-
course all over Palestine, as indeed all over the Eastern world. I
never liked the idea that we knew of Christ's own words only
through a translation of a translation. It is a delight to me to think
that as far as his conversation was concerned, Charmides might
have listened to him, and Socrates reasoned with him, and Plato
understood him: that he really said ἐγώ εἰμι ὁ ποιμήν ὁ καλός, that
when he thought of the lilies of the field and how they neither toil
nor spin, his absolute expression was κατα-μάθετε τὰ κρίνα τοῦ αγροῦ
πῶς αὔξάνει οὐ κοπιᾷ οὐδὲ νήθει, and that his last word when he
cried out, 'My life has been completed, has reached its fulfilment,
has been perfected,' was exactly as St John tells us it was:
τετέλεσται – no more

While in reading the Gospels – particularly that of St John
himself, or whatever early Gnostic took his name and mantle – I
see the continual assertion of the imagination as the basis of all
spiritual and material life, I see also that to Christ imagination was
simply a form of love, and that to him love was lord in the fullest
meaning of the phrase. Some six weeks ago I was allowed by the
doctor to have white bread to eat instead of the coarse black or
brown bread of ordinary prison fare. It is a great delicacy. It will
sound strange that dry bread could possibly be a delicacy to
anyone. To me it is so much so that at the close of each meal I
carefully eat whatever crumbs may be left on my tin plate, or have
fallen on the rough towel that one uses as a cloth so as not to soil
one's table; and I do so not from hunger – I get now quite
sufficient food – but simply in order that nothing should he
wasted of what is given to me. So one should look on love.

Christ, like all fascinating personalities, had the power of not
merely saying beautiful things himself, but of making other
people say beautiful things to him; and I love the story St Mark
tells us about the Greek woman who, when as a trial of her faith he
said to her that he could not give her the bread of the children of
Israel, answered him that the little dogs – κυνάρια, 'little dogs', it
should be rendered – who are under the table eat of the crumbs
that the children let fall. Most people live for love and admiration.
But it is by love and admiration that we should live. If any love is
shown us we should recognise that we are quite unworthy of it.

Nobody is worthy to be loved. The fact that God loves man shows us that in the divine order of ideal things it is written that eternal love is to be given to what is eternally unworthy. Or if that phrase seems to be a bitter one to bear, let us say that everyone is worthy of love, except him who thinks that he is. Love is a sacrament that should be taken kneeling, and *Domine, non sum dignus* should be on the lips and in the hearts of those who receive it.

If ever I write again, in the sense of producing artistic work, there are just two subjects on which and through which I desire to express myself: one is 'Christ as the precursor of the romantic movement in life'; the other is 'The artistic life considered in its relation to conduct'. The first is, of course, intensely fascinating, for I see in Christ not merely the essentials of the supreme romantic type, but all the accidents, the wilfulnesses even, of the romantic temperament also. He was the first person who ever said to people that they should live 'flower-like lives'. He fixed the phrase. He took children as the type of what people should try to become. He held them up as examples to their elders, which I myself have always thought the chief use of children, if what is perfect should have a use. Dante describes the soul of a man as coming from the hand of God 'weeping and laughing like a little child', and Christ also saw that the soul of each one should be *a guisa di fanciulla che piangendo e ridendo pargoleggia*. He felt that life was changeful, fluid, active, and that to allow it to be stereotyped into any form was death. He saw that people should not be too serious over material, common interests: that to be unpractical was to be a great thing: that one should not bother too much over affairs. The birds didn't, why should man? He is charming when he says, 'Take no thought for the morrow; is not the soul more than meat? Is not the body more than raiment?' A Greek might have used the latter phrase. It is full of Greek feeling. But only Christ could have said both, and so summed up life perfectly for us.

His morality is all sympathy, just what morality should be. If the only thing that he ever said had been, 'Her sins are forgiven her because she loved much,' it would have been worthwhile dying to have said it. His justice is all poetical justice, exactly what justice should be. The beggar goes to heaven because he has been unhappy. I cannot conceive a better reason for his being sent there. The people who work for an hour in the vineyard in the cool of the evening receive just as much reward as those who have toiled there all day long in the hot sun. Why shouldn't they? Probably no one deserved anything. Or perhaps they were a different kind of people. Christ had no patience with the dull lifeless mechanical systems that treat people as if they were things, and so treat everybody alike; for him there were no laws: there were exceptions merely, as if anybody, or anything, for that matter, was like aught else in the world!

That which is the very keynote of romantic art was to him the proper basis of natural life. He saw no other basis. And when they brought him one taken in the very act of sin and showed him her sentence written in the law, and asked him what was to be done, he wrote with his finger on the ground as though he did not hear them, and finally, when they pressed him again, looked up and said, 'Let him of you who has never sinned be the first to throw the stone at her.' It was worthwhile living to have said that.

Like all poetical natures, he loved ignorant people. He knew that in the soul of one who is ignorant there is always room for a great idea. But he could not stand stupid people, especially those who are made stupid by education: people who are full of opinions, not one of which they even understand, a peculiarly modern type, summed up by Christ when he describes it as the type of one who has the key of knowledge, cannot use it himself, and does not allow other people to use it, though it may be made to open the gate of God's Kingdom. His chief war was against the Philistines. That is the war every child of light has to wage. Philistinism was the note of the age and community in which he lived. In their heavy inaccessibility to ideas, their dull respectability, their tedious orthodoxy, their worship of vulgar success, their entire preoccupation with the gross materialistic side of life, and their ridiculous estimate of themselves and their importance, the Jews of Jerusalem in Christ's day were the exact counterpart of the British philistine of our own. Christ mocked at the 'whited sepulchre' of respectability, and fixed that phrase for ever. He treated worldly success as a thing absolutely to be despised. He saw nothing in it at all. He looked on wealth as an encumbrance to a man. He would not hear of life being sacrificed to any system of thought or morals. He pointed out that forms and ceremonies were made for man, not man for forms and ceremonies. He took sabbatarianism as a type of the things that should be set at nought. The cold philanthropies, the ostentatious public charities, the tedious formalisms so dear to the middle-class mind, he exposed with utter and relentless scorn. To us, what is termed orthodoxy is merely a facile unintelligent acquiescence; but to them, and in their hands, it was a terrible and paralysing tyranny. Christ swept it aside. He showed that the spirit alone was of value. He took a keen pleasure in pointing out to them that though they were always reading the law and the prophets, they had not really the smallest idea of what either of them meant. In opposition to their tithing of each separate day into the fixed routine of prescribed duties, as they tithe mint and rue, he preached the enormous importance of living completely for the moment.

Those whom he saved from their sins are saved simply for beautiful moments in their lives. Mary Magdalen, when she sees Christ, breaks the rich vase of alabaster that one of her seven lovers had given her, and spills the odorous spices over his tired dusty feet, and for that one moment's sake sits for ever with Ruth and Beatrice in the tresses of the snow-white rose of Paradise. All that Christ says to us by the way of a little warning is that every moment should be beautiful, that the soul should always be ready for the coming of the bridegroom, always waiting for the voice of the lover, philistinism being simply that side of man's nature that is not illumined by the imagination. He sees all the lovely influences of life as modes of light: the imagination itself is the world of light. The world is made by it, and yet the world cannot understand it: that is because the imagination is simply a manifestation of love, and it is love and the capacity for it that distinguishes one human being from another.

But it is when he deals with a sinner that Christ is most romantic, in the sense of most real. The world had always loved the saint as being the nearest possible approach to the perfection of God. Christ, through some divine instinct in him, seems to have always loved the sinner as being the nearest possible approach to the perfection of man. His primary desire was not to reform people, any more than his primary desire was to relieve suffering. To turn an interesting thief into a tedious honest man was not his aim. He would have thought little of the Prisoners' Aid Society and other modern movements of the kind. The conversion of a publican into a Pharisee would not have seemed to him a great achievement. But in a manner not yet understood of the world he regarded sin and suffering as being in themselves beautiful holy things and modes of perfection.

It seems a very dangerous idea. It is – all great ideas are dangerous. That it was Christ's creed admits of no doubt. That it is the true creed I don't doubt myself.

Of course the sinner must repent. But why? Simply because otherwise he would be unable to realise what he had done. The moment of repentance is the moment of initiation. More than that: it is the means by which one alters one's past. The Greeks thought that impossible. They often say in their Gnomic aphorisms, 'Even the gods cannot alter the past.' Christ showed that the commonest sinner could do it, that it was the one thing he could do. Christ, had he been asked, would have said – I feel quite certain about it – that the moment the prodigal son fell on his knees and wept, he made his having wasted his substance with harlots, his swine-herding and hungering for the husks they ate, beautiful and holy moments in his life. It is difficult for most people to grasp the idea. I dare say one has to go to prison to understand it. If so, it may be worthwhile going to prison.

There is something so unique about Christ. Of course just as there are false dawns before the dawn itself, and winter days so full of sudden sunlight that they will cheat the wise crocus into squandering its gold before its time, and make some foolish bird call to its mate to build on barren boughs, so there were Christians before Christ. For that we should be grateful. The unfortunate thing is that there have been none since. I make one exception, St Francis of Assisi. But then God had given him at his birth the soul of a poet, as he himself when quite young had in mystical marriage taken poverty as his bride: and with the soul of a poet and the body of a beggar he found the way to perfection not difficult. He understood Christ, and so he became like him. We do not require the *Liber Conformitatum* to teach us that the life of

St Francis was the true *Imitatio Christi*, a poem compared to which the book of that name is merely prose.

Indeed, that is the charm about Christ, when all is said; he is just like a work of art. He does not really teach one anything, but by being brought into his presence one becomes something. And everybody is predestined to his presence. Once at least in his life each man walks with Christ to Emmaus.

As regards the other subject, the relation of the artistic life to conduct, it will no doubt seem strange to you that I should select it. People point to Reading Gaol and say, 'That is where the artistic life leads a man.' Well, it might lead to worse places. The more mechanical people, to whom life is a shrewd speculation depending on a careful calculation of ways and means, always know where they are going, and go there. They start with the ideal desire of being the parish beadle, and in whatever sphere they are placed they succeed in being the parish beadle and no more. A man whose desire is to be something separate from himself, to be a member of Parliament, or a successful grocer, or a prominent solicitor, or a judge, or something equally tedious, invariably succeeds in being what he wants to be. That is his punishment. Those who want a mask have to wear it.

But with the dynamic forces of life, and those in whom those dynamic forces become incarnate, it is different. People whose desire is solely for self-realisation never know where they are going. They can't know. In one sense of the word it is of course necessary as the Greek oracle said to know oneself: that is the first achievement of knowledge. But to recognise that the soul of a man is unknowable, is the ultimate achievement of wisdom. The final mystery is oneself. When one has weighed the sun in the balance, and measured the steps of the moon, and mapped out the seven heavens star by star, there still remains oneself. Who can calculate the orbit of his own soul? When the son went out to look for his father's asses, he did not know that a man of God was waiting for him with the very chrism of coronation, and that his own soul was already the soul of a king.

I hope to live long enough and to produce work of such a character that I shall be able at the end of my days to say, 'Yes! this is just where the artistic life leads a man!' Two of the most perfect

lives I have come across in my own experience are the lives of
Verlaine and of Prince Kropotkin, both of them men who have
passed years in prison: the first, the one Christian poet since
Dante; the other, a man with a soul of that beautiful white Christ
which seems coming out of Russia. And for the last seven or eight
months, in spite of a succession of great troubles reaching me from
the outside world almost without intermission, I have been placed
in direct contact with a new spirit working in this prison through
men and things that has helped me beyond any possibility of
expression in words; so that while for the first year of my
imprisonment I did nothing else, and can remember doing nothing
else, but wring my hands in impotent despair, and say, 'What an
ending, what an appalling ending!' now I try to say to myself, and
sometimes when I am not torturing myself do really and sincerely
say, 'What a beginning, what a wonderful beginning!' It may really
be so. It may become so. If it does I shall owe much to this new
personality that has altered every man's life in this place.

You may realise it when I say that had I been released last May,
as I tried to be, I would have left this place loathing it and every
official in it with a bitterness of hatred that would have poisoned
my life. I have had a year longer of imprisonment, but humanity
has been in the prison along with us all, and now when I go out I
shall always remember great kindnesses that I have received here
from almost everybody, and on the day of my release I shall give
many thanks to many people, and ask to be remembered by them
in turn.

The prison style is absolutely and entirely wrong. I would give
anything to be able to alter it when I go out. I intend to try. But
there is nothing in the world so wrong but that the spirit of
humanity, which is the spirit of love, the spirit of the Christ who
is not in churches, may make it, if not right, at least possible to be
borne without too much bitterness of heart.

I know also that much is waiting for me outside that is very
delightful, from what St Francis of Assisi calls 'my brother the
wind, and my sister the rain', lovely things both of them, down to
the shop-windows and sunsets of great cities. If I made a list of all
that still remains to me, I don't know where I should stop, for,
indeed, God made the world just as much for me as for anyone

else. Perhaps I may go out with something that I had not got before. I need not tell you that to me reformations in morals are as meaningless and vulgar as Reformations in theology. But while to propose to be a better man is a piece of unscientific cant, to have become a deeper man is the privilege of those who have suffered. And such I think I have become.

If after I am free a friend of mine gave a feast, and did not invite me to it, I should not mind a bit. I can be perfectly happy by myself. With freedom, flowers, books and the moon, who could not be perfectly happy? Besides, feasts are not for me any more. I have given too many to care about them. That side of life is over for me, very fortunately, I dare say. But if after I am free a friend of mine had a sorrow and refused to allow me to share it, I should feel it most bitterly. If he shut the doors of the house of mourning against me, I would come back again and again and beg to be admitted, so that I might share in what I was entitled to share in. If he thought me unworthy, unfit to weep with him, I should feel it as the most poignant humiliation, as the most terrible mode in which disgrace could be inflicted on me. But that could not be. I have a right to share in sorrow, and he who can look at the loveliness of the world and share its sorrow, and realise something of the wonder of both, is in immediate contact with divine things, and has got as near to God's secret as anyone can get.

Perhaps there may come into my art also, no less than into my life, a still deeper note, one of greater unity of passion and directness of impulse. Not width but intensity is the true aim of modern art. We are no longer in art concerned with the type. It is with the exception that we have to do. I cannot put my sufferings into any form they took, I need hardly say. Art only begins where Imitation ends, but something must come into my work, of fuller memory of words perhaps, of richer cadences, of more curious effects, of simpler architectural order, of some aesthetic quality at any rate.

When Marsyas was 'torn from the scabbard of his limbs' – *della vagina della membre sue*, to use one of Dante's most terrible Tacitean phrases – he had no more song, the Greek said. Apollo had been victor. The lyre had vanquished the reed. But perhaps the Greeks were mistaken. I hear in much modern art the cry of

Marsyas. It is bitter in Baudelaire, sweet and plaintive in Lamartine, mystic in Verlaine. It is in the deferred resolutions of Chopin's music. It is in the discontent that haunts Burne-Jones's women. Even Matthew Arnold, whose song of Callicles tells of 'the triumph of the sweet persuasive lyre', and the 'famous final victory', in such a clear note of lyrical beauty, has not a little of it; in the troubled undertone of doubt and distress that haunts his verses, neither Goethe nor Wordsworth could help him, though he followed each in turn, and when he seeks to mourn for *Thyrsis* or to sing of the *Scholar Gipsy*, it is the reed that he has to take for the rendering of his strain. But whether or not the Phrygian faun was silent, I cannot be. Expression is as necessary to me as leaf and blossoms are to the black branches of the trees that show themselves above the prison walls and are so restless in the wind. Between my art and the world there is now a wide gulf, but between art and myself there is none. I hope at least that there is none.

To each of us different fates are meted out. My lot has been one of public infamy, of long imprisonment, of misery, of ruin, of disgrace, but I am not worthy of it – not yet at any rate. I remember that I used to say that I thought I could bear a real tragedy if it came to me with purple pall and a mask of noble sorrow, but that the dreadful thing about modernity was that it put tragedy into the raiment of comedy, so that the great realities seemed commonplace or grotesque or lacking in style. It is quite true about modernity. It has probably always been true about actual life. It is said that all martyrdoms seemed mean to the looker on. The nineteenth century is no exception to the rule.

Everything about my tragedy has been hideous, mean, repellent, lacking in style; our very dress makes us grotesque. We are the zanies of sorrow. We are clowns whose hearts are broken. We are specially designed to appeal to the sense of humour. On November 13th, 1895, I was brought down here from London. From two o'clock till half-past two on that day I had to stand on the centre platform of Clapham Junction in convict dress, and handcuffed, for the world to look at. I had been taken out of the hospital ward without a moment's notice being given to me. Of all possible objects I was the most grotesque. When people saw me they laughed. Each train as it came up swelled the audience. Nothing could exceed their amusement. That was, of course, before they knew who I was. As soon as they had been informed they laughed still more. For half an hour I stood there in the grey November rain surrounded by a jeering mob.

For a year after that was done to me I wept every day at the same hour and for the same space of time. That is not such a tragic thing as possibly it sounds to you. To those who are in prison tears are a part of every day's experience. A day in prison on which one does not weep is a day on which one's heart is hard, not a day on which one's heart is happy

Well, now I am really beginning to feel more regret for the people who laughed than for myself. Of course when they saw me I was not on my pedestal, I was in the pillory. But it is a very unimaginative nature that only cares for people on their pedestals. A pedestal may be a very unreal thing. A pillory is a terrific reality. They should have known also how to interpret sorrow better. I have said that behind sorrow there is always sorrow. It were wiser still to say that behind sorrow there is always a soul. And to mock at a soul in pain is a dreadful thing. In the strangely simple economy of the world, people only get what they give, and to those who have not enough imagination to penetrate the mere outward of things, and feel pity, what pity can be given save that of scorn?

I write this account of the mode of my being transferred here simply that it should be realised how hard it has been for me to get anything out of my punishment but bitterness and despair. I have, however, to do it, and now and then I have moments of submission and acceptance. All the spring may be hidden in the single bud, and the low ground nest of the lark may hold the joy that is to herald the feet of many rose-red dawns. So perhaps whatever beauty of life still remains to me is contained in some moment of surrender, abasement and humiliation. I can, at any rate, merely proceed on the lines of my own development, and, accepting all that has happened to me, make myself worthy of it.

People used to say of me that I was too individualistic. I must be far more of an individualist than ever I was. I must get far more out of myself than ever I got, and ask far less of the world than ever I asked. Indeed, my ruin came not from too great individualism of life, but from too little. The one disgraceful, unpardonable, and to all time contemptible action of my life was to allow myself to appeal to society for help and protection. To have made such an appeal would have been from the individualist point of view bad enough, but what excuse can there ever be put forward for having made it? Of course once I had put into motion the forces of society, society turned on me and said, 'Have you been living all this time in defiance of my laws, and do you now appeal to those laws for protection? You shall have those laws exercised to the full. You shall abide by what you have appealed to.' The result is I am in gaol. Certainly no man ever fell so ignobly, and by such ignoble instruments, as I did.

The philistine element in life is not the failure to understand art. Charming people, such as fishermen, shepherds, ploughboys, peasants and the like know nothing about art, and are the very salt of the earth. He is the philistine who upholds and aids the heavy, cumbrous, blind, mechanical forces of society and who does not recognise dynamic force when he meets it either in a man or a movement.

People thought it dreadful of me to have entertained at dinner the evil things of life, and to have found pleasure in their company. But then, from the point of view through which I, as an artist in life, approached them they were delightfully suggestive and stimulating. The danger was half the excitement . . . My business as an artist was with Ariel. I set myself to wrestle with Caliban . . .

A great friend of mine – a friend of ten years' standing – came to see me some time ago, and told me that he did not believe a single word of what was said against me, and wished me to know that he considered me quite innocent, and the victim of a hideous plot. I burst into tears at what he said, and told him that while there was much amongst the definite charges that was quite untrue and transferred to me by revolting malice, still that my life had been full of perverse pleasures, and that unless he accepted that as a fact about me and realised it to the full I could not possibly be friends with him any more, or ever be in his company. It was a terrible shock to him, but we are friends, and I have not got his friendship on false pretences.

Emotional forces, as I say somewhere in *Intentions*, are as limited in extent and duration as the forces of physical energy. The little cup that is made to hold so much, can hold so much and no more, though all the purple vats of Burgundy be filled with wine to the brim, and the treaders stand knee-deep in the gathered grapes of the stony vineyards of Spain. There is no error more common than that of thinking that those who are the causes or occasions of great tragedies share in the feelings suitable to the tragic mood: no error more fatal than expecting it of them. The martyr in his 'shirt of flame' may be looking on the face of God, but to him who is piling the faggots or loosening the logs for the blast the whole scene is no more than the slaying of an ox is to the butcher, or the felling of a tree to the charcoal burner in the forest, or the fall of a flower to one who is mowing down the grass with a scythe. Great passions are for the great of soul, and great events can be seen only by those who are on a level with them.

I know of nothing in all drama more incomparable from the point of view of art, nothing more suggestive in its subtlety of observation, than Shakespeare's drawing of Rosencrantz and Guildenstern. They are Hamlet's college friends. They have been his companions. They bring with them memories of pleasant days together. At the moment when they come across him in the play he is staggering under the weight of a burden intolerable to one of his temperament. The dead have come armed out of the grave to impose on him a mission at once too great and too mean for him. He is a dreamer, and he is called upon to act. He has the nature of the poet, and he is asked to grapple with the common complexity of cause and effect, with life in its practical realisation, of which he knows nothing, not with life in its ideal essence, of which he knows so much. He has no conception of what to do, and his folly is to feign folly. Brutus used madness as a cloak to conceal the sword of his purpose, the dagger of his will, but the Hamlet madness is a mere mask for the hiding of weakness. In the making of fancies and jests he sees a chance of delay. He keeps playing with action as an artist plays with a theory. He makes himself the spy of his proper actions, and listening to his own words knows them to be but 'words, words, words'. Instead of trying to be the hero of his own history, he seeks to be the spectator of his own tragedy. He disbelieves in everything, including himself, and yet his doubt helps him not, as it comes not from scepticism, but from a divided will.

Of all this Guildenstern and Rosencrantz realise nothing. They bow and smirk and smile, and what the one says the other echoes with sickliest intonation. When at last, by means of the play within the play and the puppets in their dalliance, Hamlet 'catches the conscience' of the king, and drives the wretched man in terror from his throne, Guildenstern and Rosencrantz see no more in his conduct than a rather painful breach of court etiquette. That is as far as they can attain to in 'the contemplation of the spectacle of life with appropriate emotions'. They are close to his very secret and know nothing of it. Nor would there be any use in telling them. They are the little cups that can hold so much and no more. Towards the close it is suggested that, caught in a cunning spring set for another, they have met, or may meet, with a violent and sudden death. But a tragic ending of this kind, though touched by Hamlet's humour with something of the surprise and justice of comedy, is really not for such as they. They never die. Horatio, who in order to 'report Hamlet and his cause aright to the unsatisfied',

> Absents him from felicity a while,
> And in this harsh world draws his breath in pain,

dies, but Guildenstern and Rosencrantz are as immortal as Angelo and Tartuffe, and should rank with them. They are what modern life has contributed to the antique ideal of friendship. He who writes a new *De Amicitia* must find a niche for them, and praise them in Tusculan prose. They are types fixed for all time. To censure them would show 'a lack of appreciation'. They are merely out of their sphere – that is all. In sublimity of soul there is no contagion. High thoughts and high emotions are by their very existence isolated.

I am to be released, if all goes well with me, towards the end of May, and hope to go at once to some little seaside village abroad with R— and M—.

The sea, as Euripides says in one of his plays about Iphigeneia, washes away the stains and wounds of the world.

I hope to be at least a month with my friends, and to gain peace and balance, and a less troubled heart and a sweeter mood. I have a strange longing for the great simple primeval things, such as the sea, to me no less of a mother than the earth. It seems to me that we all look at nature too much, and live with her too little. I discern great sanity in the Greek attitude. They never chattered about sunsets, or discussed whether the shadows on the grass were really mauve or not. But they saw that the sea was for the swimmer, and the sand for the feet of the runner. They loved the trees for the shadow that they cast, and the forest for its silence at noon. The vineyard-dresser wreathed his hair with ivy that he might keep off the rays of the sun as he stooped over the young shoots, and for the artist and the athlete, the two types that Greece gave us, they plaited with garlands the leaves of the bitter laurel and of the wild parsley, which else had been of no service to men.

We call ours a utilitarian age, and we do not know the use of any single thing. We have forgotten that water can cleanse, and fire purify, and that the earth is mother to us all. As a consequence our art is of the moon and plays with shadows, while Greek art is of the sun and deals directly with things. I feel sure that in elemental forces there is purification and I want to go back to them and live in their presence.

Of course to one so modern as I am, *enfant de mon siècle*, merely to look at the world will be always lovely. I tremble with pleasure when I think that on the very day of my leaving prison both the laburnum and the lilac will be blooming in the gardens, and that I shall see the wind stir into restless beauty the swaying gold of the one, and make the other toss the pale purple of its plumes so that all the air shall be Arabia for me. Linnaeus fell on his knees and wept for joy when he saw for the first time the long heath of some English upland made yellow with the tawny aromatic blossoms of the common furze; and I know that for me, to whom flowers are part of desire, there are tears waiting in the petals of some rose. It has always been so with me from my boyhood. There is not a single colour hidden away in the chalice of a flower, or the curve of a shell, to which, by some subtle sympathy with the very soul of things, my nature does not answer. Like Gautier, I have always been one of those *pour qui le monde visible existe*.

Still, I am conscious now that behind all this beauty, satisfying though it may be, there is some spirit hidden of which the painted forms and shapes are but modes of manifestation, and it is with this spirit that I desire to become in harmony. I have grown tired of the articulate utterances of men and things. The mystical in art, the mystical in life, the mystical in nature, this is what I am looking for. It is absolutely necessary for me to find it somewhere.

All trials are trials for one's life, just as all sentences are sentences of death; and three times have I been tried. The first time I left the box to be arrested, the second time to be led back to the house of detention, the third time to pass into a prison for two years. Society, as we have constituted it, will have no place for me, has none to offer; but nature, whose sweet rains fall on unjust and just alike, will have clefts in the rocks where I may hide, and secret valleys in whose silence I may weep undisturbed. She will hang the night with stars so that I may walk abroad in the darkness without stumbling, and send the wind over my footprints so that none may track me to my hurt: she will cleanse me in great waters, and with bitter herbs make me whole.

THE BALLAD OF READING GAOL

The Ballad of Reading Gaol

In memoriam
C. T. W., *sometime trooper of the Royal Horse Guards,*
obiit HM Prison, Reading, Berkshire, 7 *July* 1896

I

He did not wear his scarlet coat,
   For blood and wine are red,
And blood and wine were on his hands
   When they found him with the dead,
The poor dead woman whom he loved,
   And murdered in her bed.

He walked amongst the trial men
   In a suit of shabby grey;
A cricket cap was on his head,
   And his step seemed light and gay;
But I never saw a man who looked
   So wistfully at the day.

I never saw a man who looked
   With such a wistful eye
Upon that little tent of blue
   Which prisoners call the sky,
And at every drifting cloud that went
   With sails of silver by.

I walked with other souls in pain,
   Within another ring,
And was wondering if the man had done
   A great or little thing,
When a voice behind me whispered low,
   'That fellow's got to swing.'

Dear Christ! the very prison walls
   Suddenly seemed to reel,
And the sky above my head became
   Like a casque of scorching steel;
And, though I was a soul in pain,
   My pain I could not feel.

I only knew what hunted thought
   Quickened his step, and why
He looked upon the garish day
   With such a wistful eye;
The man had killed the thing he loved,
   And so he had to die.

*

Yet each man kills the thing he loves,
   By each let this be heard,
Some do it with a bitter look,
   Some with a flattering word,
The coward does it with a kiss,
   The brave man with a sword!

Some kill their love when they are young,
   And some when they are old;
Some strangle with the hands of lust,
   Some with the hands of gold:
The kindest use a knife, because
   The dead so soon grow cold.

Some love too little, some too long,
   Some sell, and others buy;
Some do the deed with many tears,
   And some without a sigh:
For each man kills the thing he loves,
   Yet each man does not die.

He does not die a death of shame
  On a day of dark disgrace,
Nor have a noose about his neck,
  Nor a cloth upon his face,
Nor drop feet foremost through the floor
  Into an empty space.

*

He does not sit with silent men
  Who watch him night and day;
Who watch him when he tries to weep,
  And when he tries to pray;
Who watch him lest himself should rob
  The prison of its prey.

He does not wake at dawn to see
  Dread figures throng his room,
The shivering chaplain robed in white,
  The sheriff stern with gloom,
And the governor all in shiny black,
  With the yellow face of doom.

He does not rise in piteous haste
  To put on convict-clothes,
While some coarse-mouthed doctor gloats,
                                    and notes
  Each new and nerve-twitched pose,
Fingering a watch whose little ticks
  Are like horrible hammer-blows.

He does not know that sickening thirst
  That sands one's throat, before
The hangman with his gardener's gloves
  Slips through the padded door,
And binds one with three leathern thongs,
  That the throat may thirst no more.

He does not bend his head to hear
   The Burial Office read,
Nor, while the terror of his soul
   Tells him he is not dead,
Cross his own coffin, as he moves
   Into the hideous shed.

He does not stare upon the air
   Through a little roof of glass;
He does not pray with lips of clay
   For his agony to pass,
Nor feel upon his shuddering cheek
   The kiss of Caiaphas.

II

Six weeks our guardsman walked the yard,
   In the suit of shabby grey:
His cricket cap was on his head,
   And his step seemed light and gay,
But I never saw a man who looked
   So wistfully at the day.

I never saw a man who looked
   With such a wistful eye
Upon that little tent of blue
   Which prisoners call the sky,
And at every wandering cloud that trailed
   Its ravelled fleeces by.

He did not wring his hands, as do
   Those witless men who dare
To try to rear the changeling Hope
   In the cave of black Despair:
He only looked upon the sun,
   And drank the morning air.

He did not wring his hands nor weep,
    Nor did he peek or pine,
But he drank the air as though it held
    Some healthful anodyne;
With open mouth he drank the sun
    As though it had been wine!

And I and all the souls in pain,
    Who tramped the other ring,
Forgot if we ourselves had done
    A great or little thing,
And watched with gaze of dull amaze
    The man who had to swing.

And strange it was to see him pass
    With a step so light and gay,
And strange it was to see him look
    So wistfully at the day,
And strange it was to think that he
    Had such a debt to pay.

*

For oak and elm have pleasant leaves
    That in the springtime shoot:
But grim to see is the gallows-tree,
    With its adder-bitten root,
And, green or dry, a man must die
    Before it bears its fruit!

The loftiest place is that seat of grace
    For which all worldlings try:
But who would stand in hempen band
    Upon a scaffold high,
And through a murderer's collar take
    His last look at the sky?

It is sweet to dance to violins
　　When love and life are fair:
To dance to flutes, to dance to lutes
　　Is delicate and rare:
But it is not sweet with nimble feet
　　To dance upon the air!

So with curious eyes and sick surmise
　　We watched him day by day,
And wondered if each one of us
　　Would end the self-same way,
For none can tell to what red hell
　　His sightless soul may stray.

At last the dead man walked no more
　　Amongst the trial men,
And I knew that he was standing up
　　In the black dock's dreadful pen,
And that never would I see his face
　　In God's sweet world again.

Like two doomed ships that pass in storm
　　We had crossed each other's way:
But we made no sign, we said no word,
　　We had no word to say;
For we did not meet in the holy night,
　　But in the shameful day.

A prison wall was round us both,
　　Two outcast men we were:
The world had thrust us from its heart,
　　And God from out His care:
And the iron gin that waits for Sin
　　Had caught us in its snare.

III

In Debtors' Yard the stones are hard,
  And the dripping wall is high,
So it was there he took the air
  Beneath the leaden sky,
And by each side a warder walked,
  For fear the man might die.

Or else he sat with those who watched
  His anguish night and day;
Who watched him when he rose to weep,
  And when he crouched to pray;
Who watched him lest himself should rob
  Their scaffold of its prey.

The governor was strong upon
  The Regulations Act;
The doctor said that death was but
  A scientific fact;
And twice a day the chaplain called,
  And left a little tract.

And twice a day he smoked his pipe,
  And drank his quart of beer:
His soul was resolute, and held
  No hiding-place for fear;
He often said that he was glad
  The hangman's hands were near.

But why he said so strange a thing
  No warder dared to ask:
For he to whom a watcher's doom
  Is given as his task,
Must set a lock upon his lips,
  And make his face a mask.

Or else he might be moved, and try
    To comfort or console:
And what should human pity do
    Pent up in murderer's hole?
What word of grace in such a place
    Could help a brother's soul?

*

With slouch and swing around the ring
    We trod the fools' parade!
We did not care: we knew we were
    The devil's own brigade:
And shaven head and feet of lead
    Make a merry masquerade.

We tore the tarry rope to shreds
    With blunt and bleeding nails;
We rubbed the doors, and scrubbed the floors,
    And cleaned the shining rails;
And, rank by rank, we soaped the plank,
    And clattered with the pails.

We sewed the sacks, we broke the stones,
    We turned the dusty drill;
We banged the tins, and bawled the hymns,
    And sweated on the mill;
But in the heart of every man
    Terror was lying still.

So still it lay that every day
    Crawled like a weed-clogged wave:
And we forgot the bitter lot
    That waits for fool and knave,
Till once, as we tramped in from work,
    We passed an open grave.

With yawning mouth the yellow hole
  Gaped for a living thing;
The very mud cried out for blood
  To the thirsty asphalt ring:
And we knew that ere one dawn grew fair
  Some prisoner had to swing.

Right in we went, with soul intent
  On death and dread and doom;
The hangman, with his little bag,
  Went shuffling through the gloom;
And each man trembled as he crept
  Into his numbered tomb.

*

That night the empty corridors
  Were full of forms of fear,
And up and down the iron town
  Stole feet we could not hear,
And through the bars that hide the stars
  White faces seemed to peer.

He lay as one who lies and dreams
  In a pleasant meadowland,
The watchers watched him as he slept,
  And could not understand
How one could sleep so sweet a sleep
  With a hangman close at hand.

But there is no sleep when men must weep
  Who never yet have wept:
So we – the fool, the fraud, the knave –
  That endless vigil kept,
And through each brain on hands of pain
    Another's terror crept.

Alas! it is a fearful thing
    To feel another's guilt!
For, right within, the sword of sin
    Pierced to its poisoned hilt,
And as molten lead were the tears we shed
    For the blood we had not spilt.

The warders with their shoes of felt
    Crept by each padlocked door,
And peeped and saw, with eyes of awe,
    Grey figures on the floor,
And wondered why men knelt to pray
    Who never prayed before.

All through the night we knelt and prayed,
    Mad mourners of a corse!
The troubled plumes of midnight were
    The plumes upon a hearse:
And bitter wine upon a sponge
    Was the savour of remorse.

*

The grey cock crew, the red cock crew,
    But never came the day:
And crooked shapes of terror crouched,
    In the corners where we lay:
And each evil sprite that walks by night
    Before us seemed to play.

They glided past, they glided fast,
    Like travellers through a mist:
They mocked the moon in a rigadoon
    Of delicate turn and twist,
And with formal pace and loathsome grace
    The phantoms kept their tryst.

With mop and mow, we saw them go,
   Slim shadows hand in hand:
About, about, in ghostly rout
   They trod a saraband:
And the damned grotesques made arabesques,
   Like the wind upon the sand!

With the pirouettes of marionettes,
   They tripped on pointed tread:
But with flutes of fear they filled the ear,
   As their grisly masque they led,
And loud they sang, and long they sang,
   For they sang to wake the dead.

'*Oho!*' they cried, '*The world is wide,*
   But fettered limbs go lame!
And once, or twice, to throw the dice
   Is a gentlemanly game,
But he does not win who plays with sin
   In the secret House of Shame.'

No things of air these antics were,
   That frolicked with such glee:
To men whose lives were held in gyves,
   And whose feet might not go free,
Ah! wounds of Christ! they were living things,
   Most terrible to see.

Around, around, they waltzed and wound;
   Some wheeled in smirking pairs:
With the mincing step of a demirep
   Some sidled up the stairs:
And with subtle sneer, and fawning leer,
   Each helped us at our prayers.

The morning wind began to moan,
   But still the night went on:
Through its giant loom the web of gloom
   Crept till each thread was spun:
And, as we prayed, we grew afraid
   Of the justice of the sun.

The moaning wind went wandering round
   The weeping prison-wall:
Till like a wheel of turning steel
   We felt the minutes crawl:
O moaning wind! what had we done
   To have such a seneschal?

At last I saw the shadowed bars,
   Like a lattice wrought in lead,
Move right across the whitewashed wall
   That faced my three-plank bed,
And I knew that somewhere in the world
   God's dreadful dawn was red.

At six o'clock we cleaned our cells,
   At seven all was still,
But the sough and swing of a mighty wing
   The prison seemed to fill,
For the Lord of Death with icy breath
   Had entered in to kill.

He did not pass in purple pomp,
   Nor ride a moon-white steed.
Three yards of cord and a sliding board
   Are all the gallows' need:
So with rope of shame the herald came
   To do the secret deed.

We were as men who through a fen
  Of filthy darkness grope:
We did not dare to breathe a prayer,
  Or to give our anguish scope:
Something was dead in each of us,
  And what was dead was hope.

For man's grim justice goes its way
  And will not swerve aside:
It slays the weak, it slays the strong,
  It has a deadly stride:
With iron heel it slays the strong,
  The monstrous parricide!

We waited for the stroke of eight;
  Each tongue was thick with thirst:
For the stroke of eight is the stroke of fate
  That makes a man accursed,
And fate will use a running noose
  For the best man and the worst.

We had no other thing to do,
  Save to wait for the sign to come:
So, like things of stone in a valley lone,
  Quiet we sat and dumb:
But each man's heart beat thick and quick,
  Like a madman on a drum!

With sudden shock the prison-clock
  Smote on the shivering air,
And from all the gaol rose up a wail
  Of impotent despair,
Like the sound that frightened marshes hear
  From some leper in his lair.

And as one sees most dreadful things
   In the crystal of a dream,
We saw the greasy hempen rope
   Hooked to the blackened beam,
And heard the prayer the hangman's snare
   Strangled into a scream.

And all the woe that moved him so
   That he gave that bitter cry,
And the wild regrets and the bloody sweats
   None knew so well as I:
For he who lives more lives than one
   More deaths than one must die.

IV

There is no chapel on the day
   On which they hang a man:
The chaplain's heart is far too sick,
   Or his face is far too wan,
Or there is that written in his eyes
   Which none should look upon.

So they kept us close till nigh on noon,
   And then they rang the bell,
And the warders with their jingling keys
   Opened each listening cell,
And down the iron stair we tramped,
   Each from his separate hell.

Out into God's sweet air we went,
   But not in wonted way,
For this man's face was white with fear,
   And that man's face was grey,
And I never saw sad men who looked
   So wistfully at the day.

I never saw sad men who looked
    With such a wistful eye
Upon that little tent of blue
    We prisoners called the sky,
And at every careless cloud that passed
    In happy freedom by.

But there were those amongst us all
    Who walked with downcast head,
And knew that, had each got his due,
    They should have died instead:
He had but killed a thing that lived,
    Whilst they had killed the dead.

For he who sins a second time
    Wakes a dead soul to pain,
And draws it from its spotted shroud,
    And makes it bleed again,
And makes it bleed great gouts of blood,
    And makes it bleed in vain!

*

Like ape or clown, in monstrous garb
    With crooked arrows starred,
Silently we went round and round
    The slippery asphalt yard;
Silently we went round and round,
    And no man spoke a word.

Silently we went round and round,
    And through each hollow mind
The memory of dreadful things
    Rushed like a dreadful wind,
And horror stalked before each man,
    And terror crept behind.

*

The warders strutted up and down,
　　And watched their herd of brutes,
Their uniforms were spick and span,
　　And they wore their Sunday suits,
But we knew the work they had been at
　　By the quicklime on their boots.

For where a grave had opened wide,
　　There was no grave at all:
Only a stretch of mud and sand
　　By the hideous prison-wall,
And a little heap of burning lime,
　　That the man should have his pall.

For he has a pall, this wretched man,
　　Such as few men can claim:
Deep down below a prison-yard,
　　Naked for greater shame,
He lies, with fetters on each foot,
　　Wrapt in a sheet of flame!

And all the while the burning lime
　　Eats flesh and bone away,
It eats the brittle bone by night,
　　And the soft flesh by day,
It eats the flesh and bone by turns,
　　But it eats the heart alway.

*

For three long years they will not sow
　　Or root or seedling there:
For three long years the unblessed spot
　　Will sterile be and bare,
And look upon the wondering sky
　　With unreproachful stare.

They think a murderer's heart would taint
   Each simple seed they sow.
It is not true! God's kindly earth
   Is kindlier than men know,
And the red rose would but blow more red,
   The white rose whiter blow.

Out of his mouth a red, red rose!
   Out of his heart a white!
For who can say by what strange way,
   Christ brings His will to light,
Since the barren staff the pilgrim bore
   Bloomed in the great Pope's sight?

But neither milk-white rose nor red
   May bloom in prison air;
The shard, the pebble and the flint
   Are what they give us there:
For flowers have been known to heal
   A common man's despair.

So never will wine-red rose or white,
   Petal by petal, fall
On that stretch of mud and sand that lies
   By the hideous prison-wall,
To tell the men who tramp the yard
   That God's Son died for all.

*

Yet though the hideous prison-wall
   Still hems him round and round,
And a spirit may not walk by night
   That is with fetters bound,
And a spirit may but weep that lies
   In such unholy ground,

He is at peace – this wretched man –
    At peace, or will be soon:
There is no thing to make him mad,
    Nor does terror walk at noon,
For the lampless earth in which he lies
    Has neither sun nor moon.

They hanged him as a beast is hanged:
    They did not even toll
A requiem that might have brought
    Rest to his startled soul,
But hurriedly they took him out,
    And hid him in a hole.

They stripped him of his canvas clothes,
    And gave him to the flies:
They mocked the swollen purple throat,
    And the stark and staring eyes:
And with laughter loud they heaped the shroud
    In which their convict lies.

The chaplain would not kneel to pray
    By his dishonoured grave:
Nor mark it with that blessed Cross
    That Christ for sinners gave,
Because the man was one of those
    Whom Christ came down to save.

Yet all is well; he has but passed
    To life's appointed bourne:
And alien tears will fill for him
    Pity's long-broken urn,
For his mourners will be outcast men,
    And outcasts always mourn.

v

I know not whether laws be right,
  Or whether laws be wrong;
All that we know who lie in gaol
  Is that the wall is strong;
And that each day is like a year,
  A year whose days are long.

But this I know, that every law
  That men have made for man,
Since first man took his brother's life,
  And the sad world began,
But straws the wheat and saves the chaff
  With a most evil fan.

This too I know – and wise it were
  If each could know the same –
That every prison that men build
  Is built with bricks of shame,
And bound with bars lest Christ should see
  How men their brothers maim.

With bars they blur the gracious moon,
  And blind the goodly sun:
And they do well to hide their hell,
  For in it things are done
That Son of God nor son of man
  Ever should look upon!

*

The vilest deeds, like poison weeds,
  Bloom well in prison-air;
It is only what is good in man
  That wastes and withers there:
Pale Anguish keeps the heavy gate,
  And the warder is Despair.

For they starve the little frightened child
    Till it weeps both night and day;
And they scourge the weak, and flog the fool,
    And gibe the old and grey,
And some grow mad, and all grow bad,
    And none a word may say.

Each narrow cell in which we dwell
    Is a foul and dark latrine,
And the fetid breath of living Death
    Chokes up each grated screen,
And all, but lust, is turned to dust
    In Humanity's machine.

The brackish water that we drink
    Creeps with a loathsome slime,
And the bitter bread they weigh in scales
    Is full of chalk and lime,
And Sleep will not lie down, but walks
    Wild-eyed, and cries to Time.

*

But though lean Hunger and green Thirst
    Like asp with adder fight,
We have little care of prison fare,
    For what chills and kills outright
Is that every stone one lifts by day
    Becomes one's heart by night.

With midnight always in one's heart,
    And twilight in one's cell,
We turn the crank, or tear the rope,
    Each in his separate hell,
And the silence is more awful far
    Than the sound of a brazen bell.

And never a human voice comes near
   To speak a gentle word:
And the eye that watches through the door
   Is pitiless and hard:
And by all forgot, we rot and rot,
   With soul and body marred.

And thus we rust life's iron chain
   Degraded and alone;
And some men curse, and some men weep,
   And some men make no moan;
But God's eternal laws are kind
   And break the heart of stone.

*

And every human heart that breaks,
   In prison-cell or yard,
Is as that broken box that gave
   Its treasure to the Lord,
And filled the unclean leper's house
   With the scent of costliest nard.

Ah! happy they whose hearts can break
   And peace of pardon win!
How else may man make straight his plan
   And cleanse his soul from sin?
How else but through a broken heart
   May Lord Christ enter in?

*

And he of the swollen purple throat,
   And the stark and staring eyes,
Waits for the holy hands that took
   The thief to Paradise;
And a broken and a contrite heart
   The Lord will not despise.

The man in red who reads the law
   Gave him three weeks of life,
Three little weeks in which to heal
   His soul of his soul's strife,
And cleanse from every blot of blood
   The hand that held the knife.

And with tears of blood he cleansed the hand,
   The hand that held the steel:
For only blood can wipe out blood,
   And only tears can heal:
And the crimson stain that was of Cain
   Became Christ's snow-white seal.

VI

In Reading gaol by Reading town
   There is a pit of shame,
And in it lies a wretched man
   Eaten by teeth of flame,
In a burning winding-sheet he lies,
   And his grave has got no name.

And there, till Christ call forth the dead,
   In silence let him lie:
No need to waste the foolish tear,
   Or heave the windy sigh:
The man had killed the thing he loved,
   And so he had to die.

And all men kill the thing they love,
   By all let this be heard,
Some do it with a bitter look,
   Some with a flattering word,
The coward does it with a kiss,
   The brave man with a sword!

THE DECAY OF LYING
An Observation

CYRIL *(coming in through the open window from the terrace):* My dear Vivian, don't coop yourself up all day in the library. It is a perfectly lovely afternoon. The air is exquisite. There is a mist upon the woods like the purple bloom upon a plum. Let us go and lie on the grass and smoke cigarettes and enjoy nature.

VIVIAN: Enjoy nature! I am glad to say that I have entirely lost that faculty. People tell us that art makes us love nature more than we loved her before; that it reveals her secrets to us; and that after a careful study of Corot and Constable we see things in her that had escaped our observation. My own experience is that the more we study art, the less we care for nature. What art really reveals to us is nature's lack of design, her curious crudities, her extraordinary monotony, her absolutely unfinished condition. Nature has good intentions, of course, but, as Aristotle once said, she cannot carry them out. When I look at a landscape I cannot help seeing all its defects. It is fortunate for us, however, that nature is so imperfect, as otherwise we should have no art at all. Art is our spirited protest, our gallant attempt to teach nature her proper place. As for the infinite variety of nature, that is a pure myth. It is not to be found in nature herself. It resides in the imagination, or fancy, or cultivated blindness of the man who looks at her.

CYRIL: Well, you need not look at the landscape. You can lie on the grass and smoke and talk.

VIVIAN: But nature is so uncomfortable. Grass is hard and lumpy and damp, and full of dreadful black insects. Why, even Morris's poorest workman could make you a more comfortable seat than the whole of nature can. Nature pales before the furniture of 'the street which from Oxford has borrowed its name', as the poet you love so much once vilely phrased it. I don't complain. If nature had been comfortable, mankind would never have invented architecture, and I prefer houses to the open air. In a house we all feel of the proper proportions. Everything is subordinated to us, fashioned for our use and our pleasure. Egotism itself, which is so necessary to a proper sense of human dignity, is entirely the result of indoor life. Out of doors one becomes abstract and impersonal. One's individuality absolutely leaves one. And then nature is so indifferent, so unappreciative. Whenever I am walking in the park here, I always feel that I am no more to her than the cattle that browse on the slope, or the burdock that blooms in the ditch. Nothing is more evident than that nature hates mind. Thinking is the most unhealthy thing in the world, and people die of it just as they die of any other disease. Fortunately, in England at any rate, thought is not catching. Our splendid physique as a people is entirely due to our national stupidity. I only hope we shall be able to keep this great historic bulwark of our happiness for many years to come; but I am afraid that we are beginning to be over-educated; at least everybody who is incapable of learning has taken to teaching – that is really what our enthusiasm for education has come to. In the meantime, you had better go back to your wearisome uncomfortable nature, and leave me to correct my proofs.

CYRIL: Writing an article! That is not very consistent after what you have just said.

VIVIAN: Who wants to be consistent? The dullard and the doctrinaire, the tedious people who carry out their principles to the bitter end of action, to the *reductio ad absurdum* of practice. Not I. Like Emerson, I write over the door of my library the word 'Whim'. Besides, my article is really a most salutary and valuable warning. If it is attended to, there may be a new renaissance of art.

CYRIL: What is the subject?

VIVIAN: I intend to call it 'The Decay of Lying: A Protest'.

CYRIL: Lying! I should have thought that our politicians kept up that habit.

VIVIAN: I assure you that they do not. They never rise beyond the level of misrepresentation, and actually condescend to prove, to discuss, to argue. How different from the temper of the true liar, with his frank, fearless statements, his superb irresponsibility, his healthy, natural disdain of proof of any kind! After all, what is a fine lie? Simply that which is its own evidence. If a man is sufficiently unimaginative to produce evidence in support of a lie, he might just as well speak the truth at once. No, the politicians won't do. Something may, perhaps, be urged on behalf of the bar. The mantle of the sophist has fallen on its members. Their feigned ardours and unreal rhetoric are delightful. They can make the worse appear the better cause, as though they were fresh from Leontine schools, and have been known to wrest from reluctant juries triumphant verdicts of acquittal for their clients, even when those clients, as often happens, were clearly and unmistakably innocent. But they are briefed by the prosaic, and are not ashamed to appeal to precedent. In spite of their endeavours, the truth will out. Newspapers, even, have degenerated. They may now be absolutely relied upon. One feels it as one wades through their columns. It is always the unreadable that occurs. I am afraid that there is not much to be said in favour of either the lawyer or the journalist. Besides, what I am pleading for is lying in art. Shall I read you what I have written? It might do you a great deal of good.

CYRIL: Certainly, if you give me a cigarette. Thanks. By the way, what magazine do you intend it for?

VIVIAN: For the *Retrospective Review*. I think I told you that the elect had revived it.

CYRIL: Whom do you mean by 'the elect'?

VIVIAN: Oh, the Tired Hedonists, of course. It is a club to which I belong. We are supposed to wear faded roses in our buttonholes when we meet, and to have a sort of cult for Domitian. I am afraid you are not eligible. You are too fond of simple pleasures.

CYRIL: I should be blackballed on the ground of animal spirits, I suppose?

VIVIAN: Probably. Besides, you are a little too old. We don't admit anybody who is of the usual age.

CYRIL: Well, I should fancy you are all a good deal bored with each other.

VIVIAN: We are. That is one of the objects of the club. Now, if you promise not to interrupt too often, I will read you my article.

CYRIL: You will find me all attention.

VIVIAN (*reading in a very clear voice*): ' "The Decay of Lying: A Protest" – One of the chief causes that can be assigned for the curiously commonplace character of most of the literature of our age is undoubtedly the decay of lying as an art, a science and a social pleasure. The ancient historians gave us delightful fiction in the form of fact; the modern novelist presents us with dull facts under the guise of fiction. The Blue-Book is rapidly becoming his ideal both for method and manner. He has his tedious *document humain*, his miserable little *coin de la création*, into which he peers with his microscope. He is to be found at the Librairie Nationale, or at the British Museum, shamelessly reading up his subject. He has not even the courage of other people's ideas, but insists on going directly to life for everything, and ultimately, between encyclopaedias and personal experience, he comes to the ground, having drawn his types from the family circle or from the weekly washerwoman, and having acquired an amount of useful information from which never, even in his most meditative moments, can he thoroughly free himself.

'The loss that results to literature in general from this false ideal of our time can hardly be overestimated. People have a careless way of talking about a "born liar", just as they talk about a "born poet". But in both cases they are wrong. Lying and poetry are arts – arts, as Plato saw, not unconnected with each other – and they require the most careful study, the most disinterested devotion. Indeed, they have their technique, just as the more material arts of painting and sculpture have, their subtle secrets of form and colour, their craft-mysteries, their deliberate artistic methods. As one knows the poet by his fine music, so one can recognise the liar by his rich rhythmic utterance, and in neither case will the casual inspiration of the moment suffice. Here, as elsewhere, practice must precede perfection. But in modern days, while the fashion of writing poetry has become far too common, and should, if possible, be discouraged, the fashion of lying has almost fallen into disrepute. Many a young man starts in life with a natural gift for exaggeration which, if nurtured in congenial and sympathetic surroundings, or by the imitation of the best models, might grow into something really great and wonderful. But, as a rule, he comes to nothing. He either falls into careless habits of accuracy – '

CYRIL: My dear fellow!

VIVIAN: Please don't interrupt in the middle of a sentence. 'He either falls into careless habits of accuracy, or takes to frequenting the society of the aged and the well informed. Both things are equally fatal to his imagination, as indeed they would be fatal to the imagination of anybody, and in a short time he develops a morbid and unhealthy faculty of truth-telling, begins to verify all statements made in his presence, has no hesitation in contradicting people who are much younger than himself, and often ends by writing novels which are so lifelike that no one can possibly believe in their probability. This is no isolated instance that we are giving. It is simply one example out of many; and if something cannot be done to check, or at least to modify, our monstrous worship of facts, art will become sterile, and beauty will pass away from the land.

'Even Mr Robert Louis Stevenson, that delightful master of delicate and fanciful prose, is tainted with this modern vice, for we know positively no other name for it. There is such a thing as robbing a story of its reality by trying to make it too true, and *The Black Arrow* is so inartistic as not to contain a single anachronism to boast of, while the transformation of Dr Jekyll reads dangerously like an experiment out of the *Lancet*. As for Mr Rider Haggard, who really has, or had once, the makings of a perfectly magnificent liar, he is now so afraid of being suspected of genius that when he does tell us anything marvellous, he feels bound to invent a personal reminiscence, and to put it into a footnote as a kind of cowardly corroboration. Nor are our other novelists much better. Mr Henry James writes fiction as if it were a painful duty, and wastes upon mean motives and imperceptible "points of view" his neat literary style, his felicitous phrases, his swift and caustic satire. Mr Hall Caine, it is true, aims at the grandiose, but then he writes at the top of his voice. He is so loud that one cannot hear what he says. Mr James Payn is an adept in the art of concealing what is not worth finding. He hunts down the obvious with the enthusiasm of a short-sighted detective. As one turns over the pages, the suspense of the author becomes almost unbearable. The horses of Mr William Black's phaeton do not soar towards the sun. They merely frighten the sky at evening into violent chromolithographic effects. On seeing them approach, the peasants take refuge in dialect. Mrs Oliphant prattles pleasantly about curates, lawn-tennis parties, domesticity, and other wearisome things. Mr Marion Crawford has immolated himself upon the altar of local colour. He is like the lady in the French comedy who keeps talking about *le beau ciel d'Italie*. Besides, he has fallen into the bad habit of uttering moral platitudes. He is always telling us that to be good is to be good, and that to be bad is to be wicked. At times he is almost edifying. *Robert Elsmere* is of course a masterpiece – a masterpiece of the *genre ennuyeux*, the one form of literature that the English people seems thoroughly to enjoy. A thoughtful young friend of ours once told us that it reminded him of the sort of conversation that goes on at a meat tea in the house of a serious Nonconformist family, and we can quite believe it. Indeed it is only in England that such a book could be produced. England is the home of lost ideas. As for that great and daily increasing school of novelists for whom the sun always rises in the East End, the only thing that can be said about them is that they find life crude, and leave it raw.

'In France, though nothing so deliberately tedious as *Robert Elsmere* has been produced, things are not much better. M. Guy de Maupassant, with his keen mordant irony and his hard vivid style, strips life of the few poor rags that still cover her, and shows us foul sore and festering wound. He writes lurid little tragedies in which everybody is ridiculous; bitter comedies at which one cannot laugh for very tears. M. Zola, true to the lofty principle that he lays down in one of his *pronunciamientos* on literature, "L'homme de génie n'a jamais d'esprit", is determined to show that, if he has not got genius, he can at least be dull. And how well he succeeds! He is not without power. Indeed at times, as in *Germinal*, there is something almost epic in his work. But his work is entirely wrong from beginning to end, and wrong not on the ground of morals, but on the ground of art. From any ethical standpoint it is just what it should be. The author is perfectly truthful, and describes things exactly as they happen. What more can any moralist desire? We have no sympathy at all with the moral indignation of our time against M. Zola. It is simply the indignation of Tartuffe on being exposed. But from the standpoint of art, what can be said in favour of the author of *L'Assommoir*, *Nana* and *Pot-Bouille*? Nothing. Mr Ruskin once described the characters in George Eliot's novels as being like the sweepings of a Pentonville omnibus, but M. Zola's characters are much worse. They have their dreary vices, and their drearier virtues. The record of their lives is absolutely without interest. Who cares what happens to them? In literature we require distinction, charm, beauty and imaginative power. We don't want to be harrowed and disgusted with an account of the doings of the lower orders. M. Daudet is better. He has wit, a light touch and an amusing style. But he has lately committed literary suicide. Nobody can possibly care for Delobelle with his "Il faut lutter pour l'art", or for Valmajour with his eternal refrain about the nightingale, or for the poet in *Jack* with his "mots cruels", now that we have learned from *Vingt Ans de Ma Vie Littéraire* that these characters were taken directly from life. To us they seem to have suddenly lost all their vitality, all the few qualities they ever possessed. The only real people are the people who never existed, and if a novelist is base enough to go to life for his personages he should at least pretend that they are creations, and not boast of them as copies. The justification of a character in a novel is not that other persons are what they are, but that the author is what he is. Otherwise the novel is not a work of art. As for M. Paul Bourget, the master of the *roman psychologique*, he commits the error of imagining that the men and women of modern life are capable of being infinitely analysed for an innumerable series of chapters. In point of fact what is interesting about people in good society – and M. Bourget rarely moves out of the Faubourg St Germain, except to come to London – is the mask that each one of them wears, not the reality that lies behind the mask. It is a humiliating confession, but we are all of us made out of the same stuff. In Falstaff there is something of Hamlet, in Hamlet there is not a little of Falstaff. The fat knight has his moods of melancholy, and the young prince his moments of coarse humour. Where we differ from each other is purely in accidentals: in dress, manner, tone of voice, religious opinions, personal appearance, tricks of habit and the like. The more one analyses people, the more all reasons for analysis disappear. Sooner or later one comes to that dreadful universal thing called human nature. Indeed, as anyone who has ever worked among the poor knows only too well, the brotherhood of man is no mere poet's dream, it is a most depressing and humiliating reality; and if a writer insists upon analysing the upper classes, he might just as well write of matchgirls and costermongers at once.'

However, my dear Cyril, I will not detain you any further just here. I quite admit that modern novels have many good points. All I insist on is that, as a class, they are quite unreadable.

CYRIL: That is certainly a very grave qualification, but I must say that I think you are rather unfair in some of your strictures. I like *The Deemster*, and *The Daughter of Heth*, and *Le Disciple*, and *Mr Isaacs*, and as for *Robert Elsmere*, I am quite devoted to it. Not that I can look upon it as a serious work. As a statement of the problems that confront the earnest Christian it is ridiculous and antiquated. It is simply Arnold's *Literature and Dogma* with the literature left out. It is as much behind the age as Paley's *Evidences*, or Colenso's method of biblical exegesis. Nor could anything be less impressive than the unfortunate hero gravely heralding a dawn that rose long ago, and so completely missing its true significance that he proposes to carry on the business of the old firm under the new name. On the other hand, it contains several clever caricatures, and a heap of delightful quotations, and Green's philosophy very pleasantly sugars the somewhat bitter pill of the author's fiction. I also cannot help expressing my surprise that you have said nothing about the two novelists whom you are always reading, Balzac and George Meredith. Surely they are realists, both of them?

VIVIAN: Ah! Meredith! Who can define him? His style is chaos illumined by flashes of lightning. As a writer he has mastered everything except language; as a novelist he can do everything, except tell a story; as an artist he is everything except articulate. Somebody in Shakespeare – Touchstone, I think – talks about a man who is always breaking his shins over his own wit, and it seems to me that this might serve as the basis for a criticism of Meredith's method. But whatever he is, he is not a realist. Or rather I would say that he is a child of realism who is not on speaking terms with his father. By deliberate choice he has made himself a romanticist. He has refused to bow the knee to Baal, and after all, even if the man's fine spirit did not revolt against the noisy assertions of realism, his style would be quite sufficient of itself to keep life at a respectful distance. By its means he has planted round his garden a hedge full of thorns, and red with wonderful roses. As for Balzac, he was a most remarkable combination of the artistic temperament with the scientific spirit. The latter he bequeathed to his disciples. The former was entirely his own. The difference between such a book as M. Zola's *L'Assommoir* and Balzac's *Illusions Perdues* is the difference between unimaginative realism and imaginative reality. 'All Balzac's characters,' said Baudelaire, 'are gifted with the same ardour of life that animated himself. All his fictions are as deeply coloured as dreams. Each mind is a weapon loaded to the muzzle with will. The very scullions have genius.' A steady course of Balzac reduces our living friends to shadows, and our acquaintances to the shadows of shades. His characters have a kind of fervent fiery-coloured existence. They dominate us, and defy scepticism. One of the greatest tragedies of my life is the death of Lucien de Rubempré. It is a grief from which I have never been able completely to rid myself. It haunts me in my moments of pleasure. I remember it when I laugh. But Balzac is no more a realist than Holbein was. He created life, he did not copy it. I admit, however, that he set far too high a value on modernity of form, and that, consequently, there is no book of his that, as an artistic masterpiece, can rank with *Salammbo* or *Esmond*, or *The Cloister and the Hearth*, or the *Vicomte de Bragelonne*.

CYRIL: Do you object to modernity of form, then?

VIVIAN: Yes. It is a huge price to pay for a very poor result. Pure modernity of form is always somewhat vulgarising. It cannot help being so. The public imagine that, because they are interested in their immediate surroundings, art should be interested in them also, and should take them as her subject-matter. But the mere fact that they are interested in these things makes them unsuitable subjects for art. The only beautiful things, as somebody once said, are the things that do not concern us. As long as a thing is useful or necessary to us, or affects us in any way, either for pain or for pleasure, or appeals strongly to our sympathies, or is a vital part of the environment in which we live, it is outside the proper sphere of art. To art's subject-matter we should be more or less indifferent. We should, at any rate, have no preferences, no prejudices, no partisan feeling of any kind. It is exactly because Hecuba is nothing to us that her sorrows are such an admirable motive for a tragedy. I do not know anything in the whole history of literature sadder than the artistic career of Charles Reade. He wrote one beautiful book, *The Cloister and the Hearth*, a book as much above *Romola* as *Romola* is above *Daniel Deronda*, and wasted the rest of his life in a foolish attempt to be modern, to draw public attention to the state of our convict prisons, and the management of our private lunatic asylums. Charles Dickens was depressing enough in all conscience when he tried to arouse our sympathy for the victims of the poor-law administration; but Charles Reade, an artist, a scholar, a man with a true sense of beauty, raging and roaring over the abuses of contemporary life like a common pamphleteer or a sensational journalist, is really a sight for the angels to weep over. Believe me, my dear Cyril, modernity of form and modernity of subject matter are entirely and absolutely wrong. We have mistaken the common livery of the age for the vesture of the Muses, and spend our days in the sordid streets and hideous suburbs of our vile cities when we should be out on the hillside with Apollo. Certainly we are a degraded race, and have sold our birthright for a mess of facts.

CYRIL: There is something in what you say, and there is no doubt that whatever amusement we may find in reading a purely model novel we have rarely any artistic pleasure in rereading it. And this is perhaps the best rough test of what is literature and what is not. If one cannot enjoy reading a book over and over again, there is no use reading it at all. But what do you say about the return to life and nature? This is the panacea that is always being recommended to us.

VIVIAN: I will read you what I say on that subject. The passage comes later on in the article, but I may as well give it to you now. 'The popular cry of our time is, "Let us return to life and nature; they will recreate art for us, and send the red blood coursing through her veins; they will shoe her feet with swiftness and make her hand strong." But, alas! we are mistaken in our amiable and well-meaning efforts. Nature is always behind the age. And as for life, she is the solvent that breaks up art, the enemy that lays waste her house.'

CYRIL: What do you mean by saying that nature is always behind the age?

VIVIAN: Well, perhaps that is rather cryptic. What I mean is this. If we take nature to mean natural simple instinct as opposed to self-conscious culture, the work produced under this influence is always old-fashioned, antiquated and out of date. One touch of nature may make the whole world kin, but two touches of nature will destroy any work of art. If, on the other hand, we regard nature as the collection of phenomena external to man, people only discover in her what they bring to her. She has no suggestions of her own. Wordsworth went to the lakes, but he was never a lake poet. He found in stones the sermons he had already hidden there. He went moralising about the district, but his good work was produced when he returned, not to nature but to poetry. Poetry gave him 'Laodamia', and the fine sonnets, and the great Ode, such as it is. Nature gave him 'Martha Ray' and 'Peter Bell', and the address to Mr Wilkinson's spade.

CYRIL: I think that view might be questioned. I am rather inclined to believe in 'the impulse from a vernal wood', though of course the artistic value of such an impulse depends entirely on the kind of temperament that receives it, so that the return to nature would come to mean simply the advance to a great personality.

You would agree with that, I fancy. However, proceed with your article.

VIVIAN (*reading*): 'Art begins with abstract decoration, with purely imaginative and pleasurable work dealing with what is unreal and non-existent. This is the first stage. Then life becomes fascinated with this new wonder, and asks to be admitted into the charmed circle. Art takes life as part of her rough material, recreates it, and refashions it in fresh forms, is absolutely indifferent to fact, invents, imagines, dreams, and keeps between herself and reality the impenetrable barrier of beautiful style, of decorative or ideal treatment. The third stage is when life gets the upper hand, and drives art out into the wilderness. This is the true decadence, and it is from this that we are now suffering.

'Take the case of the English drama. At first, in the hands of the monks, dramatic art was abstract, decorative and mythological. Then she enlisted life in her service, and using some of life's external forms she created an entirely new race of beings, whose sorrows were more terrible than any sorrow man has ever felt, whose joys were keener than any lover's joys, who had the rage of the Titans and the calm of the gods, who had monstrous and marvellous sins, monstrous and marvellous virtues. To them she gave a language different from that of actual use, a language full of resonant music and sweet rhythm, made stately by solemn cadence, or made delicate by fanciful rhyme, jewelled with wonderful words, and enriched with lofty diction. She clothed her children in strange raiment and gave them masks, and at her bidding the antique world rose from its marble tomb. A new Caesar stalked through the streets of risen Rome, and with purple sail and flute-led oars another Cleopatra passed up the river to Antioch. Old myth and legend and dream took shape and substance. History was entirely rewritten, and there was hardly one of the dramatists who did not recognise that the object of art is not simple truth but complex beauty. In this they were perfectly right. Art itself is really a form of exaggeration; and selection, which is the very spirit of art, is nothing more than an intensified mode of over-emphasis.

'But life soon shattered the perfection of the form. Even in

Shakespeare we can see the beginning of the end. It shows itself by the gradual breaking-up of the blank-verse in the later plays, by the predominance given to prose, and by the over-importance assigned to characterisation. The passages in Shakespeare – and they are many – where the language is uncouth, vulgar, exaggerated, fantastic, obscene even, are entirely due to life calling for an echo of her own voice, and rejecting the intervention of beautiful style, through which alone should life be suffered to find expression. Shakespeare is not by any means a flawless artist. He is too fond of going directly to life, and borrowing life's natural utterance. He forgets that when art surrenders her imaginative medium she surrenders everything. Goethe says, somewhere –

In der Beschränkung zeigt sich erst der Meister.

'It is in working within limits that the master reveals himself, and the limitation, the very condition of any art, is style. However, we need not linger any longer over Shakespeare's realism. *The Tempest* is the most perfect of palinodes. All that we desired to point out was that the magnificent work of the Elizabethan and Jacobean artists contained within itself the seeds of its own dissolution, and that, if it drew some of its strength from using life as rough material, it drew all its weakness from using life as an artistic method. As the inevitable result of this substitution of an imitative for a creative medium, this surrender of an imaginative form, we have the modern English melodrama. The characters in these plays talk on the stage exactly as they would talk off it; they have neither aspirations nor aspirates; they are taken directly from life and reproduce its vulgarity down to the smallest detail; they present the gait, manner, costume and accent of real people; they would pass unnoticed in a third-class railway carriage. And yet how wearisome the plays are! They do not succeed in producing even that impression of reality at which they aim, and which is their only reason for existing. As a method, realism is a complete failure.

'What is true about the drama and the novel is no less true about those arts that we call the decorative arts. The whole history of these arts in Europe is the record of the struggle between

Orientalism, with its frank rejection of imitation, its love of artistic convention, its dislike to the actual representation of any object in nature, and our own imitative spirit. Wherever the former has been paramount, as in Byzantium, Sicily and Spain, by actual contact or in the rest of Europe by the influence of the Crusades we have had beautiful and imaginative work in which the visible things of life are transmuted into artistic conventions, and the things that life has not are invented and fashioned for her delight. But wherever we have returned to life and nature, our work has always become vulgar, common and uninteresting. Modern tapestry, with its aerial effects, its elaborate perspective, its broad expanses of waste sky, its faithful and laborious realism, has no beauty whatsoever. The pictorial glass of Germany is absolutely detestable. We are beginning to weave possible carpets in England but only because we have returned to the method and spirit of the East. Our rugs and carpets of twenty years ago, with their solemn depressing truths, their inane worship of nature, their sordid reproductions of visible objects, have become, even to the philistine, a source of laughter. A cultured Mahomedan once remarked to us, "You Christians are so occupied in misinterpreting the fourth commandment that you have never thought of making an artistic application of the second." He was perfectly right, and the whole truth of the matter is this: The proper school to learn art in is not life but art.'

And now let me read you a passage which seems to me to settle the question very completely.

'It was not always thus. We need not say anything about the poets, for they, with the unfortunate exception of Mr Wordsworth, have been really faithful to their high mission, and are universally recognised as being absolutely unreliable. But in the works of Herodotus, who, in spite of the shallow and ungenerous attempts of modern sciolists to verify his history, may justly be called the "Father of Lies"; in the published speeches of Cicero and the biographies of Suetonius; in Tacitus at his best; in Pliny's *Natural History*; in Hanno's *Periplus*; in all the early chronicles; in the *Lives of the Saints*; in Froissart and Sir Thomas Malory; in the travels of Marco Polo; in Olaus Magnus and

Aldrovandus and Conrad Lycosthenes, with his magnificent *Prodigiorum et Ostentorum Chronicon*; in the autobiography of Benvenuto Cellini; in the memoirs of Casanova; in Defoe's *History of the Plague*; in Boswell's *Life of Johnson*; in Napoleon's despatches; and in the works of our own Carlyle, whose *French Revolution* is one of the most fascinating historical novels ever written, facts are either kept in their proper subordinate position, or else entirely excluded on the general ground of dullness. Now, everything is changed. Facts are not merely finding a footing-place in history, but they are usurping the domain of fancy, and have invaded the kingdom of romance. Their chilling touch is over everything. They are vulgarising mankind. The crude commercialism of America, its materialising spirit, its indifference to the poetical side of things, and its lack of imagination and of high unattainable ideals, are entirely due to that country having adopted for its national hero a man who, according to his own confession, was incapable of telling a lie, and it is not too much to say that the story of George Washington and the cherry tree has done more harm, and in a shorter space of time, than any other moral tale in the whole of literature.'

CYRIL: My dear boy!

VIVIAN: I assure you it is the case, and the amusing part of the whole thing is that the story of the cherry tree is an absolute myth. However, you must not think that I am too despondent about the artistic future either of America or of our own country. Listen to this:

'That some change will take place before this century has drawn to its close we have no doubt whatsoever. Bored by the tedious and improving conversation of those who have neither the wit to exaggerate nor the genius to romance, tired of the intelligent person whose reminiscences are always based upon memory, whose statements are invariably limited by probability, and who is at any time liable to be corroborated by the merest philistine who happens to be present, society sooner or later must return to its lost leader, the cultured and fascinating liar. Who he was who first, without ever having gone out to the rude chase, told the wandering cavemen at sunset how he had dragged the Megatherium from the purple darkness of its jasper cave, or slain the Mammoth in single combat and brought back its gilded tusks, we cannot tell, and not one of our modern anthropologists, for all their much-boasted science, has had the ordinary courage to tell us. Whatever was his name or race, he certainly was the true founder of social inter-course. For the aim of the liar is simply to charm, to delight, to give pleasure. He is the very basis of civilised society, and without him a dinner-party, even at the mansions of the great, is as dull as a lecture at the Royal Society, or a debate at the Incorporated Authors, or one of Mr Burnand's farcical comedies.

'Nor will he be welcomed by society alone. Art breaking from the prison-house of realism will run to greet him, and will kiss his false, beautiful lips, knowing that he alone is in possession of the great secret of all her manifestations, the secret that truth is entirely and absolutely a matter of style; while life – poor, probable, uninteresting human life – tired of repeating herself for the benefit of Mr Herbert Spencer, scientific historians, and the compilers of statistics in general, will follow meekly after him, and try to reproduce, in her own simple and untutored way, some of the marvels of which he talks.

'No doubt there will always be critics who, like a certain writer in the *Saturday Review*, will gravely censure the teller of fairy tales for his defective knowledge of natural history, who will measure imaginative work by their own lack of any imaginative faculty, and will hold up their ink-stained hands in horror if some honest gentleman, who has never been farther than the yew trees of his own garden, pens a fascinating book of travels like Sir John Mandeville, or, like great Raleigh, writes a whole history of the world, without knowing anything whatsoever about the past. To excuse themselves they will try and shelter under the shield of him who made Prospero the magician, and gave him Caliban and Ariel as his servants, who heard the Tritons blowing their horns round the coral reef of the Enchanted Isle, and the fairies singing to each other in a wood near Athens, who led the phantom kings in dim procession across the misty Scottish heath, and hid Hecate in a cave with the weird sisters. They will call upon Shakespeare – they always do – and will quote that hackneyed passage, forgetting that this unfortunate aphorism about art holding the mirror up to nature is deliberately said by Hamlet in order to convince the bystanders of his absolute insanity in all art-matters.'

CYRIL: Ahem! Another cigarette, please.

VIVIAN: My dear fellow, whatever you may say, it is merely a dramatic utterance, and no more represents Shakespeare's real views upon art than the speeches of Iago represent his real views upon morals. But let me get to the end of the passage:

'Art finds her own perfection within, and not outside of, herself. She is not to be judged by any external standard of resemblance. She is a veil, rather than a mirror. She has flowers that no forests know of, birds that no woodland possesses. She makes and unmakes many worlds, and can draw the moon from heaven with a scarlet thread. Hers are the "forms more real than living man", and hers the great archetypes of which things that have existence are but unfinished copies. Nature has, in her eyes, no laws, no uniformity. She can work miracles at her will, and when she calls monsters from the deep they come. She can bid the almond tree blossom in winter, and send the snow upon the ripe cornfield. At her word the frost lays its silver finger on the burning mouth of June, and the winged lions creep out from the hollows of the Lydian hills. The dryads peer from the thicket as she passes by, and the brown fauns smile strangely at her when she comes near them. She has hawk-faced gods that worship her, and the centaurs gallop at her side.'

CYRIL: I like that. I can see it. Is that the end?

VIVIAN: No. There is one more passage, but it is purely practical. It simply suggests some methods by which we could revive this lost art of lying.

CYRIL: Well, before you read it to me, I should like to ask you a question. What do you mean by saying that life, 'poor, probable, uninteresting human life', will try to reproduce the marvels of art? I can quite understand your objection to art being treated as a mirror. You think it would reduce genius to the position of a cracked looking-glass. But you don't mean to say that you seriously believe that life imitates art, that life in fact is the mirror, and art the reality?

VIVIAN: Certainly I do. Paradox though it may seem – and paradoxes are always dangerous things – it is none the less true that life imitates art far more than art imitates life. We have all seen in our own day in England how a certain curious and fascinating type of beauty, invented and emphasised by two imaginative painters, has so influenced life that whenever one goes to a private view or to an artistic salon one sees, here the mystic eyes of Rossetti's dream, the long ivory throat, the strange square-cut jaw, the loosened shadowy hair that he so ardently loved, there the sweet maidenhood of 'The Golden Stair', the blossom-like mouth and weary loveliness of the 'Laus Amoris', the passion-pale face of Andromeda, the thin hands and lithe beauty of the Vivian in 'Merlin's Dream'. And it has always been so. A great artist invents a type, and life tries to copy it, to reproduce it in a popular form, like an enterprising publisher. Neither Holbein nor Vandyck found in England what they have given us. They brought their types with them, and life with her keen imitative faculty set herself to supply the master with models. The Greeks, with their quick artistic instinct, understood this, and set in the bride's chamber the statue of Hermes or of Apollo, that she might bear children as lovely as the works of art that she looked at in her rapture or her pain. They knew that life gains from art not merely spirituality, depth of thought and feeling, soul-turmoil or soul-peace, but that she can form herself on the very lines and colours of art, and can reproduce the dignity of Pheidias as well as the grace of Praxiteles. Hence came their objection to realism. They disliked it on purely social grounds. They felt that it inevitably makes people ugly, and they were perfectly right. We try to improve the conditions of the race by means of good air, free sunlight, wholesome water, and hideous bare buildings for the better housing of the lower orders. But these things merely produce health, they do not produce beauty. For this, art is required, and the true disciples of the great artist are not his studio-imitators, but those who become like his works of art, be they plastic as in Greek days, or pictorial as in modern times; in a word, life is art's best, art's only pupil.

As it is with the visible arts, so it is with literature. The most obvious and the vulgarest form in which this is shown is in the case of the silly boys who, after reading the adventures of Jack Sheppard or Dick Turpin, pillage the stalls of unfortunate apple-women, break into sweet-shops at night, and alarm old gentlemen who are returning home from the city by leaping out on them in suburban lanes, with black masks and unloaded revolvers. This interesting phenomenon, which always occurs after the appearance of a new edition of either of the books I have alluded to, is usually attributed to the influence of literature on the imagination. But this is a mistake. The imagination is essentially creative, and always seeks for a new form. The boy-burglar is simply the inevitable result of life's imitative instinct. He is fact occupied, as fact usually is, with trying to reproduce fiction, and what we see in him is repeated on an extended scale throughout the whole of life. Schopenhauer has analysed the pessimism that characterises modern thought, but Hamlet invented it. The world has become sad because a puppet was once melancholy. The Nihilist, that strange martyr who has no faith, who goes to the stake without enthusiasm, and dies for what he does not believe in, is a purely literary product. He was invented by Turgenev, and completed by Dostoevsky. Robespierre came out of the pages of Rousseau as surely as the People's Palace rose out of the debris of a novel. Literature always anticipates life. It does not copy it, but moulds it to its purpose. The nineteenth century, as we know it, is largely an invention of Balzac. Our Luciens de Rubempré, our Rastignaes and De Marsays made their first appearance on the stage of the *Comédie Humaine*. We are merely carrying out, with footnotes and unnecessary additions, the whim or fancy or creative vision of a great novelist. I once asked a lady, who knew Thackeray intimately, whether he had had any model for Becky Sharp. She told me that Becky was an invention, but that the idea of the character had been partly suggested by a governess who lived in the neighbourhood of Kensington Square, and was the companion of a very selfish and rich old woman. I inquired what became of the governess, and she replied that, oddly enough, some years after the appearance of *Vanity Fair*, she ran away with the nephew of the lady with whom she was living, and for a short time made a great splash in society, quite in Mrs Rawdon Crawley's style, and entirely by Mrs Rawdon Crawley's methods. Ultimately she came to grief, disappeared to the Continent, and used to be occasionally seen at Monte Carlo and other gambling places. The noble gentleman from whom the same great sentimentalist drew Colonel Newcome died, a few months after *The Newcomes* had reached a fourth edition, with the word '*Adsum*' on his lips. Shortly after Mr Stevenson published his curious psychological story of transformation, a friend of mine, called Mr Hyde, was in the north of London, and being anxious to get to a railway station, took what he thought would be a short cut, lost his way, and found himself in a network of mean, evil-looking streets. Feeling rather nervous he began to walk extremely fast, when suddenly out of an archway ran a child right between his legs. It fell on the pavement, he tripped over it, and trampled upon it. Being, of course, very much frightened and a little hurt, it began to scream, and in a few seconds the whole street was full of rough people who came pouring out of the houses like ants. They surrounded him, and asked him his name. He was just about to give it when he suddenly remembered the opening incident in Mr Stevenson's story. He was so filled with horror at having realised in his own person that terrible and well-written scene, and at having done accidentally, though in fact, what the Mr Hyde of fiction had done with deliberate intent, that he ran away as hard as he could go. He was, however, very closely followed, and finally he took refuge in a surgery, the door of which happened to be open, where he explained to a young assistant, who happened to be there, exactly what had occurred. The humanitarian crowd were induced to go away on his giving them a small sum of money, and as soon as the coast was clear he left. As he passed out, the name on the brass door-plate of the surgery caught his eye. It was 'Jekyll'. At least it should have been.

Here the imitation, as far as it went, was of course accidental. In the following case the imitation was self-conscious. In the year 1879, just after I had left Oxford, I met at a reception at the house of one of the foreign ministers a woman of very curious exotic beauty. We became great friends, and were constantly together. And yet what interested me most in her was not her beauty, but her character, her entire vagueness of character. She seemed to have no personality at all, but simply the possibility of many types. Sometimes she would give herself up entirely to art, turn her drawing-room into a studio, and spend two or three days a week at picture galleries or museums. Then she would take to attending race-meetings, wear the most horsey clothes, and talk about nothing but betting. She abandoned religion for mesmerism, mesmerism for politics, and politics for the melodramatic excitements of philanthropy. In fact, she was a kind of Proteus, and as much a failure in all her transformations as was that wondrous sea-god when Odysseus laid hold of him. One day a serial began in one of the French magazines. At that time I used to read serial stories, and I well remember the shock of surprise I felt when I came to the description of the heroine. She was so like my friend that I brought her the magazine, and she recognised herself in it immediately, and seemed fascinated by the resemblance. I should tell you, by the way, that the story was translated from some dead Russian writer, so that the author had not taken his type from my friend. Well, to put the matter briefly, some months afterwards I was in Venice and finding the magazine in the reading-room of the hotel, I took it up casually to see what had become of the heroine. It was a most piteous tale, as the girl had ended by running away with a man absolutely inferior to her, not merely in social station, but in character and intellect also. I wrote to my friend that evening about my views on John Bellini, and the admirable ices at Florian's, and the artistic value of gondolas, but added a postscript to the effect that her double in the story had behaved in a very silly manner. I don't know why I added that, but I remember I had a sort of dread over me that she might do the same thing. Before my letter had reached her, she had run away with a man who deserted her in six months. I saw her in 1884 in Paris, where she was living with her mother, and I asked her whether the story had had anything to do with her action. She told me that she had felt an absolutely irresistible impulse to follow the heroine step by step in her strange and fatal progress, and that it was with a feeling of real terror that she had looked forward to the last few chapters of the story. When they appeared, it seemed to her that she was compelled to reproduce them in life, and she did so. It was a most clear example of this imitative instinct of which I was speaking, and an extremely tragic one.

However, I do not wish to dwell any further upon individual instances. Personal experience is a most vicious and limited circle. All that I desire to point out is the general principle that life imitates art far more than art imitates life, and I feel sure that if you think seriously about it you will find that it is true. Life holds the mirror up to art, and either reproduces some strange type imagined by painter or sculptor, or realises in fact what has been dreamed in fiction. Scientifically speaking, the basis of life – the energy of life, as Aristotle would call it – is simply the desire for expression, and art is always presenting various forms through which the expression can be attained. Life seizes on them and uses them, even if they be to her own hurt. Young men have committed suicide because Rolla did so, have died by their own hand because by his own hand Werther died. Think of what we owe to the imitation of Christ, of what we owe to the imitation of Caesar.

CYRIL: The theory is certainly a very curious one, but to make it complete you must show that nature, no less than life, is an imitation of art. Are you prepared to prove that?

VIVIAN: My dear fellow, I am prepared to prove anything.

CYRIL: Nature follows the landscape painter, then, and takes her effects from him?

VIVIAN: Certainly. Where, if not from the Impressionists, do we get those wonderful brown fogs that come creeping down our streets, blurring the gas-lamps and changing the houses into monstrous shadows? To whom, if not to them and their master, do we owe the lovely silver mists that brood over our river, and turn to faint forms of fading grace curved bridge and swaying barge? The extraordinary change that has taken place in the climate of London during the last ten years is entirely due to a particular school of art. You smile. Consider the matter from a scientific or a metaphysical point of view, and you will find that I am right. For what is nature? Nature is no great mother who has borne us. She is our creation. It is in our brain that she quickens to life. Things are because we see them, and what we see, and how we see it, depends on the arts that have influenced us. To look at a thing is very different from seeing a thing. One does not see anything until one sees its beauty. Then, and then only, does it come into existence. At present, people see fogs, not because there are fogs, but because poets and painters have taught them the mysterious loveliness of such effects. There may have been fogs for centuries in London. I dare say there were. But no one saw them, and so we do not know anything about them. They did not exist till art had invented them. Now, it must be admitted, fogs are carried to excess. They have become the mere manner-ism of a clique, and the exaggerated realism of their method gives dull people bronchitis. Where the cultured catch an effect, the uncultured catch cold. And so, let us be humane, and invite art to turn her wonderful eyes elsewhere. She has done so already, indeed. That white quivering sunlight that one sees now in France, with its strange blotches of mauve, and its restless violet shadows, is her latest fancy, and, on the whole, nature reproduces it quite admirably. Where she used to give us Corots and Daubignys, she gives us now exquisite Monets and entrancing Pissarros. Indeed there are moments, rare, it is true, but still to be observed from time to time, when nature becomes absolutely modern. Of course she is not always to be relied upon. The fact is that she is in this unfortunate position. Art creates an incom-parable and unique effect, and, having done so, passes on to other things. Nature, upon the other hand, forgetting that imitation can be made the sincerest form of insult, keeps on repeating this effect until we all become absolutely wearied of it. Nobody of any real culture, for instance, ever talks nowadays about the beauty of a sunset. Sunsets are quite old-fashioned. They belong to the time when Turner was the last note in art. To admire them is a distinct sign of provincialism of temperament. Upon the other hand they go on. Yesterday evening Mrs Arundel insisted on my going to the window, and looking at the glorious sky, as she called it. Of course I had to look at it. She is one of those absurdly pretty philistines to whom one can deny nothing. And what was it? It was simply a very second-rate Turner, a Turner of a bad period, with all the painter's worst faults exaggerated and over-emphasised. Of course, I am quite ready to admit that life very often commits the same error. She produces her false Renés and her sham Vautrins, just as nature gives us on one day a doubtful Cuyp and on another a more than questionable Rousseau. Still, nature irritates one more when she does things of that kind. It seems so stupid, so obvious, so unnecessary. A false Vautrin might be delightful. A doubtful Cuyp is unbearable. However, I don't want to be too hard on nature. I wish the Channel, especially at Hastings, did not look quite so often like a Henry Moore, grey pearl with yellow lights, but then, when art is more varied, nature will, no doubt, be more varied also. That she imitates art, I don't think even her worst enemy would deny now. It is the one thing that keeps her in touch with civilised man. But have I proved my theory to your satisfaction?

CYRIL: You have proved it to my dissatisfaction, which is better. But even admitting this strange imitative instinct in life and nature, surely you would acknowledge that art expresses the temper of its age, the spirit of its time, the moral and social conditions that surround it, and under whose influence it is produced

VIVIAN: Certainly not! art never expresses anything but itself. This is the principle of my new aesthetics; and it is this, more than that vital connection between form and substance, on which Mr Pater dwells, that makes basic the type of all the arts. Of course, nations and individuals, with that healthy natural vanity which is the secret of existence, are always under the impression that it is of them that the Muses are talking, always trying to find in the calm dignity of imaginative art some mirror of their own turbid passions, always forgetting that the singer of life is not Apollo but Marsyas. Remote from reality, and with her eyes turned away from the shadows of the cave, art reveals her own perfection, and the wondering crowd that watches the opening of the marvellous, many-petalled rose fancies that it is its own history that is being told to it, its own spirit that is finding expression in a new form. But it is not so. The highest art rejects the burden of the human spirit and gains more from a new medium or a fresh material than she does from any enthusiasm for art, or from any lofty passion, or from any great awakening of the human consciousness. She develops purely on her own lines. She is not symbolic of any age. It is the ages that are her symbols.

Even those who hold that art is representative of time and place and people cannot help admitting that the more imitative an art is, the less it represents to us the spirit of its age. The evil faces of the Roman emperors look out at us from the foul porphyry and spotted jasper in which the realistic artists of the day delighted to work, and we fancy that in those cruel lips and heavy sensual jaws we can find the secret of the ruin of the Empire. But it was not so. The vices of Tiberius could not destroy that supreme civilisation, any more than the virtues of the Antonines could save it. It fell for other, for less interesting reasons. The sibyls and prophets of the Sistine may indeed serve to interpret for some that new birth of the emancipated spirit that we call the Renaissance; but what do the drunken boors and bawling peasants of Dutch art tell us about the great soul of Holland? The more abstract, the more ideal an art is, the more it reveals to us the temper of its age. If we wish to understand a nation by means of its art, let us look at its architecture or its music.

CYRIL: I quite agree with you there. The spirit of an age may be best expressed in the abstract ideal arts, for the spirit itself is abstract and ideal. Upon the other hand, for the visible aspect of an age, for its look, as the phrase goes, we must of course go to the arts of imitation.

VIVIAN: I don't think so. After all, what the imitative arts really give us are merely the various styles of particular artists, or of certain schools of artists. Surely you don't imagine that the people of the Middle Ages bore any resemblance at all to the figures on mediaeval stained glass, or in mediaeval stone and wood carving, or on mediaeval metalwork or tapestries or illuminated manuscripts. They were probably very ordinary-looking people, with nothing grotesque, or remarkable, or fantastic in their appearance. The Middle Ages, as we know them in art, are simply a definite form of style and there is no reason at all why an artist with this style should not be produced in the nineteenth century. No great artist ever sees things as they really are. If he did, he would cease to be an artist. Take an example from our own day. I know that you are fond of Japanese things. Now, do you really imagine that the Japanese people, as they are presented to us in art, have any existence? If you do, you have never understood Japanese art at all. The Japanese people are the deliberate self-conscious creation of certain individual artists. If you set a picture by Hokusai, or Hokkei, or any of the great native painters, beside a real Japanese gentleman or lady, you will see that there is not the slightest resemblance between them. The actual people who live in Japan are not unlike the general run of English people; that is to say, they are extremely commonplace, and have nothing curious or extraordinary about them. In fact, the whole of Japan is a pure invention. There is no such country, there are no such people. One of our most charming painters went recently to the Land of the Chrysanthemum in the foolish hope of seeing the Japanese. All he saw, all he had the chance of painting, were a few lanterns and some fans. He was quite unable to discover the inhabitants, as his delightful exhibition at Messrs Dowdeswell's Gallery showed only too well. He did not know that the Japanese people are, as I have said, simply a mode of style, an exquisite fancy of art. And so, if you desire to see a Japanese effect, you will not behave like a tourist and go to Tokyo. On the contrary, you will stay at home and steep yourself in the work of certain Japanese artists, and then, when you have absorbed the spirit of their style, and caught their imaginative manner of vision, you will go some afternoon and sit in the park or stroll down Piccadilly, and if you cannot see an absolutely Japanese effect there, you will not see it anywhere. Or, to return again to the past, take as another instance the ancient Greeks. Do you think that Greek art ever tells us what the Greek people were like? Do you believe that the Athenian women were like the stately dignified figures of the Parthenon frieze, or like those marvellous goddesses who sat in the triangular pediments of the same building? If you judge from the art, they certainly were so.

But read an authority, like Aristophanes, for instance. You will find that the Athenian ladies laced tightly, wore high-heeled shoes, dyed their hair yellow, painted and rouged their faces, and were exactly like any silly fashionable or fallen creature of our own day. The fact is that we look back on the ages entirely through the medium of art, and art, very fortunately, has never once told us the truth.

CYRIL: But modern portraits by English painters, what of them? Surely they are like the people they pretend to represent?

VIVIAN: Quite so. They are so like them that a hundred years from now no one will believe in them. The only portraits in which one believes are portraits where there is very little of the sitter, and a very great deal of the artist. Holbein's drawings of the men and women of his time impress us with a sense of their absolute reality. But this is simply because Holbein compelled life to accept his conditions, to restrain itself within his limitations, to reproduce his type and to appear as he wished it to appear. It is style that makes us believe in a thing – nothing but style. Most of our modern portrait painters are doomed to absolute oblivion. They never paint what they see. They paint what the public sees, and the public never sees anything.

CYRIL: Well, after that I think I should like to hear the end of your article.

VIVIAN: With pleasure. Whether it will do any good I really cannot say. Ours is certainly the dullest and most prosaic century possible. Why, even sleep has played us false, and has closed up the gates of ivory and opened the gates of horn. The dreams of the great middle classes of this country, as recorded in Mr Myers's two bulky volumes on the subject, and in the *Transactions of the Psychical Society*, are the most depressing things I have ever read. There is not even a fine nightmare among them. They are commonplace, sordid and tedious. As for the church I cannot conceive anything better for the culture of a country than the presence in it of a body of men whose duty it is to believe in the supernatural, to perform daily miracles, and to keep alive that mythopoeic faculty which is so essential for the imagination. But in the English church a man succeeds, not through his capacity for belief but through his capacity for disbelief. Ours is the only church where the sceptic stands at the altar and where St Thomas is regarded as the ideal apostle. Many a worthy clergyman, who passes his life in admirable works of kindly charity, lives and dies unnoticed and unknown; but it is sufficient for some shallow uneducated passman out of either university to get up in his pulpit and express his doubts about Noah's ark, or Balaam's ass, or Jonah and the whale, for half of London to flock to hear him, and to sit open-mouthed in rapt admiration at his superb intellect. The growth of common sense in the English church is a thing very much to be regretted. It is really a degrading concession to a low form of realism. It is silly, too. It springs from an entire ignorance of psychology. Man can believe the impossible, but man can never believe the improbable. However, I must read the end of my article:

'What we have to do, what at any rate it is our duty to do, is to revive this old art of lying. Much, of course, may be done, in the way of educating the public, by amateurs, in the domestic circle, at literary lunches and at afternoon teas. But this is merely the light and graceful side of lying, such as was probably heard at Cretan dinner-parties. There are many other forms. Lying for the sake of gaining some immediate personal advantage for instance – lying with a moral purpose, as it is usually called – though of late it has been rather looked down upon, was extremely popular with the antique world. Athena laughs when Odysseus tells her "his words of sly devising", as Mr William Morris phrases it, and the glory of mendacity illumines the pale brow of the stainless hero of Euripidean tragedy, and sets among the noble women of the past the young bride of one of Horace's most exquisite odes. Later on, what at first had been merely a natural instinct was elevated into a self-conscious science. Elaborate rules were laid down for the guidance of mankind, and an important school of literature grew up round the subject. Indeed when one remembers the excellent philosophical treatise of Sanchez on the whole question, one cannot help regretting that no one has ever thought of publishing a cheap and condensed edition of the works of that great casuist. A short primer, *When to Lie and How*, if brought out in attractive and not too expensive a form, would no doubt command a large sale, and would prove of real practical service to many earnest and deep-thinking people. Lying for the sake of the improvement of the young, which is the basis of home education, still lingers amongst us, and its advantages are so admirably set forth in the early books of Plato's *Republic* that it is unnecessary to dwell upon them here. It is a mode of lying for which all good mothers have peculiar capabilities, but it is capable of still further development, and has been sadly overlooked by the school board. Lying for the sake of a monthly salary is of course well known in Fleet Street, and the profession of a political leader-writer is not without its advantages. But it is said to be a somewhat dull occupation, and it certainly does not lead to much beyond a kind of ostentatious obscurity. The only form of lying that is absolutely beyond reproach is lying for its own sake, and the highest development of this is, as we have already pointed out, lying in art. Just as those who do not love Plato more than truth cannot pass beyond the threshold of Academe, so those who do not love beauty more than truth never know the inmost shrine of art. The solid, stolid British intellect lies in the desert sands like the Sphinx in Flaubert's marvellous tale, and fantasy, *La Chimère*, dances round it, and calls to it with her false, flute-toned voice. It may not hear her now, but surely someday, when we are all bored to death with the commonplace character of modern fiction, it will hearken to her and try to borrow her wings.

'And when that day dawns, or sunset reddens, how joyous we shall all be! Facts will be regarded as discreditable, truth will be found mourning over her fetters, and romance, with her temper of wonder, will return to the land. The very aspect of the world will change to our startled eyes. Out of the sea will rise Behemoth and Leviathan, and sail round the high-pooped galleys, as they do on the delightful maps of those ages when books on geography were actually readable. Dragons will wander about the waste places and the phoenix will soar from her nest of fire into the air. We shall lay our hands upon the basilisk, and see the jewel in the toad's head. Champing his gilded oats, the hippogriff will stand in our stalls, and over our heads will float the bluebird singing of beautiful and impossible things, of things that are lovely and that never happen, of things that are not and that should be. But before this comes to pass we must cultivate the lost art of lying.'

CYRIL: Then we must entirely cultivate it at once. But in order to avoid making any error I want you to tell me briefly the doctrines of the new aesthetics.

VIVIAN: Briefly, then, they are these. Art never expresses anything but itself. It has an independent life, just as thought has, and develops purely on its own lines. It is not necessarily realistic in an age of realism, nor spiritual in an age of faith. So far from being the creation of its time, it is usually in direct opposition to it, and the only history that it preserves for us is the history of its own progress. Sometimes it returns upon its footsteps and revives some antique form, as happened in the archaistic movement of late Greek art, and in the pre-Raphaelite movement of our own day. At other times it entirely anticipates its age, and produces in one century work that it takes another century to understand, to appreciate and to enjoy. In no case does it reproduce its age. To pass from the art of a time to the time itself is the great mistake that all historians commit

The second doctrine is this. All bad art comes from returning to life and nature, and elevating them into ideals. Life and nature may sometimes be used as part of art's rough material, but before they are of any real service to art they must be translated into artistic conventions. The moment art surrenders its imaginative medium it surrenders everything. As a method Realism is a complete failure, and the two things that every artist should avoid are modernity of form and modernity of subject-matter. To us, who live in the nineteenth century, any century is a suitable subject for art except our own. The only beautiful things are the things that do not concern us. It is, to have the pleasure of quoting myself, exactly because Hecuba is nothing to us that her sorrows are so suitable a motive for a tragedy. Besides, it is only the modern that ever becomes old-fashioned. M. Zola sits down to give us a picture of the Second Empire. Who cares for the Second Empire now? It is out of date. Life goes faster than realism, but romanticism is always in front of life.

The third doctrine is that life imitates art far more than art imitates life. This results not merely from life's imitative instinct, but from the fact that the self-conscious aim of life is to find expression, and that art offers it certain beautiful forms through which it may realise that energy. It is a theory that has never been put forward before, but it is extremely fruitful, and throws an entirely new light upon the history of art.

It follows as a corollary from this, that external nature also imitates art. The only effects that she can show us are effects that we have already seen through poetry, or in paintings. This is the secret of nature's charm, as well as the explanation of nature's weakness.

The final revelation is that lying, the telling of beautiful untrue things, is the proper aim of art. But of this I think I have spoken at sufficient length. And now let us go out on the terrace, where 'droops the milk-white peacock like a ghost', while the evening star 'washes the dusk with silver'. At twilight nature becomes a wonderfully suggestive effect, and is not without loveliness, though perhaps its chief use is to illustrate quotations from the poets. Come! We have talked long enough.

THE CRITIC AS ARTIST
A Dialogue in Two Parts

Part One

PERSONS: Gilbert and Ernest.
SCENE: The library of a house in Piccadilly,
overlooking Green Park.

GILBERT (*at the piano*): My dear Ernest what are you laughing at?

ERNEST (looking up): At a capital story at I have just come across in this volume of reminiscences that I have found on your table.

GILBERT: What is the book? Ah! I see. I have not read it yet. Is it good?

ERNEST: Well, while you have been playing, I have been turning over the pages with some amusement, though, as a rule, I dislike modern memoirs. They are generally written by people who have either entirely lost their memories, or have never done anything worth remembering; which, however, is, no doubt, the true explanation of their popularity, as the English public always feels perfectly at its ease when a mediocrity is talking to it.

GILBERT: Yes; the public is wonderfully tolerant. It forgives everything except genius. But I must confess that I like all memoirs. I like them for their form, just as much as for their matter. In literature mere egotism is delightful. It is what fascinates us in the letters of personalities so different as Cicero and Balzac, Flaubert and Berlioz, Byron and Madame de Sévigné. Whenever we come across it, and, strangely enough, it is rather rare, we cannot but welcome it, and do not easily forget it. Humanity will always love Rousseau for having confessed his sins, not to a priest, but to the world, and the couchant nymphs that Cellini wrought in bronze for the castle of King Francis, the green and gold Perseus, even, that in the open Loggia at Florence shows the moon the dead terror that once turned life to stone, have not given it more pleasure than has that autobiography in which the supreme scoundrel of the Renaissance relates the story of his splendour and his shame. The opinions, the character, the achievements of the man, matter very little. He may be a sceptic like the gentle Sieur de Montaigne, or a saint like the bitter son of Monica, but when he tells us his own secrets he can always charm our ears to listening and our lips to silence. The mode of thought that Cardinal Newman represented – if that can be called a mode of thought which seeks to solve intellectual problems by a denial of the supremacy of the intellect – may not, cannot, I think, survive. But the world will never weary of watching that troubled soul in its progress from darkness to darkness. The lonely church at Littlemore, where 'the breath of the morning is damp, and worshippers are few', will always be dear to it, and whenever men see the yellow snapdragon blossoming on the wall of Trinity they will think of that gracious undergraduate who saw in the flower's sure recurrence a prophecy that he would abide for ever with the Benign Mother of his days – a prophecy that Faith, in her wisdom or her folly, suffered not to be fulfilled. Yes; autobiography is irresistible. Poor, silly, conceited Mr Secretary Pepys has chattered his way into the circle of the Immortals, and, conscious that indiscretion is the better part of valour, bustles about among them in that 'shaggy purple gown with gold buttons and looped lace' which he is so fond of describing to us, perfectly at his ease, and prattling, to his own and our infinite pleasure, of the Indian blue petticoat that he bought for his wife, of the 'good hog's harslet' and the 'pleasant French fricassee of veal' that he loved to eat, of his game of bowls with Will Joyce, and his 'gadding after beauties', and his reciting of *Hamlet* on a Sunday, and his playing of the viol on weekdays, and other wicked or trivial things. Even in actual life egotism is not without its attractions. When people talk to us about others they are usually dull. When they talk to us about themselves they are nearly always interesting, and if one could shut them up, when they become wearisome, as easily as one can shut up a book of which one has grown wearied, they would be perfect absolutely.

ERNEST: There is much virtue in that 'if', as Touchstone would say. But do you seriously propose that every man should become his own Boswell? What would become of our industrious compilers of *Lives* and *Recollections* in that case?

GILBERT: What has become of them? They are the pest of the age, nothing more and nothing less. Every great man nowadays has his disciples, and it is always Judas who writes the biography.

ERNEST: My dear fellow!

GILBERT: I am afraid it is true. Formerly we used to canonise our heroes. The modern method is to vulgarise them. Cheap editions of great books may be delightful, but cheap editions of great men are absolutely detestable.

ERNEST: May I ask, Gilbert, to whom you allude?

GILBERT: Oh! to all our second-rate *littérateurs*. We are overrun by a set of people who, when poet or painter passes away, arrive at the house along with the undertaker, and forget that their one duty is to behave as mutes. But we won't talk about them. They are the mere body-snatchers of literature. The dust is given to one, and the ashes to another, and the soul is out of their reach. And now, let me play Chopin to you, or Dvořák. Shall I play you a fantasy by Dvořák? He writes passionate, curiously-coloured things.

ERNEST: No; I don't want music just at present. It is far too indefinite. Besides, I took the Baroness Bernstein down to dinner last night, and, though absolutely charming in every other respect, she insisted on discussing music as if it were actually written in the German language. Now, whatever music sounds like, I am glad to say that it does not sound in the smallest degree like German. There are forms of patriotism that are really quite degrading. No; Gilbert, don't play any more. Turn round and talk to me. Talk to me till the white-horned day comes into the room. There is something in your voice that is wonderful.

GILBERT (*rising from the piano*): I am not in a mood for talking tonight. How horrid of you to smile! I really am not. Where are the cigarettes? Thanks. How exquisite these single daffodils are! They seem to be made of amber and cool ivory. They are like

Greek things of the best period. What was the story in the confessions of the remorseful Academician that made you laugh? Tell it to me. After playing Chopin, I feel as if I had been weeping over sins that I had never committed, and mourning over tragedies that were not my own. Music always seems to me to produce that effect. It creates for one a past of which one has been ignorant, and fills one with a sense of sorrows that have been hidden from one's tears. I can fancy a man who had led a perfectly commonplace life, hearing by chance some curious piece of music, and suddenly discovering that his soul, without his being conscious of it, had passed through terrible experiences, and known fearful joys, or wild romantic loves, or great renunciations. And so tell me this story, Ernest. I want to be amused.

ERNEST: Oh! I don't know that it is of any importance. But I thought it a really admirable illustration of the true value of ordinary art-criticism. It seems that a lady once gravely asked the remorseful Academician, as you call him, if his celebrated picture of *A Spring-Day at Whiteley's*, or *Waiting for the Last Omnibus*, or some subject of that kind, was all painted by hand.

GILBERT: And was it?

ERNEST: You are quite incorrigible. But, seriously speaking, what is the use of art-criticism? Why cannot the artist be left alone, to create a new world if he wishes it or, if not, to shadow forth the world which we already know, and of which, I fancy, we would each one of us be wearied if art, with her fine spirit of choice and delicate instinct of selection, did not, as it were, purify it for us, and give to it a momentary perfection. It seems to me that the imagination spreads, or should spread, a solitude around it, and works best in silence and in isolation. Why should the artist be troubled by the shrill clamour of criticism? Why should those who cannot create take upon themselves to estimate the value of creative work? What can they know about it? If a man's work is easy to understand, an explanation is unnecessary . . .

GILBERT: And if his work is incomprehensible, an explanation is wicked.

ERNEST: I did not say that.

GILBERT: Ah! but you should have. Nowadays, we have so few

mysteries left to us that we cannot afford to part with one of them. The members of the Browning Society, like the theologians of the Broad Church Party, or the authors of Mr Walter Scott's Great Writers Series, seem to me to spend their time in trying to explain their divinity away. Where one had hoped that Browning was a mystic they have sought to show that he was simply inarticulate. Where one had fancied that he had something to conceal, they have proved that he had but little to reveal. But I speak merely of his incoherent work. Taken as a whole the man was great. He did not belong to the Olympians, and had all the incompleteness of the Titan. He did not survey and it was but rarely that he could sing. His work is marred by struggle, violence and effort, and he passed not from emotion to form, but from thought to chaos. Still, he was great. He has been called a thinker, and was certainly a man who was always thinking, and always thinking aloud; but it was not thought that fascinated him, but rather the processes by which thought moves. It was the machine he loved, not what the machine makes. The method by which the fool arrives at his folly was as dear to him as the ultimate wisdom of the wise. So much, indeed, did the subtle mechanism of mind fascinate him that he despised language, or looked upon it as an incomplete instrument of expression. Rhyme, that exquisite echo which in the Muse's hollow hill creates and answers its own voice; rhyme, which in the hands of the real artist becomes not merely a material element of metrical beauty, but a spiritual element of thought and passion also, waking a new mood, it may be, or stirring a fresh train of ideas, or opening by mere sweetness and suggestion of sound some golden door at which the Imagination itself had knocked in vain; rhyme, which can turn man's utterance to the speech of gods; rhyme, the one chord we have added to the Greek lyre, became in Robert Browning's hands a grotesque, misshapen thing, which at times made him masquerade in poetry as a low comedian, and ride Pegasus too often with his tongue in his cheek. There are moments when he wounds us by monstrous music. Nay if he can only get his music by breaking the strings of his lute, he breaks them, and they snap in discord, and no Athenian tettix, making melody from tremulous wings, lights on the ivory horn to make the movement perfect, or the interval less harsh. Yet he was great: and though he turned language into ignoble clay, he made from it men and women that live. He is the most Shakespearian creature since Shakespeare. If Shakespeare could sing with myriad lips, Browning could stammer through a thousand mouths. Even now as I am speaking, and speaking not against him but for him, there glides through the room the pageant of his persons. There creeps Fra Lippo Lippi with his cheeks still burning from some girl's hot kiss. There stands dread Saul with the lordly male-sapphires gleaming in his turban. Mildred Tresham is there, and the Spanish monk, yellow with hatred, and Blougram, and Ben Ezra, and the Bishop of St Praxed's. The spawn of Setebos gibbers in the corner, and Sebald, hearing Pippa pass by, looks on Ottima's haggard face, and loathes her and his own sin, and himself. Pale as the white satin of his doublet, the melancholy king watches with dreamy treacherous eyes too-loyal Strafford pass forth to his doom, and Andrea shudders as he hears the cousins whistle in the garden, and bids his perfect wife go down. Yes, Browning was great. And as what will he be remembered? As a poet? Ah, not as a poet! He will be remembered as a writer of fiction, as the most supreme writer of fiction, it may be, that we have ever had. His sense of dramatic situation was unrivalled, and, if he could not answer his own problems, he could at least put problems forth, and what more should an artist do? Considered from the point of view of a creator of character he ranks next to him who made Hamlet. Had he been articulate, he might have sat beside him. The only man who can touch the hem of his garment is George Meredith. Meredith is a prose Browning, and so is Browning. He used poetry as a medium for writing in prose.

ERNEST: There is something in what you say, but there is not everything in what you say. In many points you are unjust.

GILBERT: It is difficult not to be unjust to what one loves. But let us return to the particular point at issue. What was it that you said?

ERNEST: Simply this: that in the best days of art there were no art-critics.

GILBERT: I seem to have heard that observation before, Ernest. It has all the vitality of error and all the tediousness of an old friend.

ERNEST: It is true. Yes: there is no use your tossing your head in that petulant manner. It is quite true. In the best days of art there was no art-criticism. The sculptor hewed from the marble block the great white-limbed Hermes that slept within it. The waxers and gilders of images gave tone and texture to the statue, and the world, when it saw it, worshipped and was dumb. He poured the glowing bronze into the mould of sand, and the river of red metal cooled into noble curves and took the impress of the body of a god. With enamel or polished jewels he gave sight to the sightless eyes. The hyacinth-like curls grew crisp beneath his graver. And when, in some dim frescoed fane, or pillared sunlit portico, the child of Leto stood upon his pedestal, those who passed by, διὰ λαμπροτάτου βαίνοντες ἀβρῶς αἰθέρος, became conscious of a new influence that had come across their lives, and dreamily, or with a sense of strange and quickening joy, went to their homes or daily labour, or wandered, it may be, through the city gates to that nymph-haunted meadow while young Phaedrus bathed his feet, and, lying there on the soft grass, beneath the tall wind-whispering planes and flowering *agnus castus*, began to think of the wonder of beauty, and grew silent with unaccustomed awe. In those days the artist was free. From the river valley he took the fine clay in his fingers, and with a little tool of wood or bone, fashioned it into forms so exquisite that the people gave them to the dead as their playthings, and we find them still in the dusty tombs on the yellow hillside by Tanagra, with the faint gold and the fading crimson still lingering about hair and lips and raiment. On a wall of fresh plaster, stained with bright sandyx or mixed with milk and saffron, he pictured one who trod with tired feet the purple white-starred fields of asphodel, one 'in whose eyelids lay the whole of the Trojan War', Polyxena, the daughter of Priam; or figured Odysseus, the wise and cunning, bound by tight cords to the mast-step, that he might listen without hurt to the singing of the Sirens, or wandering by the clear river of Acheron, where the ghosts of fishes flitted over the pebbly bed; or showed the Persian in trews and mitre flying before the Greek at Marathon, or the galleys clashing their beaks of brass in the little Salaminian bay. He drew with silver-point and charcoal upon parchment and prepared cedar. Upon ivory and rose-coloured terracotta he painted with wax, making the wax fluid with juice of olives, and with heated irons making it firm. Panel and marble and linen canvas became wonderful as his brush swept across them; and life, seeing her own image, was still, and dared not speak. All life, indeed, was his, from the merchants seated in the market-place to the cloaked shepherd lying on the hill; from the nymph hidden in the laurels and the faun that pipes at noon, to the king whom, in long green-curtained litter, slaves bore upon oil-bright shoulders, and fanned with peacock fans. Men and women, with pleasure or sorrow in their faces, passed before him. He watched them, and their secret became his. Through form and colour he recreated a world.

All subtle arts belonged to him also. He held the gem against the revolving disc, and the amethyst became the purple couch for Adonis, and across the veined sardonyx sped Artemis with her hounds. He beat out the gold into roses, and strung them together for necklace or armlet. He beat out the gold into wreaths for the conqueror's helmet, or into palmates for the Tyrian robe, or into masks for the royal dead. On the back of the silver mirror he graved Thetis borne by her Nereids, or love-sick Phaedra with her nurse, or Persephone, weary of memory, putting poppies in her hair. The potter sat in his shed, and, flower-like from the silent wheel, the vase rose up beneath his hands. He decorated the base and stem and ears with pattern of dainty olive-leaf, of foliated acanthus, or curved and crested wave. Then in black or red he painted lads wrestling, or in the race; knights in full armour, with strange heraldic shields and curious visors, leaning from shell-shaped chariot over rearing steeds; the gods seated at the feast or working their miracles; the heroes in their victory or in their pain. Sometimes he would etch in thin vermilion lines upon a ground of white the languid bridegroom and his bride, with Eros hovering round them – an Eros like one of Donatello's angels, a little laughing thing with gilded or with azure wings. On the curved side he would write the name of his friend. ΚΑΛΟΣ ΑΛΚΙΒΙΑΔΗΣ or ΚΑΛΟΣ ΧΑΡΜΙΔΗΣ tells us the story of his days. Again, on the rim of the wide flat cup he would draw the stag browsing, or the lion at rest, as his fancy willed it. From the tiny perfume-bottle laughed Aphrodite at her toilet, and, with bare-limbed Maenads in his train, Dionysus danced round the wine-jar on naked must-stained feet, while, satyr-like, the old Silenus sprawled upon the bloated skins or shook that magic spear which was tipped with a fretted fir-cone, and wreathed with dark ivy. And no one came to trouble the artist at his work. No irresponsible chatter disturbed him. He was not worried by opinions. By the Ilyssus, says Arnold somewhere, there was no Higginbotham. By the Ilyssus, my dear Gilbert, there were no silly art congresses bringing provincialism to the provinces and teaching the mediocrity how to mouth. By the Ilyssus there were no tedious magazines about art, in which the industrious prattle of what they do not understand. On the reed-grown banks of that little stream strutted no ridiculous journalism monopolising the seat of judgement when it should be apologising in the dock. The Greeks had no art-critics.

GILBERT: Ernest, you are quite delightful, but your views are terribly unsound. I am afraid that you have been listening to the conversation of someone older than yourself. That is always a dangerous thing to do and if you allow it to degenerate into a habit you will find it absolutely fatal to any intellectual development. As for modern journalism, it is not my business to defend it. It justifies its own existence by the great Darwinian principle of the survival of the vulgarest. I have merely to do with literature.

ERNEST: But what is the difference between literature and journalism?

GILBERT: Oh! journalism is unreadable, and literature is not read. That is all. But with regard to your statement that the Greeks had no art-critics, I assure you that is quite absurd. It would be more just to say that the Greeks were a nation of art-critics.

ERNEST: Really?

GILBERT: Yes, a nation of art-critics. But I don't wish to destroy the delightfully unreal picture that you have drawn of the relation of the Hellenic artist to the intellectual spirit of his age. To give an accurate description of what has never occurred is not merely the proper occupation of the historian, but the inalienable privilege of any man of parts and culture. Still less do I desire to talk learnedly. Learned conversation is either the affectation of the ignorant or the profession of the mentally unemployed. And, as for what is called improving conversation, that is merely the foolish method by which the still more foolish philanthropist feebly tries to disarm the just rancour of the criminal classes. No; let me play to you some mad scarlet thing by Dvořák. The pallid figures on the tapestry are smiling at us, and the heavy eyelids of my bronze Narcissus are folded in sleep. Don't let us discuss anything solemnly. I am but too conscious of the fact that we are born in an age when only the dull are treated seriously, and I live in terror of not being misunderstood. Don't degrade me into the position of giving you useful information. Education is an admirable thing, but it is well to remember from time to time that nothing that is worth knowing can be taught. Through the parted curtains of the window I see the moon like a clipped piece of silver. Like gilded bees the stars cluster round her. The sky is a hard hollow sapphire. Let us go out into the night. Thought is wonderful, but adventure is more wonderful still. Who knows but we may meet Prince Florizel of Bohemia, and hear the fair Cuban tell us that she is not what she seems?

ERNEST: You are horribly wilful. I insist on your discussing this matter with me. You have said that the Greeks were a nation of art-critics. What art-criticism have they left us?

GILBERT: My dear Ernest, even if not a single fragment of art-criticism had come down to us from Hellenic or Hellenistic days, it would be none the less true that the Greeks were a nation of art-critics, and that they invented the criticism of art just as they invented the criticism of everything else. For, after all, what is our primary debt to the Greeks? Simply the critical spirit. And, this spirit, which they exercised on questions of religion and science, of ethics and metaphysics, of politics and education, they exercised on questions of art also, and, indeed, of the two supreme and highest arts, they have left us the most flawless system of criticism that the world has ever seen.

ERNEST: But what are the two supreme and highest arts?

GILBERT: Life and literature, life and the perfect expression of life. The principles of the former, as laid down by the Greeks, we may not realise in an age so marred by false ideals as our own. The principles of the latter as they laid them down are, in many cases, so subtle that we can hardly understand them. Recognising that the most perfect art is that which most fully mirrors man in all his infinite variety, they elaborated the criticism of language, considered in the light of the mere material of that art, to a point to which we, with our accentual system of reasonable or emotional emphasis, can barely if at all attain; studying, for instance, the metrical movements of a prose as scientifically as a modern musician studies harmony and counterpoint, and, I need hardly say, with much keener aesthetic instinct. In this they were right, as they were right in all things. Since the introduction of printing, and the fatal development of the habit of reading amongst the middle and lower classes of this country, there has been a tendency in literature to appeal more and more to the eye and less and less to the ear, which is really the sense which, from the standpoint of pure art, it should seek to please, and by whose canons of pleasure it should abide always. Even the work of Mr Pater, who is, on the whole, the most perfect master of English prose now creating amongst us, is often far more like a piece of mosaic than a passage in music, and seems here and there, to lack the true rhythmical life of words and the fine freedom and richness of effect that such rhythmical life produces. We, in fact, have made writing a definite mode of composition and have treated it as a form of elaborate design. The Greeks, upon the other hand, regarded writing simply as a method of chronicling. Their test was always the spoken word in its musical and metrical relations. The voice was the medium, and the ear the critic. I have sometimes thought that the story of Homer's blindness might be really an artistic myth, created in critical days, and serving to remind us, not merely that the great poet is always a seer, seeing less with the eyes of the body than he does with the eyes of the soul, but he is a true singer also, building his song out of music, repeating each line over and over again to himself till he has caught the secret of its melody, chaunting in darkness the words that are winged with light. Certainly, whether this be so or not, it was to his blindness, as an occasion, if not as a cause, that England's great poet owed much of the majestic movement and sonorous splendour of his late verse. When Milton could no longer write he began to sing. Who would match the measures of

Comus with the measures of *Samson Agonistes*, or of *Paradise Lost* or *Regained*? When Milton became blind he composed, as everyone should compose, with the voice purely, and so the pipe or reed of earlier days became that mighty many-stopped organ whose rich reverberant music has all the stateliness of Homeric verse, if it seeks not to have its swiftness, and is the one imperishable inheritance of English literature sweeping through all the ages, because above them, and abiding with us ever, being immortal in its form. Yes: writing has done much harm to writers. We must return to the voice. That must be our test, and perhaps then we shall be able to appreciate some of the subtleties of Greek art-criticism.

As it now is, we cannot do so. Sometimes, when I have written a piece of prose that I have been modest enough to consider absolutely free from fault, a dreadful thought comes over me that I may have been guilty of the immoral effeminacy of using trochaic and tribrachic movements, a crime for which a learned critic of the Augustan age censures with most just severity the brilliant if somewhat paradoxical Hegesias. I grow cold when I think of it, and wonder to myself if the admirable ethical effect of the prose of that charming writer, who once in a spirit of reckless generosity towards the uncultivated portion of our community proclaimed the monstrous doctrine that conduct is three-fourths of life, will not someday be entirely annihilated by the discovery that the paeons have been wrongly placed.

ERNEST: Ah! now you are flippant.

GILBERT: Who would not be flippant when he is gravely told that the Greeks had no art-critics? I can understand it being said that the constructive genius of the Greeks lost itself in criticism, but not that the race to whom we owe the critical spirit did not criticise. You will not ask me to give you a survey of Greek art-criticism from Plato to Plotinus. The night is too lovely for that, and the moon, if she heard us, would put more ashes on her face than are there already. But think merely of one perfect little work of aesthetic criticism, Aristotle's *Treatise on Poetry*. It is not perfect in form, for it is badly written, consisting perhaps of notes dotted down for an art lecture, or of isolated fragments destined for some larger book, but in temper and treatment it is perfect, absolutely. The ethical effect of art, its importance to culture, and its place in the formation of character, had been done once for all by Plato; but here we have art treated, not from the moral, but from the purely aesthetic point of view. Plato had, of course, dealt with many definitely artistic subjects, such as the importance of unity on a work of art, the necessity for tone and harmony, the aesthetic value of appearances, the relation of the visible arts to the external world, and the relation of fiction to fact. He first perhaps stirred in the soul of man that desire that we have not yet satisfied, the desire to know the connection between beauty and truth, and the place of beauty in the moral and intellectual order of the Cosmos. The problems of idealism and realism, as he sets them forth, may seem to many to be somewhat barren of result in the metaphysical sphere of abstract being in which he places them, but transfer them to the sphere of art, and you will find that they are still vital and full of meaning. It may be that it is as a critic of beauty that Plato is destined to live, and that by altering the name of the sphere of his speculation we shall find a new philosophy. But Aristotle, like Goethe, deals with art primarily in its concrete manifestations, taking tragedy, for instance, and investigating the material it uses, which is language, its subject-matter, which is life, the method by which it works, which is action, the conditions under which it reveals itself, which are those of theatric presentation, its logical structure, which is plot, and its final aesthetic appeal, which is to the sense of beauty realised through the passions of pity and awe. That purification and spiritualism of the nature which he calls κάθαρσις is, as Goethe saw, essentially aesthetic, and is not moral, as Lessing fancied. Concerning himself primarily with the impression that the work of art produces, Aristotle sets himself to analyse that impression, to investigate its source, to see how it is engendered. As a physiologist and psychologist, he knows that the health of a function resides in energy. To have a capacity for a passion and not to realise it, is to make oneself incomplete and limited. The mimic spectacle of life that tragedy affords cleanses the bosom of much 'perilous stuff', and by presenting high and worthy objects for the exercise of the emotions purifies and spiritualises the man; nay, not merely does it spiritualise him, but it initiates him also into noble feelings of which he might else have known nothing, the word κάθαρσις having, it has sometimes seemed to me, a definite allusion to the rite of initiation, if indeed that be not, as I am occasionally tempted to fancy, its true and only meaning here. This is of course a mere outline of the book. But you see what a perfect piece of aesthetic criticism it is. Who indeed but a Greek could have analysed art so well? After reading it, one does not wonder any longer that Alexandria devoted itself so largely to art-criticism, and that we find the artistic temperaments of the day investigating every question of style and manner, discussing the great academic schools of painting, for instance, such as the school of Sicyon, that sought to preserve the dignified traditions of the antique mode, or the realistic and impressionist schools that aimed at reproducing actual life, or the elements of ideality in portraiture, or the artistic value of the epic form in an age so modern as theirs, or the proper subject-matter for the artist. Indeed, I fear that the inartistic temperaments of the day busied themselves also in matters of literature and art, for the accusations of plagiarism were endless, and such accusations proceed either from the thin colourless lips of impotence, or from the grotesque mouths of those who, possessing nothing of their own, fancy that they can gain a reputation for wealth by crying out that they have been robbed. And I assure you, my dear Ernest, that the Greeks chattered about painters quite as much as people do nowadays, and had their private views, and shilling exhibitions, and Arts and Crafts guilds, and Pre-Raphaelite movements, and movements towards realism, and lectured about art, and wrote essays on art, and produced their art-historians, and their archaeologists, and all the rest of it. Why, even the theatrical managers of travelling companies brought their dramatic critics with them when they went on tour, and paid them very handsome salaries for writing laudatory notices. Whatever, in fact, is modern in our life we owe to the Greeks. Whatever is an anachronism is due to mediaevalism. It is the Greeks who have given us the whole system of art-criticism, and how fine their critical instinct was may be seen from the fact that the material they criticised with most care was, as I have already said, language. For the material that painter or sculptor uses is meagre in comparison with that of words. Words have not merely music as sweet as that of viol and lute, colour as rich and vivid as any that makes lovely for us the canvas of the Venetian or the Spaniard, and plastic form no less sure and certain than that which reveals itself in marble or in bronze, but thought and passion and spirituality are theirs also, are theirs indeed alone. If the Greeks had criticised nothing but language, they would still have been the great art-critics of the world. To know the principles of the highest art is to know the principles of all the arts.

But I see that the moon is hiding behind a sulphur-coloured cloud. Out of a tawny mane or drift she gleams like a lion's eye. She is afraid that I will talk to you of Lucian and Longinus, of Quinctilian and Dionysius, of Pliny and Fronto and Pausanias, of all those who in the antique world wrote or lectured upon art matters. She need not be afraid. I am tired of my expedition into the dim, dull abyss of facts. There is nothing left for me now but the divine μονόχρονος ἡδονή of another cigarette. Cigarettes have at least the charm of leaving one unsatisfied.

ERNEST: Try one of mine. They are rather good, I get them direct from Cairo. The only use of our *attachés* is that they supply their friends with excellent tobacco. And as the moon has hidden herself, let us talk a little longer. I am quite ready to admit that I was wrong in what I said about the Greeks. They were as you have pointed out, a nation of art-critics. I acknowledge it, and I feel a little sorry for them. For the creative faculty is higher than the critical. There is really no comparison between them.

GILBERT: The antithesis between them is entirely arbitrary. Without the critical faculty, there is no artistic creation at all, worthy of the name. You spoke a little while ago of that fine spirit of choice and delicate instinct of selection by which the artist realises life for us, and gives to it a momentary perfection. Well, that spirit of choice, that subtle tact of omission, is really the critical faculty in one of its most characteristic moods, and no one who does not possess this critical faculty can create anything at all in art. Arnold's definition of literature as a criticism of life was not very felicitous in form, but it showed how keenly he recognised the importance of the critical element in all creative work.

ERNEST: I should have said that great artists work unconsciously, that they were 'wiser than they knew', as, I think, Emerson remarks somewhere.

GILBERT: It is really not so, Ernest. All fine imaginative work is self-conscious and deliberate. No poet sings because he must sing. At least, no great poet does. A great poet sings because he chooses to sing. It is so now, and it has always been so. We are sometimes apt to think that the voices that sounded at the dawn of poetry were simpler, fresher, and more natural than ours, and that the world which the early poets looked at, and through which they walked, had a kind of poetical quality of its own, and almost without changing could pass into song. The snow lies thick now upon Olympus, and its steep scarped sides are bleak and barren, but once, we fancy, the white feet of the Muses brushed the dew from the anemones in the morning, and at evening came Apollo to sing to the shepherds in the vale. But in this we are merely lending to other ages what we desire, or think we desire for our own. Our historical sense is at fault. Every century that produces poetry is, so far, an artificial century, and the work that seems to us to be the most natural and simple product of its time is always the result of the most self-conscious effort. Believe me, Ernest, there is no fine art without self-consciousness and self-consciousness and the critical spirit are one.

ERNEST: I see what you mean, and there is much in it. But surely you would admit that the great poems of the early world, the primitive, anonymous collective poems, were the result of the imagination of races, rather than of the imagination of individuals?

GILBERT: Not when they became poetry. Not when they received a beautiful form. For there is no art where there is no style, and no style where there is no unity, and unity is of the individual. No doubt Homer had old ballads and stories to deal with, as Shakespeare had chronicles and plays and novels from which to work, but they were merely his rough material. He took them,

and shaped them into song. They become his, because he made
them lovely. They were built out of music,

> And so not built at all,
> And therefore built for ever.

The longer one studies life and literature, the more strongly one
feels that behind everything that is wonderful stands the individual, and that it is not the moment that makes the man, but the
man who creates the age. Indeed, I am inclined to think that each
myth and legend that seems to us to spring out of the wonder, or
terror, or fancy of tribe and nation, was in its origin the invention
of one single mind. The curiously limited number of the myths
seems to me to point to this conclusion. But we must not go off
into questions of comparative mythology. We must keep to
criticism. And what I want to point out is this. An age that has no
criticism is either an age in which art is immobile, hieratic, and
confined to the reproduction of formal types, or an age that
possesses no art at all. There have been critical ages that have not
been creative, in the ordinary sense of the word, ages in which the
spirit of man has sought to set in order the treasures of his
treasure-house, to separate the gold from the silver, and the silver
from the lead, to count over the jewels, and to give names to the
pearls. But there has never been a creative age that has not been
critical also. For it is the critical faculty that invents fresh forms.
The tendency of creation is to repeat itself. It is to the critical
instinct that we owe each new school that springs up, each new
mould that art finds ready to its hand. There is really not a single
form that art now uses that does not come to us from the critical
spirit of Alexandria, where these forms were either stereotyped or
invented or made perfect. I say Alexandria, not merely because it
was there that the Greek spirit became most self-conscious, and
indeed ultimately expired in scepticism and theology, but because
it was to that city, and not to Athens, that Rome turned for her
models, and it was through the survival, such as it was, of the
Latin language that culture lived at all. When, at the Renaissance,
Greek literature dawned upon Europe, the soil had been in some
measure prepared for it. But, to get rid of the details of history,
which are always wearisome and usually inaccurate, let us say

generally, that the forms of art have been due to the Greek critical spirit. To it we owe the epic, the lyric, the entire drama in every one of its developments, including burlesque, the idyll, the romantic novel, the novel of adventure, the essay, the dialogue, the oration, the lecture, for which perhaps we should not forgive them, and the epigram, in all the wide meaning of that word. In fact, we owe it everything, except the sonnet, to which, however, some curious parallels of thought-movement may be traced in the *Anthology*, American journalism, to which no parallel can be found anywhere, and the ballad in sham Scotch dialect, which one of our most industrious writers has recently proposed should be made the basis for a final and unanimous effort on the part of our second-rate poets to make themselves really romantic. Each new school, as it appears, cries out against criticism, but it is to the critical faculty in man that it owes its origin. The mere creative instinct does not innovate, but reproduces.

ERNEST: You have been talking of criticism as an essential part of the creative spirit, and I now fully accept your theory. But what of criticism outside creation? I have a foolish habit of reading periodicals, and it seems to me that most modern criticism is perfectly valueless.

GILBERT: So is most modern creative work also. Mediocrity weighing mediocrity in the balance, and incompetence applauding its brother – that is the spectacle which the artistic activity of England affords us from time to time. And yet, I feel I am a little unfair in this matter. As a rule the critics – I speak, of course, of the higher class, of those, in fact, who write for the sixpenny papers – are far more cultured than the people whose work they are called upon to review. This is, indeed, only what one would expect, for criticism demands infinitely more cultivation than creation does.

ERNEST: Really?

GILBERT: Certainly. Anybody can write a three-volumed novel. It merely requires a complete ignorance of both life and literature. The difficulty that I should fancy the reviewer feels is the difficulty of sustaining any standard. Where there is no style, a standard must be impossible. The poor reviewers are apparently reduced to be the reporters of the police-court of literature, the chroniclers of the doings of the habitual criminals of art. It is sometimes said of them that they do not read all through the works they are called upon to criticise. They do not. Or at least they should not. If they did so, they would become confirmed misanthropes, or if I may borrow a phrase from one of the pretty Newnham graduates, confirmed womanthropes for the rest of their lives. Nor is it necessary. To know the vintage and quality of a wine one need not drink the whole cask. It must be perfectly easy in half an hour to say whether a book is worth anything or worth nothing. Ten minutes are really sufficient, if one has the instinct for form. Who wants to wade through a dull volume? One tastes it, and that is quite enough – more than enough, I should imagine. I am aware that there are many honest workers in painting as well as in literature who object to criticism entirely. They are quite right. Their work stands in no intellectual relation to their age. It brings us no new element of pleasure. It suggests no fresh departure of thought, or passion, or beauty. It should not be spoken of. It should be left to the oblivion that it deserves.

ERNEST: But, my dear fellow excuse me for interrupting you – you seem to me to be allowing your passion for criticism to lead you a great deal too far. For, after all, even you must admit that it is much more difficult to do a thing than to talk about it.

GILBERT: More difficult to do a thing than to talk about it? Not at all. That is a gross popular error. It is very much more difficult to talk about a thing than to do it. In the sphere of actual life that is of course obvious. Anybody can make history. Only a great man can write it. There is no mode of action, no form of emotion, that we do not share with the lower animals. It is only by language that we rise above them, or above each other – by language, which is the parent, and not the child, of thought. Action, indeed, is always easy, and when presented to us in its most aggravated, because most continuous form, which I take to be that of real industry, becomes simply the refuge of people who have nothing whatso-ever to do. No, Ernest, don't talk about action. It is a blind thing dependent on external influences, and moved by an impulse of whose nature it is unconscious. It is a thing incomplete in its essence, because limited by accident and ignorant of its direction, being always at variance with its aim. Its basis is the lack of imagination. It is the last resource of those who know not how to dream.

ERNEST: Gilbert, you treat the world as if it were a crystal ball. You hold it in your hand, and reverse it to please a wilful fancy. You do nothing but rewrite history.

GILBERT: The one duty we owe to history is to rewrite it. That is not the least of the tasks in store for the critical spirit. When we have fully discovered the scientific laws that govern life, we shall realise that the one person who has more illusions than the dreamer is the man of action. He, indeed, knows neither the origin of his deeds nor their results. From the field in which he thought that he had sown thorns, we have gathered our vintage, and the fig tree that he planted for our pleasure is as barren as the thistle, and more bitter. It is because humanity has never known where it was going that it has been able to find its way.

ERNEST: You think, then, that in the sphere of action a conscious aim is a delusion?

GILBERT: It is worse than a delusion. If we lived long enough to see the results of our actions it may be that those who call themselves good would be sickened with a dull remorse, and those whom the world calls evil stirred by a noble joy. Each little thing that we do passes into the great machine of life which may grind our virtues to powder and make them worthless, or transform our sins into elements of a new civilisation, more marvellous and more splendid than any that has gone before. But men are the slaves of words. They rage against materialism, as they call it, forgetting that there has been no material improvement that has not spiritualised the world, and that there have been few, if any, spiritual awakenings that have not wasted the world's faculties in barren hopes, and fruitless aspirations, and empty or trammelling creeds. What is termed sin is an essential element of progress. Without it the world would stagnate, or grow old, or become colourless. By its curiosity sin increases the experience of the race. Through its intensified assertion of individualism, it saves us from monotony of type. In its rejection of the current notions about morality, it is one with the higher ethics. And as for the virtues! What are the virtues? Nature, M. Renan tells us, cares little about chastity, and it may be that it is to the shame of the Magdalen, and not to their own purity, that the Lucretias of modern life owe their freedom from stain. Charity, as even those of whose religion it makes a formal part have been compelled to acknowledge, creates a multitude of evils. The mere existence of conscience, that faculty of which people prate so much nowadays, and are so ignorantly proud, is a sign of our imperfect development. It must be merged in instinct before we become fine. Self-denial is simply a method by which man arrests his progress, and self-sacrifice a survival of the mutilation of the savage, part of that old worship of pain which is so terrible a factor in the history of the world, and which even now makes its victims day by day, and has its altars in the land. Virtues! Who knows what the virtues are? Not you. Not I. Not anyone. It is well for our vanity that we slay the criminal, for if we suffered him to live he might show us what we had gained by his crime. It is well for his peace that the saint goes to his martyrdom. He is spared the sight of the horror of his harvest.

ERNEST: Gilbert, you sound too harsh a note. Let us go back to the more gracious fields of literature. What was it you said? That it was more difficult to talk about a thing than to do it?

GILBERT (*after a pause*): Yes; I believe I ventured upon that simple truth. Surely you see now that I am right? When man acts he is a puppet. When he describes he is a poet. The whole secret lies in that. It was easy enough on the sandy plains by windy Ilion to send the notched arrow from the painted bow, or to hurl against the shield of hide and flame-like brass the long ash-handled spear. It was easy for the adulterous queen to spread the Tyrian carpets for her lord, and then, as he lay couched in the marble bath, to throw over his head the purple net, and call to her smooth-faced lover to stab through the meshes at the heart that should have broken at Aulis. For Antigone even, with Death waiting for her as her bridegroom, it was easy to pass through the tainted air at noon and climb the hill, and strew with kindly earth the wretched naked corse that had no tomb. But what of those who wrote about these things? What of those who gave them reality, and made them live for ever? Are they not greater than the men and women they sing of? 'Hector that sweet knight is dead', and Lucian tells us how in the dim underworld Menippus saw the bleaching skull of Helen, and marvelled that it was for so grim a favour that all those horned ships were launched, those beautiful mailed men laid low, those towered cities brought to dust. Yet, every day the swan-like daughter of Leda comes out on the battlements, and looks down at the tide of war. The grey-beards wonder at her loveliness, and she stands by the side of the king. In his chamber of stained ivory lies her leman. He is polishing his dainty armour, and combing the scarlet plume. With squire and page, her husband passes from tent to tent. She can see his bright hair, and hears, or fancies that she hears, that clear cold voice. In the courtyard below, the son of Priam is buckling on his brazen cuirass. The white arms of Andromache are around his neck. He sets his helmet on the ground, lest their babe should be frightened. Behind the embroidered curtains of his pavilion sits Achilles, in perfumed raiment, while in harness of gilt and silver the friend of his soul arrays himself to go forth to the fight. From a curiously carven chest that his mother Thetis had brought to his ship-side, the Lord of the Myrmidons takes out that mystic chalice that the lip of man had never touched, and cleanses it with brimstone, and with fresh water cools it, and, having washed his hands, fills with black wine its burnished hollow, and spills the thick grape-blood upon the ground in honour of Him whom at Dodona bare-footed prophets worshipped, and prays to Him, and knows not that he prays in vain, and that by the hands of two knights from Troy, Panthous' son, Euphorbus, whose love-locks were looped with gold, and the Priamid, the lion-hearted, Patroclus, the comrade of comrades, must meet his doom. Phantoms, are they? Heroes of mist and mountain? Shadows in a song? No; they are real. Action! What is action? It dies at the moment of its energy. It is a base concession to fact. The world is made by the singer for the dreamer.

ERNEST: While you talk it seems to me to be so.

GILBERT: It is so in truth. On the mouldering citadel of Troy lies the lizard like a thing of green bronze. The owl has built her nest in the palace of Priam. Over the empty plain wander shepherd and goatherd with their flocks, and where, on the wine-surfaced, oily sea – οἶνοψ πόντος, as Homer calls it – copper-prowed and streaked with vermilion, the great galleys of the Danaoi came in their gleaming crescent, the lonely tunny-fisher sits in his little boat and watches the bobbing corks of his net. Yet, every morning the doors of the city are thrown open, and on foot, or in horse-drawn chariot, the warriors go forth to battle, and mock their enemies from behind their iron masks. All day long the fight rages, and when night comes the torches gleam by the tents, and the cresset burns in the hall. Those who live in marble or on painted panel know of life but a single exquisite instant, eternal indeed in its beauty, but limited to one note of passion or one mood of calm. Those whom the poet makes live have their myriad emotions of joy and terror, of courage and despair, of pleasure and of suffering. The seasons come and go in glad or saddening pageant, and with winged or leaden feet the years pass by before them. They have their youth and their manhood, they are children, and they grow old. It is always dawn for St Helena, as Veronese saw her at the window. Through the still morning air the angels bring her the symbol of God's pain. The cool breezes of the morning lift the gilt threads from her brow. On that little hill by the city of Florence, where the lovers of Giorgione are lying, it is always the solstice of noon, of noon made so languorous by summer suns that hardly can the slim naked girl dip into the marble tank the round bubble of clear glass, and the long fingers of the lute-player rest idly upon the chords. It is twilight always for the dancing nymphs whom Corot set free among the silver poplars of France. In eternal twilight they move, those frail diaphanous figures, whose tremulous white feet seem not to touch the dew-drenched grass they tread on. But those who walk in epos, drama or romance see through the labouring months the young moons wax and wane, and watch the night from evening unto morning star, and from sunrise unto sunsetting can note the shifting day with all its gold and shadow. For them, as for us, the flowers bloom and wither, and the Earth, that Green-tressed Goddess, as Coleridge calls her, alters her raiment for their pleasure. The statue is concentrated to one moment of perfection. The image stained upon the canvas possesses no spiritual element of growth or change. If they know nothing of death, it is because they know little of life, for the secrets of life and death belong to those, and those only, whom the sequence of time affects, and who possess not merely the present but the future, and can rise or fall from a past of glory or of shame. Movement, that problem of the visible arts, can be truly realised by literature alone. It is literature that shows us the body in its swiftness and the soul in its unrest.

ERNEST: Yes, I see now what you mean. But surely, the higher you place the creative artist, the lower must the critic rank.

GILBERT: Why so?

ERNEST: Because the best that he can give us will be but an echo of rich music, a dim shadow of clear-outlined form. It may, indeed, be that life is chaos, as you tell me that it is; that its martyrdoms are mean and its heroisms ignoble; and that it is the function of literature to create, from the rough material of actual existence, a new world that will be more marvellous, more enduring, and more true than the world that common eyes look upon, and through which common natures seek to realise their perfection. But surely, if this new world has been made by the spirit and touch of a great artist, it will be a thing so complete and perfect that there will be nothing left for the critic to do. I quite understand now, and indeed admit most readily, that it is far more difficult to talk about a thing than to do it. But it seems to me that this sound and sensible maxim, which is really extremely soothing to one's feelings, and should be adopted as its motto by every Academy of Literature all over the world, applies only to the relations that exist between art and life, and not to any relations that there may be between art and criticism.

GILBERT: But, surely, criticism is itself an art. And just as artistic creation implies the working of the critical faculty, and, indeed, without it cannot be said to exist at all, so criticism is really creative in the highest sense of the word. Criticism is, in fact, both creative and independent.

ERNEST: Independent?

GILBERT: Yes; independent. Criticism is no more to be judged by any low standard of imitation or resemblance than is the work of poet or sculptor. The critic occupies the same relation to the work of art that he criticises as the artist does to the visible world of form and colour, or the unseen world of passion and of thought. He does not even require for the perfection of his art the finest materials. Anything will serve his purpose. And just as out of the sordid and sentimental *amours* of the silly wife of a small country doctor in the squalid village of Yonville-l'Abbaye near Rouen, Gustave Flaubert was able to create a classic and make a master-piece of style, so, from subjects of little or of no importance, such as the pictures in this year's Royal Academy, or in any year's Royal Academy for that matter, Mr Lewis Morris's poems, M. Ohnet's novels or the plays of Mr Henry Arthur Jones, the true critic can, if it be his pleasure so to direct or waste his faculty of contem-plation, produce work that will be flawless in beauty and instinct with intellectual subtlety. Why not? Dullness is always an irresist-ible temptation for brilliancy, and stupidity is the permanent *Bestia Trionfans* that calls wisdom from its cave. To an artist so creative as the critic what does subject-matter signify? No more and no less than it does to the novelist and the painter. Like them, he can find his motives everywhere. Treatment is the test. There is nothing that has not in it suggestion or challenge.

ERNEST: But is criticism really a creative art?

GILBERT: Why should it not be? It works with materials, and puts them into a form that is at once new and delightful. What more can one say of poetry? Indeed, I would call criticism a creation within a creation. For just as the great artists, from Homer and Aeschylus, down to Shakespeare and Keats, did not go directly to life for their subject-matter, but sought for it in myth, and legend, and ancient tale, so the critic deals with materials that others have, as it were, purified for him, and to which imaginative form and colour have been already added. Nay, more, I would say that the highest criticism, being the purest form of personal impres-sion, is in its way more creative than creation, as it has least reference to any standard external to itself, and is, in fact, its own reason for existing, and, as the Greeks would put it, in itself, and to itself, an end. Certainly, it is never trammelled by any shackles of verisimilitude. No ignoble considerations of probability, that cowardly concession to the tedious repetitions of domestic or public life, affect it ever. One may appeal from fiction unto fact. But from the soul there is no appeal.

ERNEST: From the soul?

GILBERT: Yes, from the soul. That is what the highest criticism really is, the record of one's own soul. It is more fascinating than history, as it is concerned simply with oneself. It is more delightful than philosophy, as its subject is concrete and not abstract, real and not vague. It is the only civilised form of autobiography, as it deals not with the events, but with the thoughts of one's life; not with life's physical accidents of deed or circumstance, but with the spiritual moods and imaginative passions of the mind. I am always amused by the silly vanity of those writers and artists of our day who seem to imagine that the primary function of the critic is to chatter about their second-rate work. The best that one can say of most modern creative art is that it is just a little less vulgar than reality, and so the critic, with his fine sense of distinction and sure instinct of delicate refinement, will prefer to look into the silver mirror or through the woven veil, and will turn his eyes away from the chaos and clamour of actual existence, though the mirror be tarnished and the veil be torn. His sole aim is to chronicle his own impressions. It is for him that pictures are painted, books written and marble hewn into form.

ERNEST: I seem to have heard another theory of criticism.

GILBERT: Yes; it has been said by one whose gracious memory we all revere, and the music of whose pipe once lured Proserpina from her Sicilian fields, and made those white feet stir, and not in vain, the Cumnor cowslips, that the proper aim of criticism is to see the object as in itself it really is. But this is a very serious error, and takes no cognisance of criticism's most perfect form, which is in its essence purely subjective, and seeks to reveal its own secret and not the secret of another. For the highest criticism deals with art not as expressive but as impressive purely.

ERNEST: But is that really so?

GILBERT: Of course it is. Who cares whether Mr Ruskin's views on Turner are sound or not? What does it matter? That mighty and majestic prose of his, so fervid and so fiery-coloured in its noble eloquence, so rich in its elaborate symphonic music, so sure and certain, at its best, in subtle choice of word and epithet, is at least as great a work of art as any of those wonderful sunsets that bleach or rot on their corrupted canvases in England's gallery; greater indeed, one is apt to think at times, not merely because its equal beauty is more enduring, but on account of the fuller variety of its appeal, soul speaking to soul in those long-cadenced lines, not through form and colour alone, though through these, indeed, completely and without loss, but with intellectual and emotional utterance, with lofty passion and with loftier thought, with imaginative insight, and with poetic aim; greater, I always think, even as literature is the greater art. Who, again, cares whether Mr Pater has put into the portrait of Mona Lisa something that Leonardo never dreamed of? The painter may have been merely the slave of an archaic smile, as some have fancied, but whenever I pass into the cool galleries of the Palace of the Louvre, and stand before that strange figure 'set in its marble chair in that cirque of fantastic rocks, as in some faint light under sea', I murmur to myself:

> She is older than the rocks among which she sits; like the vampire, she has been dead many times, and learned the secrets of the grave; and has been a diver in deep seas, and keeps their fallen day about her; and trafficked for strange webs with Eastern merchants; and, as Leda, was the mother of Helen of Troy, and, as St Anne, the mother of Mary; and all this has been to her but as the sound of lyres and flutes, and lives only in the delicacy with which it has moulded the changing lineaments, and tinged the eyelids and the hands.

And I say to my friend, 'The presence that thus so strangely rose beside the waters is expressive of what in the ways of a thousand years man had come to desire;' and he answers me, 'Hers is the head upon which all "the ends of the world are come", and the eyelids are a little weary.'

And so the picture becomes more wonderful to us than it really is, and reveals to us a secret of which, in truth, it knows nothing, and the music of the mystical prose is as sweet in our ears as was that flute-player's music that lent to the lips of La Gioconda those subtle and poisonous curves. Do you ask me what Leonardo would have said had anyone told him of this picture that 'all the thoughts and experience of the world had etched and moulded therein that which they had of power to refine and make expressive the outward form, the animalism of Greece, the lust of Rome, the reverie of the Middle Age with its spiritual ambition and imaginative loves, the return of the pagan world, the sins of the Borgias?' He would probably have answered that he had contemplated none of these things, but had concerned himself simply with certain arrangements of lines and masses, and with new and curious colour-harmonies of blue and green. And it is for this very reason that the criticism which I have quoted is criticism of the highest kind. It treats the work of art simply as a starting-point for a new creation. It does not confine itself – let us at least suppose so for the moment – to discovering the real intention of the artist and accepting that as final. And in this it is right, for the meaning of any beautiful created thing is, at least, as much in the soul of him who looks at it, as it was in his soul who wrought it. Nay, it is rather the beholder who lends to the beautiful thing its myriad meanings, and makes it marvellous for us, and sets it in some new relation to the age, so that it becomes a vital portion of our lives, and a symbol of what we pray for, or perhaps of what, having prayed for, we fear that we may receive. The longer I study, Ernest, the more clearly I see that the beauty of the visible arts is, as the beauty of music, impressive primarily, and that it may be marred, and indeed often is so, by any excess of intellectual intention on the part of the artist. For when the work is finished it has, as it were, an independent life of its own, and may deliver a message far other than that which was put into its lips to say. Sometimes, when I listen to the overture to *Tannhäuser*, I seem indeed to see that comely knight treading delicately on the flower-strewn grass, and to hear the voice of Venus calling to him from the caverned hill. But at other times it speaks to me of a thousand different things, of myself, it may be, and my own life, or of the lives of others whom one has loved and grown weary of loving, or of the passions that man has known, or of the passions that man has not known, and so has sought for. Tonight it may fill one with that ΕΡΩΣ ΤΩΝ ΑΔΓΝΑΤΩΝ, that *Amour de l'Impossible*, which falls like a madness on many who think they live securely and out of reach of harm, so that they sicken suddenly with the poison of unlimited desire, and, in the infinite pursuit of what they may not obtain, grow faint and swoon or stumble. Tomorrow, like the music of which Aristotle and Plato tell us, the noble Dorian music of the Greek, it may perform the office of a physician, and give us an anodyne against pain, and heal the spirit that is wounded, and 'bring the soul into harmony with all right things'. And what is true about music is true about all the arts. Beauty has as many meanings as man has moods. Beauty is the symbol of symbols. Beauty reveals everything, because it expresses nothing. When it shows us itself, it shows us the whole fiery-coloured world.

ERNEST: But is such work as you have talked about really criticism?

GILBERT: It is the highest criticism, for it criticises not merely the individual work of art, but beauty itself, and fills with wonder a form which the artist may have left void, or not understood, or understood incompletely.

ERNEST: The highest criticism, then, is more creative than creation, and the primary aim of the critic is to see the object as in itself it really is not; that is your theory, I believe?

GILBERT: Yes, that is my theory. To the critic the work of art is simply a suggestion for a new work of his own, that need not necessarily bear any obvious resemblance to the thing it criticises. The one characteristic of a beautiful form is that one can put into it whatever one wishes, and see in it whatever one chooses to see; and the beauty, that gives to creation its universal and aesthetic element, makes the critic a creator in his turn, and whispers of a thousand different things which were not present in the mind of him who carved the statue or painted the panel or graved the gem.

It is sometimes said by those who understand neither the nature of the highest criticism nor the charm of the highest art, that the pictures that the critic loves most to write about are those that belong to the anecdotage of painting, and that deal with scenes taken out of literature or history. But this is not so. Indeed, pictures of this kind are far too intelligible. As a class, they rank with illustrations, and even considered from this point of view are failures, as they do not stir the imagination, but set definite bounds to it. For the domain of the painter is, as I suggested before, widely different from that of the poet. To the latter belongs life in its full and absolutely entirety; not merely the beauty that men look at, but the beauty that men listen to also; not merely the momentary grace of form or the transient gladness of colour, but the whole sphere of feeling, the perfect cycle of thought. The painter is so far limited that it is only through the mask of the body that he can show us the mystery of the soul; only through conventional images that he can handle ideas; only through its physical equivalents that he can deal with psychology. And how inadequately does he do it then, asking us to accept the torn turban of the Moor for the noble rage of Othello, or a dotard in a storm for the wild madness of Lear! Yet it seems as if nothing could stop him. Most of our elderly English painters spend their wicked and wasted lives in poaching upon the domain of the poets, marring their motives by clumsy treatment, and striving to render, by visible form or colour, the marvel of what is invisible, the splendour of what is not seen. Their pictures are, as a natural consequence, insufferably tedious. They have degraded the invisible arts into the obvious arts, and the one thing not worth looking at is the obvious. I do not say that poet and painter may not treat of the same subject. They have always done so, and will always do so. But while the poet can be pictorial or not, as he chooses, the painter must be pictorial always. For a painter is limited, not to what he sees in nature, but to what upon canvas may be seen.

And so, my dear Ernest, pictures of this kind will not really fascinate the critic. He will turn from them to such works as made him brood and dream and fancy, to works that possess the subtle quality of suggestion, and seem to tell one that even from them there is an escape into a wider world. It is sometimes said that the tragedy of an artist's life is that he cannot realise his ideal. But the true tragedy that dogs the steps of most artists is that they realise their ideal too absolutely. For, when the ideal is realised, it is robbed of its wonder and its mystery and becomes simply a new starting-point for an ideal that is other than itself. This is the reason why music is the perfect type of art. Music can never reveal its ultimate secret. This, also, is the explanation of the value of limitations in art. The sculptor gladly surrenders imitative colour, and the painter the actual dimensions of form, because by such renunciations they are able to avoid too definite a presentation of the real, which would be mere imitation, and too definite a realisation of the ideal, which would be too purely intellectual. It is through its very incompleteness that art becomes complete in beauty, and so addresses itself, not to the faculty of recognition nor to the faculty of reason, but to the aesthetic sense alone, which, while accepting both reason and recognition as stages of apprehension, subordinates them both to a pure synthetic impression of the work of art as a whole, and, taking whatever alien emotional elements the work may possess, uses their very complexity as a means by which a richer unity may be added to the ultimate impression itself. You see, then, how it is that the aesthetic critic rejects these obvious modes of art that have but one message to deliver and having delivered it become dumb and sterile, and seeks rather for such modes as suggest reverie and mood, and by their imaginative beauty make all interpretations true, and no interpretation final. Some resemblance, no doubt, the creative work of the critic will have to the work that has stirred him to creation, but it will be such resemblance as exists not between nature and the mirror that the painter of landscape or figure may be supposed to hold up to her, but between nature and the work of the decorative artist. Just as on the flowerless carpets of Persia, tulip and rose blossom indeed and are lovely to look on, though they are not reproduced in visible shape or line; just as the pearl and purple of the seashell is echoed in the church of St Mark at Venice; just as the vaulted ceiling of the wondrous chapel at Ravenna is made gorgeous by the gold and green and sapphire of the peacock's tail, though the birds of Juno fly not across it; so the critic reproduces the work that he criticises in a mode that is never imitative, and part of whose charm may really consist in the rejection of resemblance, and shows us in this way not merely the meaning but also the mystery of beauty and, by transforming each art into literature, solves once for all the problem of art's unity.

But I see it is time for supper. After we have discussed some Chambertin and a few ortolans, we will pass on to the question of the critic considered in the light of the interpreter.

ERNEST: Ah! you admit, then, that the critic may occasionally be allowed to see the object as in itself it really is.

GILBERT: I am not quite sure. Perhaps I may admit it after supper. There is a subtle influence in supper.

Part Two

WITH SOME REMARKS UPON THE
IMPORTANCE OF DISCUSSING EVERYTHING

PERSONS: The same.
SCENE: The same.

ERNEST: The ortolans were delightful, and the Chambertin perfect, and now let us return to the point at issue.

GILBERT: Ah! don't let us do that. Conversation should touch everything but should concentrate itself on nothing. Let us talk about Moral Indignation, its Cause and Cure, a subject on which I think of writing; or about The Survival of Thersites, as shown by the English comic papers; or about any topic that may turn up.

ERNEST: No; I want to discuss the critic and criticism. You have told me that the highest criticism deals with art, not as expressive, but as impressive purely, and is consequently both creative and independent, is in fact an art by itself, occupying the same relation to creative work that creative work does to the visible world of form and colour, or the unseen world of passion and of thought. Well, now, tell me, will not the critic be sometimes a real interpreter?

GILBERT: Yes; the critic will be an interpreter, if he chooses. He can pass from his synthetic impression of the work of art as a whole, to an analysis or exposition of the work itself, and in this lower sphere, as I hold it to be, there are many delightful things to be said and done. Yet his object will not always be to explain the work of art. He may seek rather to deepen its mystery, to raise round it, and round its maker, that mist of wonder which is dear to both gods and worshippers alike. Ordinary people are 'terribly at ease in Zion'. They propose to walk arm in arm with the poets, and have a glib ignorant way of saying, 'Why should we read what is written about Shakespeare and Milton? We can read the plays and the poems. That is enough.' But an appreciation of Milton is, as the late Rector of Lincoln remarked once, the reward of consummate scholarship. And he who desires to understand Shakespeare truly must understand the relations in which Shakespeare stood to the Renaissance and the Reformation, to the age of Elizabeth and the age of James; he must be familiar with the history of the struggle for supremacy between the old classical forms and the new spirit of romance, between the school of Sidney, and Daniel, and Johnson, and the school of Marlowe and Marlowe's greater son; he must know the materials that were at Shakespeare's disposal, and the method in which he used them, and the conditions of theatric presentation in the sixteenth and seventeenth century, their limitations and their opportunities for freedom, and the literary criticism of Shakespeare's day, its aims and modes and canons; he must study the English language in its progress, and blank or rhymed verse in its various developments; he must study the Greek drama, and the connection between the art of the creator of the *Agamemnon* and the art of the creator of *Macbeth*; in a word, he must be able to bind Elizabethan London to the Athens of Pericles, and to learn Shakespeare's true position in the history of European drama and the drama of the world. The critic will certainly be an interpreter, but he will not treat art as a riddling Sphinx whose shallow secret may be guessed and revealed by one whose feet are wounded and who knows not his name. Rather, he will look upon art as a goddess whose mystery it is his province to intensify, and whose majesty his privilege to make more marvellous in the eyes of men.

And here, Ernest, this strange thing happens. The critic will indeed be an interpreter, but he will not be an interpreter in the sense of one who simply repeats in another form a message that has been put into his lips to say. For, just as it is only by contact with the art of foreign nations that the art of a country gains that individual and separate life that we call nationality, so, by curious inversion, it is only by intensifying his own personality that the critic can interpret the personality and work of others, and the more strongly this personality enters into the interpretation, the more real the interpretation becomes, the more satisfying, the more convincing and the more true.

ERNEST: I would have said that personality would have been a disturbing element.

GILBERT: No, it is an element of revelation. If you wish to understand others you must intensify your own individualism.

ERNEST: What, then is the result?

GILBERT: I will tell you, and perhaps I can tell you best by definite example. It seems to me that, while the literary critic stands of course first, as having the wider range, and larger vision, and nobler material, each of the arts has a critic, as it were, assigned to it. The actor is a critic of the drama. He shows the poet's work under new conditions, and by a method special to himself. He takes the written word, and action, gesture and voice become the media of revelation. The singer or the player on lute and viol is the critic of music. The etcher of a picture robs the painting of its fair colours, but shows us by the use of a new material its true colour-quality, its tones and values, and the relations of its masses, and so is, in his way, a critic of it, for the critic is he who exhibits to us a work of art in a form different from that of the work itself and the employment of a new material is a critical as well as a creative element. Sculpture, too, has its critic, who may be either the carver of a gem, as he was in Greek days, or some painter like Mantegna, who sought to reproduce on canvas the beauty of plastic line and the symphonic dignity of processional bas-relief. And in the case of all these creative critics of art it is evident that personality is an absolute essential for any real interpretation. When Rubinstein plays to us the *Sonata Appassionata* of Beethoven he gives us not merely Beethoven, but also himself, and so gives us Beethoven absolutely – Beethoven reinterpreted through a rich artistic nature, and made vivid and wonderful to us by a new and intense personality. When a great actor plays Shakespeare we have the same experience. His own individuality becomes a vital part of the interpretation. People sometimes say that actors give us their own Hamlets, and not Shakespeare's; and this fallacy – for it is a fallacy – is, I regret to say, repeated by that charming and graceful writer who has lately deserted the turmoil of literature for the peace of the House of Commons, I mean the author of *Obiter Dicta*. In point of fact, there is no such thing as Shakespeare's Hamlet. If Hamlet has something of the definiteness of a work of art, he has also all the obscurity that belongs to life. There are as many Hamlets as there are melancholies.

ERNEST: As many Hamlets as there are melancholies?

GILBERT: Yes; and as art springs from personality, so it is only to personality that it can be revealed, and from the meeting of the two comes right interpretative criticism.

ERNEST: The critic then, considered as the interpreter, will give no less than he receives, and lend as much as he borrows?

GILBERT: He will be always showing us the work of art in some new relation to our age. He will always be reminding us that great works of art are living things – are, in fact, the only things that live. So much, indeed, will he feel this, that I am certain that, as civilisation progresses and we become more highly organised, the elect spirits of each age, the critical and cultured spirits, will grow less and less interested in actual life, and *will seek to gain their impressions almost certainly from what art has touched*. For life is terribly deficient in form. Its catastrophes happen in the wrong way and to the wrong people. There is a grotesque horror about its comedies, and its tragedies seem to culminate in farce. One is always wounded when one approaches it. Things last either too long, or not long enough.

ERNEST: Poor life! Poor human life! Are you not even touched by the tears that the Roman poet tells us are part of its essence.

GILBERT: Too quickly touched by them, I fear. For when one looks back upon the life that was so vivid in its emotional intensity, and filled with such fervent moments of ecstasy or of joy, it all seems to be a dream and an illusion. What are the unreal things, but the passions that once burned one like fire? What are the incredible things, but the things that one has faithfully believed? What are the improbable things? The things that one has done oneself. No Ernest; life cheats us with shadows, like a puppet-master. We ask it for pleasure. It gives it to us, with bitterness and disappointment in its train. We come across some noble grief that we think will lend the purple dignity of tragedy to our days, but it passes away from us, and things less noble take its place, and on some grey windy dawn, or odorous eve of silence and of silver, we find ourselves looking with callous wonder, or dull heart of stone, at the tress of gold-flecked hair that we had once so wildly worshipped and so madly kissed.

ERNEST: Life then is a failure?

GILBERT: From the artistic point of view certainly. And the chief thing that makes life a failure from this artistic point of view is the thing that lends to life its sordid security, the fact that one can never repeat exactly the same emotion. How different it is in the world of art! On a shelf of the bookcase behind you stands the *Divine Comedy*, and I know that, if I open it at a certain place, I shall be filled with a fierce hatred of someone who has never wronged me, or stirred by a great love for someone whom I shall never see. There is no mood of passion that art cannot give us, and those of us who have discovered her secret can settle beforehand what our experiences are going to be. We can choose our day and select our hour. We can say to ourselves, 'Tomorrow, at dawn, we shall walk with grave Virgil through the valley of the shadow of death,' and lo! the dawn finds us in the obscure wood, and the Mantuan stands by our side. We pass through the gate of the legend fatal to hope, and with pity or with joy behold the horror of another world. The hypocrites go by, with their painted faces and their cowls of gilded lead. Out of the ceaseless winds that drive them, the carnal look at us, and we watch the heretic rending his flesh, and the glutton lashed by the rain. We break the withered branches from the tree in the grove of the Harpies, and each dull-hued poisonous twig bleeds with red blood before us, and cries aloud with bitter cries. Out of a horn of fire Odysseus speaks to us, and when from his sepulchre of flame the great Ghibelline rises, the pride that triumphs over the torture of that bed becomes ours for a moment. Through the dim purple air fly those who have stained the world with the beauty of their sin, and in the pit of loathsome disease, dropsy-stricken and swollen of body into the semblance of a monstrous lute, lies Adamo di Brescia, the coiner of false coin. He bids us listen to his misery; we stop and with dry and gaping lips he tells us how he dreams day and night of the brooks of clear water that in cool dewy channels gush down the green Casentine hills. Sinon, the false Greek of Troy, mocks at him. He smites him in the face, and they wrangle. We are fascinated by their shame, and loiter, till Virgil chides us and leads us away to that city turreted by giants where great Nimrod blows his horn. Terrible things are in store for us, and we go to meet them in Dante's raiment and with Dante's heart. We traverse the marches of the Styx, and Argenti swims to the boat through the slimy waves. He calls to us, and we reject him. When we hear the voice of his agony we are glad, and Virgil praises us for the bitterness of our scorn. We tread upon the cold crystal of Cocytus, in which traitors stick like straws in glass. Our foot strikes against the head of Bocca. He will not tell us his name, and we tear the hair in handfuls from the screaming skull. Alberigo prays us to break the ice upon his face that he may weep a little. We pledge our word to him, and when he has uttered his dolorous tale we deny the word that we have spoken, and pass from him; such cruelty being courtesy indeed, for who more base than he who has mercy for the condemned of God? In the jaws of Lucifer we see the man who sold Christ, and in the jaws of Lucifer the men who slew Caesar. We tremble, and come forth to re-behold the stars.

In the land of Purgation the air is freer, and the holy mountain rises into the pure light of day. There is peace for us, and for those who for a season abide in it there is some peace also, though, pale from the poison of the Maremma, Madonna Pia passes before us, and Ismene, with the sorrow of earth still lingering about her, is there. Soul after soul makes us share in some repentance or some joy. He whom the mourning of his widow taught to drink the sweet wormwood of pain, tells us of Nella praying in her lonely bed, and we learn from the mouth of Buonconte how a single tear may save a dying sinner from the fiend. Sordello, that noble and disdainful Lombard, eyes us from afar like a couchant lion. When he learns that Virgil is one of Mantua's citizens, he falls upon his neck, and when he learns that he is the singer of Rome he falls before his feet. In that valley whose grass and flowers are fairer than cleft emerald and Indian wood, and brighter than scarlet and silver, they are singing who in the world were kings; but the lips of Rudolph of Hapsburg do not move to the music of the others, and Philip of France beats his breast and Henry of England sits alone. On and on we go, climbing the marvellous stair, and the stars become larger than their wont, and the song of the kings grows faint, and at length we reach the seven trees of gold and the garden of the Earthly Paradise. In a griffin-drawn chariot appears one whose brows are bound with olive, who is veiled in white, and mantled in green, and robed in a vesture that is coloured like live fire. The ancient flame wakes within us. Our blood quickens through terrible pulses. We recognise her. It is Beatrice, the woman we have worshipped. The ice congealed about our heart melts. Wild tears of anguish break from us, and we bow our forehead to the ground, for we know that we have sinned. When we have done penance, and are purified, and have drunk of the fountain of Lethe and bathed in the fountain of Eunoe, the mistress of our soul raises us to the Paradise of Heaven. Out of that eternal pearl, the moon, the face of Piccarda Donati leans to us. Her beauty troubles us for a moment, and when, like a thing that falls through water, she passes away, we gaze after her with wistful eyes. The sweet planet of Venus is full of lovers. Cunizza, the sister of Ezzelin, the lady of Sordello's heart, is there, and Folco, the passionate singer of Provence, who in sorrow for Azalais forsook the world, and the Canaanitish harlot whose soul was the first that Christ redeemed. Joachim of Flora stands in the sun, and, in the sun, Aquinas recounts the story of St Francis and Bonaventure the story of St Dominic. Through the burning rubies of Mars, Cacciaguida approaches. He tells us of the arrow that is shot from the bow of exile, and how salt tastes the bread of another, and how steep are the stairs in the house of a stranger. In Saturn the soul sings not, and even she who guides us dare not smile. On a ladder of gold the flames rise and fall. At last, we see the pageant of the Mystical Rose. Beatrice fixes her eyes upon the face of God to turn them not again. The beatific vision is granted to us; we know the love that moves the sun and all the stars.

Yes, we can put the earth back six hundred courses and make ourselves one with the great Florentine, kneel at the same altar with him, and share his rapture and his scorn. And if we grow tired

of an antique time, and desire to realise our own age in all its
weariness and sin, are there not books that can make us live more
in one single hour than life can make us live in a score of shameful
years? Close to your hand lies a little volume, bound in some Nile-
green skin that has been powdered with gilded nenuphars and
smoothed with hard ivory. It is the book that Gautier loved, it is
Baudelaire's masterpiece. Open it at that sad madrigal that begins

> Que m'importe que tu sois sage?
> Sois belle! et sois triste!

and you will find yourself worshipping sorrow as you have never
worshipped joy. Pass on to the poem on the man who tortures
himself, let its subtle music steal into your brain and colour your
thoughts, and you will become for a moment what he was who
wrote it, nay, not for a moment only, but for many barren
moonlit nights and sunless sterile days will a despair that is not
your own make its dwelling within you, and the misery of
another gnaw your heart away. Read the whole book, suffer it to
tell even one of its secrets to your soul, and your soul will grow
eager to know more, and will feed upon poisonous honey, and
seek to repent of strange crimes of which it is guiltless and to
make atonement for terrible pleasures that it has never known.
And then, when you are tired of these flowers of evil, turn to the
flowers that grow in the garden of Perdita, and in their dew-
drenched chalices cool your fevered brow, and let their loveliness heal and restore your soul; or wake from his forgotten tomb
the sweet Syrian, Meleager, and bid the lover of Heliodore make
you music, for he too has flowers in his song, red pomegranate
blossoms, and irises that smell of myrrh, ringed daffodils and
dark-blue hyacinths, and marjoram and crinkled ox-eyes. Dear
to him was the perfume of the bean-field at evening and dear to
him the odorous eared-spikenard that grew on the Syrian hills,
and the fresh green thyme, the wine-cup's charm. The feet of his
love as she walked in the garden were like lilies set upon lilies.
Softer than sleep-laden poppy petals were her lips, softer than
violets and as scented. The flame-like crocus sprang from the
grass to look at her. For her the slim narcissus stored the cool
rain; and for her the anemones forgot the Sicilian winds that

wooed them. And neither crocus, nor anemone, nor narcissus was as fair as she was.

It is a strange thing, this transference of emotion. We sicken with the same maladies as the poets, and the singer lends us his pain. Dead lips have their message for us, and hearts that have fallen to dust can communicate their joy. We run to kiss the bleeding mouth of Fantine, and we follow Manon Lescaut over the whole world. Ours is the love-madness of the Tyrian, and the terror of Orestes is ours also. There is no passion that we cannot feel, no pleasure that we may not gratify, and we can choose the time of our initiation and the time of our freedom also. Life! Life! Don't let us go to life for our fulfilment or our experience. It is a thing narrowed by circumstances, incoherent in its utterance, and without that fine correspondence of form and spirit which is the only thing that can satisfy the artistic and critical temperament. It makes us pay too high a price for its wares, and we purchase the meanest of its secrets at a cost that is monstrous and infinite.

ERNEST: Must we go, then, to art for everything?

GILBERT: For everything. Because art does not hurt us. The tears that we shed at a play are a type of the exquisite sterile emotions that it is the function of art to awaken. We weep, but we are not wounded. We grieve, but our grief is not bitter. In the actual life of man, sorrow, as Spinoza says somewhere, is a passage to a lesser perfection. But the sorrow with which art fills us both purifies and initiates, if I may quote once more from the great art critic of the Greeks. It is through art, and through art only, that we can realise our perfection; through art, and through art only that we can shield ourselves from the sordid perils of actual existence. This results not merely from the fact that nothing that one can imagine is worth doing, and that one can imagine everything, but from the subtle law that emotional forces, like the forces of the physical sphere, are limited in extent and energy. One can feel so much, and no more. And how can it matter with what pleasure life tries to tempt one, or with what pain it seeks to maim and mar one's soul, if in the spectacle of the lives of those who have never existed one has found the true secret of joy, and wept away one's tears over their deaths who, like Cordelia and the daughter of Brabantio, can never die?

ERNEST: Stop a moment. It seems to me that in everything that you have said there is something radically immoral.

GILBERT: All art is immoral.

ERNEST: All art?

GILBERT: Yes. For emotion for the sake of emotion is the aim of art, and emotion for the sake of action is the aim of life, and of that practical organisation of life that we call society. Society, which is the beginning and basis of morals, exists simply for the concentration of human energy, and in order to ensure its own continuance and healthy stability it demands, and no doubt rightly demands, of each of its citizens that he should contribute some form of productive labour to the common weal, and toil and travail that the day's work may be done. Society often forgives the criminal; it never forgives the dreamer. The beautiful sterile emotions that art excites in us are hateful in its eyes, and so completely are people dominated by the tyranny of this dreadful social ideal that they are always coming shamelessly up to one at private views and other places that are open to the general public, and saying in a loud stentorian voice, 'What are you doing?' whereas 'What are you thinking?' is the only question that any single civilised being should ever be allowed to whisper to another. They mean well, no doubt, these honest beaming folk. Perhaps that is the reason why they are so excessively tedious. But someone should teach them that while in the opinion of society, contemplation is the gravest sin of which any citizen can be guilty, in the opinion of the highest culture it is the proper occupation of man.

ERNEST: Contemplation?

GILBERT: Contemplation. I said to you some time ago that it was far more difficult to talk about a thing than to do it. Let me say to you now that to do nothing at all is the most difficult thing in the world, the most difficult and the most intellectual. To Plato, with his passion for wisdom, this was the noblest form of energy. To Aristotle, with his passion for knowledge, this was the noblest form of energy also. It was to this that the passion for holiness led the saint and the mystic of mediaeval days.

ERNEST: We exist, then, to do nothing?

GILBERT: It is to do nothing that the elect exist. Action is limited and relative. Unlimited and absolute is the vision of him who sits at ease and watches, who walks in loneliness and dreams. But we who are born at the close of this wonderful age are at once too cultured and too critical, too intellectually subtle and too curious of exquisite pleasures, to accept any speculations about life in exchange for life itself. To us the *città divina* is colourless, and the *fruitio Dei* without meaning. Metaphysics do not satisfy our temperaments, and religious ecstasy is out of date. The world through which the academic philosopher becomes 'the spectator of all time and of all existence' is not really an ideal world, but simply a world of abstract ideas. When we enter it, we starve amidst the chill mathematics of thought. The courts of the city of God are not open to us now. Its gates are guarded by ignorance, and to pass them we have to surrender all that in our nature is most divine. It is enough that our fathers believed. They have exhausted the faith-faculty of the species. Their legacy to us is the scepticism of which they were afraid. Had they put it into words, it might not live within us as thought. No, Ernest, no. We cannot go back to the saint. There is far more to be learned from the sinner. We cannot go back to the philosopher, and the mystic leads us astray. Who, as Mr Pater suggests somewhere, would exchange the curve of a single rose-leaf for that formless intangible Being which Plato rates so high? What to us is the Illumination of Philo, the Abyss of Eckhart, the Vision of Böhme, the monstrous heaven itself that was revealed to Swedenborg's blinded eyes? Such things are less than the yellow trumpet of one daffodil of the field, far less than the meanest of the visible arts; for, just as nature is matter struggling into mind, so art is mind expressing itself under the conditions of matter, and thus, even in the lowliest of her manifestations, she speaks to both sense and soul alike. To the aesthetic temperament the vague is always repellent. The Greeks were a nation of artists because they were spared the sense of the infinite. Like Aristotle, like Goethe after he had read Kant, we desire the concrete, and nothing but the concrete can satisfy us.

ERNEST: What then do you propose?

GILBERT: It seems to me that with the development of the critical spirit we shall be able to realise, not merely our own lives, but the collective life of the race, and so to make ourselves absolutely modern, in the true meaning of the word modernity. For he to whom the present is the only thing that is present, knows nothing of the age in which he lives. To realise the nineteenth century, one must realise every century that has preceded it and that has contributed to its making. To know anything about oneself one must know all about others. There must be no mood with which one cannot sympathise, no dead mode of life that one cannot make alive. Is this impossible? I think not. By revealing to us the absolute mechanism of all action, and so freeing us from the self-imposed and trammelling burden of moral responsibility, the scientific principle of heredity has become, as it were, the warrant for the contemplative life. It has shown us that we are never less free than when we try to act. It has hemmed us round with the nets of the hunter, and written upon the wall the prophecy of our doom. We may not watch it, for it is within us. We may not see it, save in a mirror that mirrors the soul. It is Nemesis without her mask. It is the last of the Fates, and the most terrible. It is the only one of the gods whose real name we know.

And yet, while in the sphere of practical and external life it has robbed energy of its freedom and activity of its choice, in the subjective sphere, where the soul is at work, it comes to us, this terrible shadow, with many gifts in its hands, gifts of strange temperaments and subtle susceptibilities, gifts of wild ardours and chill moods of indifference, complex multiform gifts of thoughts that are at variance with each other, and passions that war against themselves. And so it is not our own life that we live but the lives of the dead and the soul that dwells within us is no single spiritual entity, making us personal and individual, created for our service, and entering into us for our joy. It is something that has dwelt in fearful places, and in ancient sepulchres has made its abode. It is sick with many maladies, and has memories of curious sins. It is wiser than we are, and its wisdom is bitter. It fills us with impossible desires, and makes us follow what we know we cannot gain. One thing, however, Ernest, it can do for us. It can lead us away from surroundings whose beauty is dimmed to us by the mist of familiarity, or whose ignoble ugliness and sordid claims are marring the perfection of our development. It can help us to leave the age in which we were born, and to pass into other ages, and find ourselves not exiled from their air. It can teach us how to escape from our experience, and to realise the experiences of those who are greater than we are. The pain of Leopardi crying out against life becomes our pain. Theocritus blows on his pipe and we laugh with the lips of nymph and shepherd. In the wolfskin of Pierre Vidal we flee before the hounds, and in the armour of Lancelot we ride from the bower of the queen. We have whispered the secret of our love beneath the cowl of Abelard, and in the stained raiment of Villon have put our shame into song. We can see the dawn through Shelley's eyes, and when we wander with Endymion, the moon grows amorous of our youth. Ours is the anguish of Atys, and ours the weak rage and noble sorrows of the Dane. Do you think that it is the imagination that enables us to live these countless lives? Yes, it is the imagination; and the imagination is the result of heredity. It is simply concentrated race-experience.

ERNEST: But where in this is the function of the critical spirit?

GILBERT: The culture that this transmission of racial experiences makes possible can be made perfect by the critical spirit alone, and indeed may be said to be one with it. For who is the true critic but he who bears within himself the dreams, and ideas, and feelings of myriad generations, and he to whom no form of thought is alien, no emotional impulse obscure? And who the true man of culture, if not he who by fine scholarship and fastidious rejection has made instinct self-conscious and intelligent, and can separate the work that has distinction from the work that has it not, and so by contact and comparison makes himself master of the secrets of style and school, and understands their meanings, and listens to their voices, and develops that spirit of disinterested curiosity which is the real root, as it is the real flower, of the intellectual life, and thus attains to intellectual clarity, and, having learned 'the best that is known and thought in the world', lives – it is not fanciful to say so – with those who are the Immortals.

Yes, Ernest: the contemplative life, the life that has for its aim not *doing* but *being*, and not *being* merely, but *becoming* – that is what the critical spirit can give us. The gods live thus: either brooding over their own perfection, as Aristotle tells us, or, as Epicurus fancied, watching with the calm eyes of the spectator the tragi-comedy of the world that they have made. We, too, might live like them and set ourselves to witness with appropriate emotions the varied scenes that man and nature afford. We might make ourselves spiritual by detaching ourselves from action, and become perfect by the rejection of energy. It has often seemed to me that Browning felt something of this. Shakespeare hurls Hamlet into active life, and makes him realise his mission by effort. Browning might have given us a Hamlet who would have realised his mission by thought. Incident and event were to him unreal or unmeaning. He made the soul the protagonist of life's tragedy, and looked on action as the one undramatic element of a play. To us, at any rate, the ΒΙΟΣ ΘΕΩΡΗΤΙΚΟΣ is the true ideal. From the high tower of thought we can look out at the world. Calm, and self-centred, and complete, the aesthetic critic contemplates life, and no arrow drawn at a venture can pierce between the joints of his harness. He at least is safe. He has discovered how to live.

Is such a mode of life immoral? Yes all the arts are immoral, except those baser forms of sensual or didactic art that seek to excite to action of evil or of good. For action of every kind belongs to the sphere of ethics. The aim of art is simply to create a mood. Is such a mode of life unpractical? Ah! it is not so easy to be unpractical as the ignorant philistine imagines. It were well for England if it were so. There is no country in the world so much in need of unpractical people as this country of ours. With us, thought is degraded by its constant association with practice. Who that moves in the stress and turmoil of actual existence, noisy politician or brawling social reformer or poor narrow-minded priest blinded by the sufferings of that unimportant section of the community among whom he has cast his lot, can seriously claim to be able to form a disinterested intellectual judgement about any one thing? Each of the professions means a prejudice. The necessity for a career forces everyone to take sides. We live in the age of the overworked, and the under-educated; the age in which people are so industrious that they become absolutely stupid. And, harsh though it may sound, I cannot help saying that such people deserve their doom. The sure way of knowing nothing about life is to try to make oneself useful.

ERNEST: A charming doctrine, Gilbert.

GILBERT: I am not sure about that, but it has at least the minor merit of being true. That the desire to do good to others produces a plentiful crop of prigs is the least of the evils of which it is the cause. The prig is a very interesting psychological study, and though of all poses a moral pose is the most offensive, still to have a pose at all is something. It is a formal recognition of the importance of treating life from a definite and reasoned stand-point. That humanitarian sympathy wars against nature, by securing the survival of the failure, may make the man of science loathe its facile virtues. The political economist may cry out against it for putting the improvident on the same level as the provident, and so robbing life of the strongest, because most sordid, incentive to industry. But in the eyes of the thinker the real harm that emotional sympathy does is that it limits knowledge, and so prevents us from solving any single social problem. We are trying at present to stave off the coming crisis, the coming revolution, as my friends the Fabianists call it, by means of doles and alms. Well, when the revolution or crisis arrives, we shall be powerless, because we shall know nothing. And so, Ernest, let us not be deceived. England will never be civilised till she has added Utopia to her dominions. There is more than one of her colonies that she might with advantage surrender for so fair a land. What we want are unpractical people who see beyond the moment, and think beyond the day. Those who try to lead the people can only do so by following the mob. It is through the voice of one crying in the wilderness that the ways of the gods must be prepared.

But perhaps you think that in beholding for the mere joy of beholding, and contemplating for the sake of contemplation, there is something that is egotistic. If you think so, do not say so.

It takes a thoroughly selfish age, like our own, to deify self-sacrifice. It takes a thoroughly grasping age, such as that in which we live, to set above the fine intellectual virtues those shallow and emotional virtues that are an immediate practical benefit to itself. They miss their aim, too, these philanthropists and sentimentalists of our day who are always chattering to one about one's duty to one's neighbour. For the development of the race depends on the development of the individual, and where self-culture has ceased to be the ideal the intellectual standard is instantly lowered, and, often, ultimately lost. If you meet at dinner a man who has spent his life in educating himself – a rare type in our time, I admit, but still one occasionally to be met with – you rise from table richer, and conscious that a high ideal has for a moment touched and sanctified your days. But oh! my dear Ernest, to sit next to a man who has spent his life in trying to educate others! What a dreadful experience that is! How appalling is that ignorance which is the inevitable result of the fatal habit of imparting opinions! How limited in range the creature's mind proves to be! How it wearies us, and must weary himself, with its endless repetitions and sickly reiteration! How lacking it is in any element of intellectual growth! In what a vicious circle it always moves!

ERNEST: You speak with strange feeling, Gilbert. Have you had this dreadful experience, as you call it, lately?

GILBERT: Few of us escape it. People say that the schoolmaster is abroad. I wish to goodness he were. But the type of which, after all, he is only one, and certainly the least important, of the representatives, seems to me to be really dominating our lives, and just as the philanthropist is the nuisance of the ethical sphere, so the nuisance of the intellectual sphere is the man who is so occupied in trying to educate others that he has never had any time to educate himself. No, Ernest, self-culture is the true ideal of man. Goethe saw it, and the immediate debt that we owe to Goethe is greater than the debt we owe to any man since Greek days. The Greeks saw it, and have left us, as their legacy to modern thought, the conception of the contemplative life as well as the critical method by which alone can that life be truly realised. It was the one thing that made the Renaissance great, and gave us Humanism. It is the one thing that could make our own age great also; for the real weakness of England lies, not in incomplete armaments or unfortified coasts, not in the poverty that creeps through sunless lanes, or the drunkenness that brawls in loathsome courts, but simply in the fact that her ideals are emotional and not intellectual.

I do not deny that the intellectual ideal is difficult of attainment, still less that it is, and perhaps will be for years to come, unpopular with the crowd. It is so easy for people to have sympathy with suffering. It is so difficult for them to have sympathy with thought. Indeed, so little do ordinary people understand what thought really is, that they seem to imagine that, when they have said that a theory is dangerous, they have pronounced its condemnation, whereas it is only such theories that have any true intellectual value. An idea that is not dangerous is unworthy of being called an idea at all.

ERNEST: Gilbert, you bewilder me. You have told me that all art is, in its essence, immoral. Are you going to tell me now that all thought is, in its essence, dangerous?

GILBERT: Yes, in the practical sphere it is so. The security of society lies in custom and unconscious instinct, and the basis of the stability of society, as a healthy organism, is the complete absence of any intelligence amongst its members. The great majority of people being fully aware of this, rank themselves naturally on the side of that splendid system that elevates them to the dignity of machines, and rage so wildly against the intrusion of the intellectual faculty into any question that concerns life, that one is tempted to define man as a rational animal who always loses his temper when he is called upon to act in accordance with the dictates of reason. But let us turn from the practical sphere, and say no more about the wicked philanthropists, who, indeed, may well be left to the mercy of the almond-eyed sage of the Yellow River, Chuang Tsŭ the Wise, who has proved that such well-meaning and offensive busybodies have destroyed the simple and spontaneous virtue that there is in man. They are a wearisome topic, and I am anxious to get back to the sphere in which criticism is free.

ERNEST: The sphere of the intellect?

GILBERT: Yes. You remember that I spoke of the critic as being in his own way as creative as the artist whose work, indeed, may be merely of value in so far as it gives to the critic a suggestion for some new mood of thought and feeling which he can realise with equal, or perhaps greater, distinction of form and through the use of a fresh medium of expression make differently beautiful and more perfect. Well you seemed to be a little sceptical about the theory. But perhaps I wronged you?

ERNEST: I am not really sceptical about it, but I must admit that I feel very strongly that such work as you describe the critic producing – and creative such work must undoubtedly be admitted to be – is of necessity, purely subjective, whereas the greatest work is objective always, objective and impersonal.

GILBERT: The difference between objective and subjective work is one of external form merely. It is accidental, not essential. All artistic creation is absolutely subjective. The very landscape that Corot looked at was, as he said himself, but a mood of his own mind; and those great figures of Greek or English drama that seem to us to possess an actual existence of their own, apart from the poets who shaped and fashioned them, are, in their ultimate analysis, simply the poets themselves, not as they thought they were, but as they thought they were not; and by such thinking came in strange manner, though but for a moment, really so to be. For out of ourselves we can never pass, nor can there be in creation what in the creator was not. Nay, I would say that the more objective a creation appears to be, the more subjective it really is. Shakespeare might have met Rosencrantz and Guildenstern in the white streets of London, or seen the serving-men of rival houses bite their thumbs at each other in the open square; but Hamlet came out of his soul, and Romeo out of his passion. They were elements of his nature to which he gave visible form, impulses that stirred so strongly within him that he had, as it were perforce, to suffer them to realise their energy, not on the lower plane of actual life, where they would have been trammelled and constrained and so made imperfect, but on that imaginative plane of art where love can indeed find in death its rich fulfilment, where one can stab the eavesdropper behind the arras, and wrestle in a new-made grave, and make a guilty king drink his own hurt, and see one's father's spirit, beneath the glimpses of the moon, stalking in complete steel from misty wall to wall. Action being limited would have left Shakespeare unsatisfied and unexpressed; and, just as it is because he did nothing that he has been able to achieve everything, so it is because he never speaks to us of himself in his plays that his plays reveal him to us absolutely, and show us his true nature and temperament far more completely than do those strange and exquisite sonnets, even, in which he bares to crystal eyes the secret closet of his heart. Yes, the objective form is the most subjective in matter. Man is least himself when he talks in his own person. Give him a mask, and he will tell you the truth.

ERNEST: The critic, then, being limited to the subjective form, will necessarily be less able fully to express himself than the artist, who has always at his disposal the forms that are impersonal and objective.

GILBERT: Not necessarily, and certainly not at all if he recognises that each mode of criticism is, in its highest development, simply a mood, and that we are never more true to ourselves than when we are inconsistent. The aesthetic critic, constant only to the principle of beauty in all things, will ever be looking for fresh impressions, winning from the various schools the secret of their charm, bowing, it may be, before foreign altars, or smiling, if it be his fancy, at strange new gods. What other people call one's past has, no doubt, everything to do with them, but has absolutely nothing to do with oneself. The man who regards his past is a man who deserves to have no future to look forward to. When one has found expression for a mood, one has done with it. You laugh; but believe me it is so. Yesterday it was Realism that charmed one. One gained from it that *nouveau frisson* which it was its aim to produce. One analysed it, explained it, and wearied of it. At sunset came the *Luministe* in painting and the *Symboliste* in poetry, and the spirit of mediaevalism, that spirit which belongs not to time but to temperament, woke suddenly in wounded Russia and stirred us for a moment by the terrible fascination of pain. Today the cry is for Romance, and already the leaves are tremulous in the valley, and on the purple hill-tops walks beauty with slim gilded feet. The old modes of creation linger, of course. The artists reproduce either themselves or each other with wearisome iteration. But criticism is always moving on, and the critic is always developing

Nor, again, is the critic really limited to the subjective form of expression. The method of the drama is his, as well as the method of the epos. He may use dialogue, as he did who set Milton talking to Marvel on the nature of comedy and tragedy, and made Sidney and Lord Brooke discourse on letters beneath the Penshurst oaks; or adopt narration, as Mr Pater is fond of doing, each of whose imaginary portraits – is not that the title of the book? – presents to us, under the fanciful guise of fiction, some fine and exquisite piece of criticism, one on the painter Watteau, another on the philosophy of Spinoza, a third on the pagan elements of the early Renaissance, and the last, and in some respects the most suggestive, on the source of that *Aufklärung*, that enlightening which dawned on Germany in the last century, and to which our own culture owes so great a debt. Dialogue, certainly, that wonderful literary form which, from Plato to Lucian, and from Lucian to Giordano Bruno, and from Bruno to that grand old pagan in whom Carlyle took such delight, the creative critics of the world have always employed, can never lose for the thinker its attraction as a mode of expression. By its means he can both reveal and conceal himself, and give form to every fancy and reality to every mood. By its means he can exhibit the object from each point of view, and show it to us in the round, as a sculptor shows us things, gaining in this manner all the richness and reality of effect that comes from those side issues that are suddenly suggested by the central idea in its progress, and really illumine the idea more completely, or from those felicitous after-thoughts that give a fuller completeness to the central scheme, and yet convey something of the delicate charm of chance.

ERNEST: By its means, too, he can invent an imaginary antagonist, and convert him when he chooses by some absurdly sophistical argument.

GILBERT: Ah! it is so easy to convert others. It is so difficult to convert oneself. To arrive at what one really believes, one must speak through lips different from one's own. To know the truth one must imagine myriads of falsehoods. For what is truth? In matters of religion, it is simply the opinion that has survived. In matters of science, it is the ultimate sensation. In matters of art, it is one's last mood. And you see now, Ernest, that the critic has at his disposal as many objective forms of expression as the artist has. Ruskin put his criticism into imaginative prose, and is superb in his changes and contradictions, and Browning put his into blank verse and made painter and poet yield us their secret; and M. Renan uses dialogue, and Mr Pater fiction, and Rossetti translated into sonnet-music the colour of Giorgione and the design of Ingres and his own design and colour also, feeling, with the instinct of one who had many modes of utterance, that the ultimate art is literature, and the finest and fullest medium that of words.

ERNEST: Well, now that you have settled that the critic has at his disposal all objective forms, I wish you would tell me what are the qualities that should characterise the true critic.

GILBERT: What would you say they were?

ERNEST: Well, I should say that a critic should above all things be fair.

GILBERT: Ah! not fair. A critic cannot be fair in the ordinary sense of the word. It is only about things that do not interest one that one can give a really unbiassed opinion, which is no doubt the reason why an unbiassed opinion is always absolutely valueless. The man who sees both sides of a question, is a man who sees absolutely nothing at all. Art is a passion and, in matters of art, thought is inevitably coloured by emotion, and so is fluid rather than fixed, and, depending upon fine moods and exquisite moments, cannot be narrowed into the rigidity of a scientific formula or a theological dogma. It is to the soul that art speaks, and the soul may be made the prisoner of the mind as well as of the body. One should, of course, have no prejudices; but, as a great Frenchman remarked a hundred years ago, it is one's business in such matters to have preferences, and when one has preferences one ceases to be fair. It is only an auctioneer who can equally and impartially admire all schools of art. No; fairness is not one of the qualities of the true critic. It is not even a condition of criticism. Each form of art with which we come in contact dominates us for the moment to the exclusion of every other form. We must surrender ourselves absolutely to the work in question, whatever it may be, if we wish to gain its secret. For the time, we must think of nothing else, can think of nothing else, indeed.

ERNEST: The true critic will be rational, at any rate, will he not?

GILBERT: Rational? There are two ways of disliking art, Ernest. One is to dislike it. The other, to like it rationally. For art, as Plato saw, and not without regret, creates in listener and spectator a form of divine madness. It does not spring from inspiration but it makes others inspired. Reason is not the faculty to which it appeals. If one loves art at all, one must love it beyond all other things in the world, and against such love, the reason, if one listened to it would cry out. There is nothing sane about the worship of beauty. It is too splendid to be sane. Those of whose lives it forms the dominant note will always seem to the world to be pure visionaries.

ERNEST: Well, at least, the critic will be sincere.

GILBERT: A little sincerity is a dangerous thing, and a great deal of it is absolutely fatal. The true critic will, indeed, always be sincere in his devotion to the principle of beauty, but he will seek for beauty in every age and in each school, and will never suffer himself to be limited to any settled custom of thought or stereotyped mode of looking at things. He will realise himself in many forms, and by a thousand different ways, and will ever be curious of new sensations and fresh points of view. Through constant change, and through constant change alone, he will find his true identity. He will not consent to be the slave of his own opinions. For what is mind but motion in the intellectual sphere? The essence of thought, as the essence of life, is growth. You must not be frightened by words, Ernest. What people call insincerity is simply a method by which we can multiply our personalities.

ERNEST: I am afraid I have not been fortunate in my suggestions.

GILBERT: Of the three qualifications you mentioned, two, sincerity and fairness, were, if not actually moral, at least on the borderland of morals, and the first condition of criticism is that the critic should be able to recognise that the sphere of art and the sphere of ethics are absolutely distinct and separate. When they are confused, chaos has come again. They are too often confused in England now, and though our modern puritans cannot destroy a beautiful thing, yet, by means of their extraordinary prurience, they can almost taint beauty for a moment. It is chiefly, I regret to say, through journalism that such people find expression. I regret it because there is much to be said in favour of modern journalism. By giving us the opinions of the uneducated, it keeps us in touch with the ignorance of the community. By carefully chronicling the current events of contemporary life, it shows us of what very little importance such events really are. By invariably discussing the unnecessary, it makes us understand what things are requisite for culture, and what are not. But it should not allow poor Tartuffe to write articles upon modern art. When it does this it stultifies itself. And yet Tartuffe's articles and Chadband's notes do this good, at least. They serve to show how extremely limited is the area over which ethics, and ethical considerations, can claim to exercise influence. Science is out of the reach of morals, for her eyes are fixed upon eternal truths. Art is out of the reach of morals, for her eyes are fixed upon things beautiful and immortal and ever-changing. To morals belong the lower and less intellectual spheres. However, let these mouthing puritans pass; they have their comic side. Who can help laughing when an ordinary journalist seriously proposes to limit the subject-matter at the disposal of the artist? Some limitation might well, and will soon, I hope, be placed upon some of our newspapers and newspaper writers. For they give us the bald, sordid, disgusting facts of life. They chronicle, with degrading avidity, the sins of the second-rate, and with the conscientiousness of the illiterate give us accurate and prosaic details of the doings of people of absolutely no interest whatsoever. But the artist, who accepts the facts of life, and yet transforms them into shapes of beauty, and makes them vehicles of pity or of awe, and shows their colour-element, and their wonder, and their true ethical import also, and builds out of them a world more real than reality itself, and of loftier and more noble import – who shall set limits to him? Not the apostles of that new journalism which is but the old vulgarity 'writ large'. Not the apostles of that new puritanism which is but the whine of the hypocrite and is both writ and spoken badly. The mere suggestion is ridiculous. Let us leave these wicked people, and proceed to the discussion of the artistic qualifications necessary for the true critic.

ERNEST: And what are they? Tell me yourself.

GILBERT: Temperament is the primary requisite for the critic – a temperament exquisitely susceptible to beauty, and to the various impressions that beauty gives us. Under what conditions and by what means this temperament is engendered in race or individual we will not discuss at present. It is sufficient to note that it exists, and that there is in us a beauty-sense separate from the other senses and above them, separate from the reason and of nobler import, separate from the soul and of equal value – a sense that leads some to create, and others, the finer spirits as I think, to contemplate merely. But to be purified and made perfect this sense requires some form of exquisite environment. Without this it starves, or is dulled. You remember that lovely passage in which Plato describes how a young Greek should be educated, and with what insistence he dwells upon the importance of surroundings, telling us how the lad is to be brought up in the midst of fair sights and sounds, so that the beauty of material things may prepare his soul for the reception of the beauty that is spiritual. Insensibly, and without knowing the reason why, he is to develop that real love of beauty which, as Plato is never weary of reminding us, is the true aim of education. By slow degrees there is to be engendered in him such a temperament as will lead him naturally and simply to choose the good in preference to the bad, and, rejecting what is vulgar and discordant, to follow by fine instinctive taste all that possesses grace and charm and loveliness. Ultimately, in its due course, this taste is to become critical and self-conscious, but at first it is to exist purely as a cultivated instinct, and 'he who has received this true culture of the inner man will with clear and certain vision perceive the omissions and faults in art or nature, and with a taste that cannot err, while he praises, and finds his pleasure in what is good, and receives it into his soul, and so becomes good and noble, he will rightly blame and hate the bad, now in the days of his youth, even before he is able to know the reason why': and so, when, later on, the critical and self-conscious spirit develops in him, he 'will recognise and salute it as a friend with whom his education has made him long familiar'. I need hardly say, Ernest, how far we in England have fallen short of this ideal, and I can imagine the smile that would illuminate the glossy face of the philistine if one ventured to suggest to him that the true aim of education was the love of beauty, and that the methods by which education should work were the development of temperament, the cultivation of taste and the creation of the critical spirit.

Yet, even for us, there is left some loveliness of environment, and the dullness of tutors and professors matters very little when one can loiter in the grey cloisters at Magdalen, and listen to some flute-like voice singing in Waynfleete's chapel, or lie in the green meadow, among the strange snake-spotted fritillaries, and watch the sunburnt noon smite to a finer gold the tower's gilded vanes, or wander up the Christ Church staircase beneath the vaulted ceiling's shadowy fans, or pass through the sculptured gateway of Laud's building in the College of St John. Nor is it merely at Oxford or Cambridge that the sense of beauty can be formed and trained and perfected. All over England there is a renaissance of the decorative arts. Ugliness has had its day. Even in the houses of the rich there is taste and the houses of those who are not rich have been made gracious and comely and sweet to live in. Caliban, poor noisy Caliban, thinks that when he has ceased to make mows at a thing the thing ceases to exist. But if he mocks no longer it is because he has been met with mockery swifter and keener than his own, and for a moment has been bitterly schooled into that silence which should seal for ever his uncouth distorted lips. What has been done up to now has been chiefly in the clearing of the way. It is always more difficult to destroy than it is to create, and when what one has to destroy is vulgarity and stupidity, the task of destruction needs not merely courage but also contempt. Yet it seems to me to have been, in a measure, done. We have got rid of what was bad. We have now to make what is beautiful. And though the mission of the aesthetic movement is to lure people to contemplate, not to lead them to create, yet, as the creative instinct is strong in the Celt, and it is the Celt who leads in art, there is no reason why in future years this strange renaissance should not become almost as mighty in its way as was that new birth of art that woke many centuries ago in the cities of Italy.

Certainly, for the cultivation of temperament, we must turn to the decorative arts: to the arts that touch us, not to the arts that teach us. Modern pictures are, no doubt, delightful to look at. At least some of them are. But they are quite impossible to live with; they are too clever, too assertive, too intellectual. Their meaning is too obvious, and their method too clearly defined. One exhausts what they have to say in a very short time, and then they become as tedious as one's relations. I am very fond of the work of many of the Impressionist painters of Paris and London. Subtlety and distinction have not yet left the school. Some of their arrangements and harmonies serve to remind one of the unapproachable beauty of Gautier's immortal *Symphonie en Blanc Majeur*, that flawless masterpiece of colour and music which may have suggested the type as well as the titles of many of their best pictures. For a class that welcomes the incompetent with sympathetic eagerness, and that confuses the bizarre with the beautiful, and vulgarity with truth, they are extremely accomplished. They can do etchings that have the brilliancy of epigrams, pastels that are as fascinating as paradoxes, and as for their portraits, whatever the commonplace may say against them, no one can deny that they possess that unique and wonderful charm which belongs to works of pure fiction. But even the Impressionists, earnest and industrious as they are, will not do. I like them. Their white keynote, with its variations in lilac, was an era in colour. Though the moment does not make the man, the moment certainly makes the Impressionist and for the moment in art, and the 'moment's monument', as Rossetti phrased it, what may not be said? They are suggestive also. If they have not opened the eyes of the blind, they have at least given great encouragement to the short-sighted, and while their leaders may have all the inexperience of old age, their young men are far too wise to be ever sensible. Yet they will insist on treating painting as if it were a mode of autobiography invented for the use of the illiterate, and are always prating to us on their coarse gritty canvases of their unnecessary selves and their unnecessary opinions, and spoiling by a vulgar over-emphasis that fine contempt of nature which is the best and only modest thing about them. One tires, at the end, of the work of individuals whose individuality is always noisy, and generally uninteresting. There is a far more to be said in favour of that newer school at Paris, the *Archaicistes*, as they call themselves, who, refusing to leave the artist entirely at the mercy of the weather, do not find the ideal of art in mere atmospheric effect, but seek rather for the imaginative beauty of design and the loveliness of fair colour, and rejecting the tedious realism of those who merely paint what they see, try to see something worth seeing, and to see it not merely with actual and physical vision, but with that nobler vision of the soul which is as far wider in spiritual scope as it is far more splendid in artistic purpose. They, at any rate, work under those decorative conditions that each art requires for its perfection, and have sufficient aesthetic instinct to regret those sordid and stupid limitations of absolute modernity of form which have proved the ruin of so many of the Impressionists. Still, the art that is frankly decorative is the art to live with. It is, of all our visible arts, the one art that creates in us both mood and temperament. Mere colour, unspoiled by meaning, and unallied with definite form, can speak to the soul in a thousand different ways. The harmony that resides in the delicate proportions of lines and masses becomes mirrored in the mind. The repetitions of pattern give us rest. The marvels of design stir the imagination. In the mere loveliness of the materials employed there are latent elements of culture. Nor is this all. By its deliberate rejection of nature as the ideal of beauty, as well as of the imitative method of the ordinary painter, decorative art not merely prepares the soul for the reception of true imaginative work, but develops in it that sense of form which is the basis of creative no less than of critical achievement. For the real artist is he who proceeds, not from feeling to form, but from form to thought and passion. He does not first conceive an idea, and then say to himself, 'I will put my idea into a complex metre of fourteen lines', but, realising the beauty of the sonnet-scheme, he conceives certain modes of music and methods of rhyme, and the mere form suggests what is to fill it and make it intellectually and emotionally complete. From time to time the world cries out against some charming artistic poet, because, to use its hackneyed and silly phrase, he has 'nothing to say'. But if he had something to say, he would probably say it, and the result would be tedious. It is just because he had no new message, that he can do beautiful work. He gains his inspiration from form, and from form purely, as an artist should. A real passion would ruin him. Whatever actually occurs is spoiled for art. All bad poetry springs from genuine feeling. To be natural is to be obvious, and to be obvious is to be inartistic.

ERNEST: I wonder do you really believe what you say?

GILBERT: Why should you wonder? It is not merely in art that the body is the soul. In every sphere of life form is the beginning of things. The rhythmic harmonious gestures of dancing convey, Plato tells us, both rhythm and harmony into the mind. Forms are the food of faith, cried Newman in one of those great moments of sincerity that make us admire and know the man. He was right, though he may not have known how terribly right he was. The Creeds are believed, not because they are rational, but because they are repeated. Yes; form is everything. It is the secret of life. Find expression for a sorrow, and it will become dear to you. Find expression for a joy, and you intensify its ecstasy. Do you wish to love? Use *Love's Litany*, and the words will create the yearning from which the world fancies that they spring. Have you a grief that corrodes your heart? Steep yourself in the language of grief, learn its utterance from Prince Hamlet and Queen Constance, and you will find that mere expression is a mode of consolation, and that form, which is the birth of passion, is also the death of pain. And so, to return to the sphere of art, it is form that creates not merely the critical temperament, but also the aesthetic instinct, that unerring instinct that reveals to one all things under their conditions of beauty. Start with the worship of form, and there is no secret in art that will not be revealed to you, and remember that in criticism, as in creation, temperament is everything, and that it is not by the time of their production but by the temperaments to which they appeal that the schools of art should be historically grouped.

ERNEST: Your theory of education is delightful. But what influence will your critic, brought up in these exquisite surroundings, possess? Do you really think that any artist is ever affected by criticism?

GILBERT: The influence of the critic will be the mere fact of his own existence. He will represent the flawless type. In him the culture of the century will see itself realised. You must not ask of him to have any aim other than the perfecting of himself. The demand of the intellect, as has been well said, is simply to feel itself alive. The critic may, indeed, desire to exercise influence; but, if so, he will concern himself not with the individual, but with the age, which he will seek to wake into consciousness, and to make responsive, creating in it new desires and appetites, and lending it his larger vision and his nobler moods. The actual art of today will occupy him less than the art of tomorrow, far less than the art of yesterday, and as for this or that person at present toiling away, what do the industrious matter? They do their best, no doubt, and consequently we get the worst from them. It is always with the best intentions that the worst work is done. And besides, my dear Ernest, when a man reaches the age of forty, or becomes a Royal Academician, or is elected a member of the Athenaeum Club, or is recognised as a popular novelist whose books are in great demand at surburban railway stations, one may have the amusement of exposing him, but one cannot have the pleasure of reforming him. And this is, I dare say, very fortunate for him; for I have no doubt that reformation is a much more painful process than punishment, is indeed punishment in its most aggravated and moral form – a fact which accounts for our entire failure as a community to reclaim that interesting phenomenon who is called the confirmed criminal.

ERNEST: But may it not be that the poet is the best judge of poetry, and the painter of painting? Each art must appeal primarily to the artist who works in it. His judgement will surely be the most valuable?

GILBERT: The appeal of all art is simply to the artistic temperament. Art does not address herself to the specialist. Her claim is that she is universal, and that in all her manifestations she is one. Indeed, so far from its being true that the artist is the best judge of art, a really great artist can never judge of other people's work at all, and can hardly, in fact, judge of his own. That very concentration of vision that makes a man an artist, limits by its sheer intensity his faculty of fine appreciation. The energy of creation hurries him blindly on to his own goal. The wheels of his chariot raise the dust as a cloud around him. The gods are hidden from each other. They can recognise their worshippers. That is all.

ERNEST: You say that a great artist cannot recognise the beauty of work different from his own.

GILBERT: It is impossible for him to do so. Wordsworth saw in *Endymion* merely a pretty piece of paganism, and Shelley, with his dislike of activity, was deaf to Wordsworth's message, being repelled by its form, and Byron, that great passionate human incomplete creature, could appreciate neither the poet of the cloud nor the poet of the lake, and the wonder of Keats was hidden from him. The realism of Euripides was hateful to Sophocles. Those droppings of warm tears had no music for him. Milton, with his sense of the grand style, could not understand the method of Shakespeare, any more than could Sir Joshua the method of Gainsborough. Bad artists always admire each other's work. They call it being large-minded and free from prejudice. But a truly great artist cannot conceive of life being shown, or beauty fashioned, under any conditions other than those that he has selected. Creation employs all its critical faculty within its own sphere. It may not use it in the sphere that belongs to others. It is exactly because a man cannot do a thing that he is the proper judge of it.

ERNEST: Do you really mean that?

GILBERT: Yes, for creation limits, while contemplation widens, the vision.

ERNEST: But what about technique? Surely each art has its separate technique?

GILBERT: Certainly: each art has its grammar and its materials. There is no mystery about either, and the incompetent can always be correct. But, while the laws upon which art rests may be fixed and certain, to find their true realisation they must be touched by the imagination into such beauty that they will seem an exception, each one of them. Technique is really personality. That is the reason why the artist cannot teach it, why the pupil cannot learn it, and why the aesthetic critic can understand it. To the great poet, there is only one method of music – his own. To the great painter, there is only one manner of painting – that which he himself employs. The aesthetic critic, and the aesthetic critic alone, can appreciate all forms and modes. It is to him that art makes her appeal.

ERNEST: Well, I think I have put all my questions to you. And now I must admit –

GILBERT: Ah! don't say that you agree with me. When people agree with me I always feel that I must be wrong.

ERNEST: In that case I certainly won't tell you whether I agree with you or not. But I will put another question. You have explained to me that criticism is a creative art. What future has it?

GILBERT: It is to criticism that the future belongs. The subject-matter at the disposal of creation becomes every day more limited in extent and variety. Providence and Mr Walter Besant have exhausted the obvious. If creation is to last at all, it can only do so on the condition of becoming far more critical than it is at present. The old roads and dusty highways have been traversed too often. Their charm has been worn away by plodding feet, and they have lost that element of novelty or surprise which is so essential for romance. He who would stir us now by fiction must either give us an entirely new background, or reveal to us the soul of man in its innermost workings. The first is for the moment being done for us by Mr Rudyard Kipling. As one turns over the pages of his *Plain Tales from the Hills*, one feels as if one were seated under a palm tree reading life by superb flashes of vulgarity. The bright colours of the bazaars dazzle one's eyes.

The jaded, second-rate Anglo-Indians are in exquisite incongruity with their surroundings. The mere lack of style in the storyteller gives an odd journalistic realism to what he tells us. From the point of view of literature Mr Kipling is a genius who drops his aspirates. From the point of view of life, he is a reporter who knows vulgarity better than anyone has ever known it. Dickens knew its clothes and its comedy. Mr Kipling knows its essence and its seriousness. He is our first authority on the second-rate, and has seen marvellous things through keyholes, and his backgrounds are real works of art. As for the second condition, we have had Browning, and Meredith is with us. But there is still much to be done in the sphere of introspection. People sometimes say that fiction is getting too morbid. As far as psychology is concerned, it has never been morbid enough. We have merely touched the surface of the soul, that is all. In one single ivory cell of the brain there are stored away things more marvellous and more terrible than even they have dreamed of, who, like the author of *Le Rouge et le Noir*, have sought to track the soul into its most secret places, and to make life confess its dearest sins. Still, there is a limit even to the number of untried backgrounds, and it is possible that a further development of the habit of introspection may prove fatal to that creative faculty to which it seeks to supply flesh material. I myself am inclined to think that creation is doomed. It springs from too primitive, too natural an impulse. However this may be, it is certain that the subject-matter at the disposal of creation is always diminishing, while the subject matter of criticism increases daily. There are always new attitudes for the mind, and new points of view. The duty of imposing form upon chaos does not grow less as the world advances. There was never a time when criticism was more needed than it is now. It is only by its means that humanity can become conscious of the point at which it has arrived.

Hours ago, Ernest, you asked me the use of criticism. You might just as well have asked me the use of thought. It is criticism, as Arnold points out, that creates the intellectual atmosphere of the age. It is criticism, as I hope to point out myself some day, that makes the mind a fine instrument. We, in our educational system, have burdened the memory with a load of unconnected facts, and laboriously striven to impart our laboriously acquired knowledge. We teach people how to remember, we never teach them how to grow. It has never occurred to us to try and develop in the mind a more subtle quality of apprehension and discernment. The Greeks did this, and when we come in contact with the Greek critical intellect, we cannot but be conscious that, while our subject-matter is in every respect larger and more varied than theirs, theirs is the only method by which this subject-matter can be interpreted. England has done one thing; it has invented and established public opinion, which is an attempt to organise the ignorance of the community, and to elevate it to the dignity of physical force. But wisdom has always been hidden from it. Considered as an instrument of thought, the English mind is coarse and undeveloped. The only thing that can purify it is the growth of the critical instinct.

It is criticism, again, that, by concentration, makes culture possible. It takes the cumbersome mass of creative work, and distils it into a finer essence. Who that desires to retain any sense of form could struggle through the monstrous multitudinous books that the world has produced, books in which thought stammers or ignorance brawls? The thread that is to guide us across the wearisome labyrinth is in the hands of criticism. Nay more, where there is no record, and history is either lost, or was never written, criticism can recreate the past for us from the very smallest fragment of language or art, just as surely as the man of science can from some tiny bone, or the mere impress of a foot upon a rock, recreate for us the winged dragon or Titan lizard that once made the earth shake beneath its tread, can call Behemoth out of his cave, and make Leviathan swim once more across the startled sea. Prehistoric history belongs to the philological and archaeological critic. It is to him that the origins of things are revealed. The self-conscious deposits of an age are nearly always misleading. Through philological criticism alone we know more of the centuries of which no actual record has been preserved than we do of the centuries that have left us their scrolls. It can do for us what can be done neither by physics nor metaphysics. It can give us the exact science of mind in the progress of becoming. It can do for us what history cannot do. It can tell us what man thought before he learned how to write. You have asked me about the influence of criticism. I think I have answered that question already; but there is this also to be said. It is criticism that makes us cosmopolitan. The Manchester school tried to make men realise the brotherhood of humanity by pointing out the commercial advantages of peace. It sought to degrade the wonderful world into a common market-place for the buyer and the seller. It addressed itself to the lowest instincts, and it failed. War followed upon war, and the tradesman's creed did not prevent France and Germany from clashing together in blood-stained battle. There are others of our own day who seek to appeal to mere emotional sympathies, or to the shallow dogmas of some vague system of abstract ethics. They have their Peace Societies, so dear to the sentimentalists, and their proposals for unarmed International Arbitration, so popular among those who have never read history. But mere emotional sympathy will not do. It is too variable, and too closely connected with the passions; and a board of arbitrators who, for the general welfare of the race, are to be deprived of the power of putting their decisions into execution, will not be of much avail. There is only one thing worse than Injustice, and that is Justice without her sword in her hand. When right is not might, it is evil.

No: the emotions will not make us cosmopolitan, any more than the greed for gain could do so. It is only by the cultivation of the habit of intellectual criticism that we shall be able to rise superior to race-prejudices. Goethe – you will not misunderstand what I say – was a German of the Germans. He loved his country – no man more so. Its people were dear to him; and he led them. Yet, when the iron hoof of Napoleon trampled upon vineyard and cornfield, his lips were silent. 'How can one write songs of hatred without hating?' he said to Eckermann, 'and how could I, to whom culture and barbarism are alone of importance, hate a nation which is among the most cultivated of the earth, and to which I owe so great a part of my own cultivation?' This note, sounded in the modern world by Goethe first, will become, I think, the starting point for the cosmopolitanism of the future. Criticism will annihilate race-prejudices by insisting upon the unity of the human mind in the variety of its forms. If we are tempted to make war upon another nation, we shall remember that we are seeking to destroy an element of our own culture, and possibly its most important element. As long as war is regarded as wicked, it will always have its fascination. When it is looked upon as vulgar, it will cease to be popular. The change will, of course, be slow, and people will not be conscious of it. They will not say, 'We will not war against France because her prose is perfect,' but because the prose of France is perfect, they will not hate the land. Intellectual criticism will bind Europe together in bonds far closer than those that can be forged by shopman or sentimentalist. It will give us the peace that springs from understanding.

Nor is this all. It is criticism that, recognising no position as final, and refusing to bind itself by the shallow shibboleths of any sect or school, creates that serene philosophic temper which loves truth for its own sake, and loves it not the less because it knows it to be unattainable. How little we have of this temper in England, and how much we need it! The English mind is always in a rage. The intellect of the race is wasted in the sordid and stupid quarrels of second-rate politicians or third-rate theologians. It was reserved for a man of science to show us the supreme example of that 'sweet reasonableness' of which Arnold spoke so wisely, and, alas! to so little effect. The author of the *Origin of Species* had, at any rate, the philosophic temper. If one contemplates the ordinary pulpits and platforms of England, one can but feel the contempt of Julian, or the indifference of Montaigne. We are dominated by the fanatic, whose worst vice is his sincerity. Anything approaching to the free play of the mind is practically unknown amongst us. People cry out against the sinner, yet it is not the sinful, but the stupid, who are our shame. There is no sin except stupidity.

ERNEST: Ah! what an antinomian you are!

GILBERT: The artistic critic, like the mystic, is an antinomian always. To be good, according to the vulgar standard of goodness, is obviously quite easy. It merely requires a certain amount of sordid terror, a certain lack of imaginative thought, and a certain low passion for middle-class respectability. Aesthetics are higher than ethics. They belong to a more spiritual sphere. To discern the beauty of a thing is the finest point to which we can arrive. Even a colour-sense is more important, in the development of the individual, than a sense of right and wrong. Aesthetics, in fact, are to ethics in the sphere of conscious civilisation, what, in the sphere of the external world, sexual is to natural selection. Ethics, like natural selection, make existence possible. Aesthetics, like sexual selection, make life lovely and wonderful, fill it with new forms, and give it progress, and variety and change. And when we reach the true culture that is our aim, we attain to that perfection of which the saints have dreamed, the perfection of those to whom sin is impossible, not because they make the renunciations of the ascetic, but because they can do everything they wish without hurt to the soul, and can wish for nothing that can do the soul harm, the soul being an entity so divine that it is able to transform into elements of a richer experience, or a finer susceptibility, or a newer mode of thought, acts or passions that with the common would be commonplace, or with the uneducated ignoble, or with the shameful vile. Is this dangerous? Yes; it is dangerous – all ideas, as I told you, are so. But the night wearies, and the light flickers in the lamp. One more thing I cannot help saying to you. You have spoken against criticism as being a sterile thing. The nineteenth century is a turning point in history, simply on account of the work of two men, Darwin and Renan, the one the critic of the book of nature, the other the critic of the books of God. Not to recognise this is to miss the meaning of one of the most important eras in the progress of the world. Creation is always behind the age. It is criticism that leads us. The critical spirit and the world-spirit are one.

ERNEST: And he who is in possession of this spirit, or whom this spirit possesses, will, I suppose, do nothing?

GILBERT: Like the Persephone of whom Landor tells us, the sweet pensive Persephone around whose white feet the asphodel and amaranth are blooming, he will sit contented 'in that deep, motionless quiet which mortals pity, and which the gods enjoy'. He will look out upon the world and know its secret. By contact with divine things he will become divine. His will be the perfect life, and his only.

ERNEST: You have told me many strange things tonight, Gilbert. You have told me that it is more difficult to talk about a thing than to do it, and that to do nothing at all is the most difficult thing in the world; you have told me that all art is immoral, and all thought dangerous; that criticism is more creative than creation, and that the highest criticism is that which reveals in the work of art what the artist had not put there; that it is exactly because a man cannot do a thing that he is the proper judge of it; and that the true critic is unfair, insincere and not rational. My friend, you are a dreamer.

GILBERT: Yes: I am a dreamer. For a dreamer is one who can only find his way by moonlight, and his punishment is that he sees the dawn before the rest of the world.

ERNEST: His punishment?

GILBERT: And his reward. But, see, it is dawn already. Draw back the curtains and open the windows wide. How cool the morning air is! Piccadilly lies at our feet like a long riband of silver. A faint purple mist hangs over the park, and the shadows of the white houses are purple. It is too late to sleep. Let us go down to Covent Garden and look at the roses. Come! I am tired of thought.

THE SOUL OF MAN
UNDER SOCIALISM

The chief advantage that would result from the establishment of Socialism is, undoubtedly, the fact that Socialism would relieve us from that sordid necessity of living for others which, in the present condition of things, presses so hardly upon almost everybody. In fact, scarcely anyone at all escapes.

Now and then, in the course of the century, a great man of science, like Darwin; a great poet like Keats; a fine critical spirit like M. Renan; a supreme artist like Flaubert, has been able to isolate himself, to keep himself out of reach of the clamorous claims of others, to stand 'under the shelter of the wall', as Plato puts it, and so to realise the perfection of what was in him, to his own incomparable gain, and to the incomparable and lasting gain of the whole world. These, however, are exceptions. The majority of people spoil their lives by an unhealthy and exaggerated altruism – are forced, indeed, so to spoil them. They find themselves surrounded by hideous poverty, by hideous ugliness, by hideous starvation. It is inevitable that they should be strongly moved by all this. The emotions of man are stirred more quickly than man's intelligence; and, as I pointed out some time ago in an article on the function of criticism, it is much more easy to have sympathy with suffering than it is to have sympathy with thought. Accordingly, with admirable, though misdirected intentions, they very seriously and very sentimentally set themselves to the task of remedying the evils that they see. But their remedies do not cure the disease: they merely prolong it. Indeed, their remedies are part of the disease.

They try to solve the problem of poverty, for instance, by keeping the poor alive; or, in the case of a very advanced school, by amusing the poor.

But this is not a solution: it is an aggravation of the difficulty. The proper aim is to try and reconstruct society on such a basis that poverty will be impossible. And the altruistic virtues have really prevented the carrying out of this aim. Just as the worst slave-owners were those who were kind to their slaves and so prevented the horror of the system being realised by those who suffered from it, and understood by those who contemplated it, so, in the present state of things in England, the people who do most harm are the people who try to do most good; and at last we have had the spectacle of men who have really studied the problem and know the life – educated men who live in the East End – coming forward and imploring the community to restrain its altruistic impulses of charity, benevolence and the like. They do so on the ground that such charity degrades and demoralises. They are perfectly right. Charity creates a multitude of sins.

There is also this to be said. It is immoral to use private property in order to alleviate the horrible evils that result from the institution of private property. It is both immoral and unfair.

Under Socialism all this will, of course, be altered. There will be no people living in fetid dens and fetid rags, and bringing up unhealthy, hunger-pinched children in the midst of impossible and absolutely repulsive surroundings. The security of society will not depend, as it does now, on the state of the weather. If a frost comes we shall not have a hundred thousand men out of work, tramping about the streets in a state of disgusting misery, or whining to their neighbours for alms, or crowding round the doors of loathsome shelters to try and secure a hunch of bread and a night's unclean lodging. Each member of the society will share in the general prosperity and happiness of the society, and if a frost comes no one will practically be anything the worse.

Upon the other hand, Socialism itself will be of value simply because it will lead to individualism.

Socialism, Communism or whatever one chooses to call it, by converting private property into public wealth, and substituting co-operation for competition will restore society to its proper condition of a thoroughly healthy organism, and ensure the material well-being of each member of the community. It will, in fact, give life its proper basis and its proper environment. But, for the full development of life to its highest mode of perfection, something more is needed. What is needed is individualism. If the Socialism is authoritarian; if there are governments armed with economic power as they are now with political power; if, in a word, we are to have industrial tyrannies, then the last state of man will be worse than the first. At present, in consequence of the existence of private property, a great many people are enabled to develop a certain very limited amount of individualism. They are either under no necessity to work for their living, or are enabled to choose the sphere of activity that is really congenial to them and gives them pleasure. These are the poets, the philosophers, the men of science, the men of culture – in a word, the real men, the men who have realised themselves, and in whom all humanity gains a partial realisation. Upon the other hand, there are a great many people who, having no private property of their own, and being always on the brink of sheer starvation, are compelled to do the work of beasts of burden, to do work that is quite uncongenial to them and to which they are forced by the peremptory, unreasonable, degrading tyranny of want. These are the poor; and amongst them there is no grace of manner, or charm of speech, or civilisation or culture, or refinement in pleasures or joy of life. From their collective force humanity gains much in material prosperity. But it is only the material result that it gains, and the man who is poor is in himself absolutely of no importance. He is merely the infinitesimal atom of a force that, so far from regarding him, crushes him: indeed, prefers him crushed, as in that case he is far more obedient.

Of course, it might be said that the individualism generated under conditions of private property is not always, or even as a rule, of a fine or wonderful type, and that the poor, if they have not culture and charm, have still many virtues. Both these statements would be quite true. The possession of private property is very often extremely demoralising, and that is of course one of the reasons why Socialism wants to get rid of the institution. In fact, property is really a nuisance. Some years ago people went about the country saying that property has duties. They said it so often and so tediously that, at last, the church has begun to say it. One hears it now from every pulpit. It is perfectly true. Property not merely has duties, but has so many duties that its possession to any large extent is a bore. It involves endless claims upon one, endless attention to business, endless bother. If property had simply pleasures, we could stand it; but its duties make it unbearable. In the interest of the rich we must get rid of it. The virtues of the poor may be readily admitted, and are much to be regretted. We are often told that the poor are grateful for charity. Some of them are, no doubt, but the best amongst the poor are never grateful. They are ungrateful, discontented, disobedient and rebellious. They are quite right to be so. Charity they feel to be a ridiculously inadequate mode of partial restitution, or a sentimental dole, usually accompanied by some impertinent attempt on the part of the sentimentalist to tyrannise over their private lives. Why should they be grateful for the crumbs that fall from the rich man's table? They should be seated at the board, and are beginning to know it. As for being discontented, a man who would not be discontented with such surroundings and such a low mode of life would be a perfect brute. Disobedience, in the eyes of anyone who has read history, is man's original virtue. It is through disobedience that progress has been made, through disobedience and through rebellion. Sometimes the poor are praised for being thrifty. But to recommend thrift to the poor is both grotesque and insulting. It is like advising a man who is starving to eat less. For a town or country labourer to practise thrift would be absolutely immoral. Man should not be ready to show that he can live like a badly fed animal. He should decline to live like that, and should either steal or go on the rates, which is considered by many to be a form of stealing. As for begging, it is safer to beg than to take, but it is finer to take than to beg. No: a poor man who is ungrateful, unthrifty, discontented and rebellious, is probably a real personality, and has much in him. He is at any rate a healthy protest. As for the virtuous poor, one can pity them, of course, but one cannot possibly admire them. They have made private terms with the enemy, and sold their birthright for very bad pottage. They must also be extraordinarily stupid. I can quite understand a man accepting laws that protect private property, and admit of its accumulation, as long as he himself is able under those conditions to realise some form of beautiful and intellectual life. But it is almost incredible to me how a man whose life is marred and made hideous by such laws can possibly acquiesce in their continuance.

However, the explanation is not really difficult to find. It is simply this. Misery and poverty are so absolutely degrading, and exercise such a paralysing effect over the nature of men, that no class is ever really conscious of its own suffering. They have to be told of it by other people, and they often entirely disbelieve them. What is said by great employers of labour against agitators is unquestionably true. Agitators are a set of interfering, meddling people, who come down to some perfectly contented class of the community and sow the seeds of discontent amongst them. That is the reason why agitators are so absolutely necessary. Without them, in our incomplete state, there would be no advance towards civilisation. Slavery was put down in America, not in consequence of any action on the part of the slaves, or even any express desire on their part that they should be free. It was put down entirely through the grossly illegal conduct of certain agitators in Boston and elsewhere, who were not slaves themselves, nor owners of slaves, nor had anything to do with the question really. It was, undoubtedly, the Abolitionists who set the torch alight, who began the whole thing. And it is curious to note that from the slaves themselves they received, not merely very little assistance, but hardly any sympathy even; and when at the close of the war the slaves found themselves free, found themselves indeed so absolutely free that they were free to starve, many of them bitterly regretted the new state of things. To the thinker, the most tragic fact in the whole of the French Revolution is not that Marie Antoinette was killed for being a queen, but that the starved peasant of the Vendée voluntarily went out to die for the hideous cause of feudalism.

It is clear, then, that no authoritarian Socialism will do. For while under the present system a very large number of people can lead lives of a certain amount of freedom and expression and happiness, under an industrial-barrack system, or a system of economic tyranny, nobody would be able to have any such freedom at all. It is to be regretted that a portion of our community should be practically in slavery, but to propose to solve the problem by enslaving the entire community is childish. Every man must be left quite free to choose his own work. No form of compulsion must be exercised over him. If there is, his work will not be good for him, will not be good in itself, and will not be good for others. And by work I simply mean activity of any kind.

I hardly think that any Socialist, nowadays, would seriously propose that an inspector should call every morning at each house to see that each citizen rose up and did manual labour for eight hours. Humanity has got beyond that stage, and reserves such a form of life for the people whom, in a very arbitrary manner, it chooses to call criminals. But I confess that many of the socialistic views that I have come across seem to me to be tainted with ideas of authority, if not of actual compulsion. Of course, authority and compulsion are out of the question. All association must be quite voluntary. It is only in voluntary associations that man is fine.

But it may be asked how individualism, which is now more or less dependent on the existence of private property for its development, will benefit by the abolition of such private property. The answer is very simple. It is true that, under existing conditions, a few men who have had private means of their own, such as Byron, Shelley, Browning, Victor Hugo, Baudelaire and others, have been able to realise their personality, more or less completely. Not one of these men ever did a single day's work for hire. They were relieved from poverty. They had an immense advantage. The question is whether it would be for the good of individualism that such an advantage should be taken away. Let us suppose that it is taken away. What happens then to individualism? How will it benefit?

It will benefit in this way. Under the new conditions individualism will be far freer, far finer and far more intensified than it is now. I am not talking of the great imaginatively realised individualism of such poets as I have mentioned, but of the great actual individualism latent and potential in mankind generally. For the recognition of private property has really harmed individualism, and obscured it, by confusing a man with what he possesses. It has led individualism entirely astray. It has made gain, not growth, its aim. So that man thought that the important thing was to have, and did not know that the important thing is to be. The true perfection of man lies, not in what man has, but in what man is.

Private property has crushed true individualism, and set up an individualism that is false. It has debarred one part of the community from being individual by starving them. It has debarred the other part of the community from being individual by putting them on the wrong road, and encumbering them. Indeed, so completely has man's personality been absorbed by his possessions that the English law has always treated offences against a man's property with far more severity than offences against his person, and property is still the test of complete citizenship. The industry necessary for the making of money is also very demoralising. In a community like ours, where property confers immense distinction, social position, honour, respect, titles, and other pleasant things of the kind, man, being naturally ambitious, makes it his aim to accumulate this property, and goes on wearily and tediously accumulating it long after he has got far more than he wants, or can use, or enjoy, or perhaps even know of. Man will kill himself by overwork in order to secure property, and really, considering the enormous advantages that property brings, one is hardly surprised. One's regret is that society should be constructed on such a basis that man has been forced into a groove in which he cannot freely develop what is wonderful, and fascinating and delightful in him – in which, in fact, he misses the true pleasure and joy of living. He is also, under existing conditions, very insecure. An enormously wealthy merchant may be – often is – at every moment of his life at the mercy of things that are not under his control. If the wind blows an extra point or so, or the weather suddenly changes, or some trivial thing happens, his ship may go down, his speculations may go wrong, and he finds himself a poor man, with his social position quite gone. Now, nothing should be able to harm a man except himself. Nothing should be able to rob a man at all. What a man really has, is what is in him. What is outside of him should be a matter of no importance.

With the abolition of private property, then, we shall have true, beautiful, healthy individualism. Nobody will waste his life in accumulating things and the symbols for things. One will live. To live is the rarest thing in the world. Most people exist, that is all.

It is a question whether we have ever seen the full expression of a personality, except on the imaginative plane of art. In action, we never have. Caesar, says Mommsen, was the complete and perfect man. But how tragically insecure was Caesar! Wherever there is a man who exercises authority, there is a man who resists authority. Caesar was very perfect, but his perfection travelled by too dangerous a road. Marcus Aurelius was the perfect man, says Renan. Yes, the great emperor was a perfect man. But how intolerable were the endless claims upon him! He staggered under the burden of the empire. He was conscious how inadequate one man was to bear the weight of that Titan and too vast orb. What I mean by a perfect man is one who develops under perfect conditions; one who is not wounded, or worried, or maimed, or in danger. Most personalities have been obliged to be rebels. Half their strength has been wasted in friction. Byron's personality, for instance, was terribly wasted in its battle with the stupidity and hypocrisy and philistinism of the English. Such battles do not always intensify strength; they often exaggerate weakness. Byron was never able to give us what he might have given us. Shelley escaped better. Like Byron, he got out of England as soon as possible. But he was not so well known. If the English had realised what a great poet he really was, they would have fallen on him with tooth and nail, and made his life as unbearable to him as they possibly could. But he was not a remarkable figure in society, and consequently he escaped, to a certain degree. Still, even in Shelley the note of rebellion is sometimes too strong. The note of the perfect personality is not rebellion, but peace.

It will be a marvellous thing – the true personality of man – when we see it. It will grow naturally and simply, flowerlike, or as a tree grows. It will not be at discord. It will never argue or dispute. It will not prove things. It will know everything. And yet it will not busy itself about knowledge. It will have wisdom. Its value will not be measured by material things. It will have nothing. And yet it will have everything, and whatever one takes from it, it will still have, so rich will it be. It will not be always meddling with others, or asking them to be like itself. It will love them because they will be different. And yet while it will not meddle with others, it will help all, as a beautiful thing helps us, by being what it is. The personality of man will be very wonderful. It will be as wonderful as the personality of a child.

In its development it will be assisted by Christianity, if men desire that, but if men do not desire that, it will develop none the less surely. For it will not worry itself about the past, nor care whether things happened or did not happen. Nor will it admit any laws but its own laws; nor any authority but its own authority. Yet it will love those who sought to intensify it, and speak often of them. And of these Christ was one.

'Know thyself!' was written over the portal of the antique world. Over the portal of the new world, 'Be thyself' shall be written. And the message of Christ to man was simply, 'Be thyself.' That is the secret of Christ.

When Jesus talks about the poor he simply means personalities, just as when he talks about the rich he simply means people who have not developed their personalities. Jesus moved in a community that allowed the accumulation of private property, just as ours does, and the gospel that he preached was not that in such a community is it an advantage for a man to live on scanty, unwholesome food, to wear ragged, unwholesome clothes, to sleep in horrid, unwholesome dwellings, and a disadvantage for a man to live under healthy, pleasant and decent conditions. Such a view would have been wrong there and then, and would, of course, be still more wrong now and in England; for as man moves northward the material necessities of life become of more vital importance and our society is infinitely more complex and displays far greater extremes of luxury and pauperism than any society of the antique world. What Jesus meant was this. He said to man, 'You have a wonderful personality. Develop it. Be yourself. Don't imagine that your perfection lies in accumulating or possessing external things. Your affection is inside of you. If only you could realise that, you would not want to be rich. Ordinary riches can be stolen from a man. Real riches cannot. In the treasury-house of your soul, there are infinitely precious things, that may not be taken from you. And so, try to so shape your life that external things will not harm you. And try also to get rid of personal property. It involves sordid preoccupation, endless industry, continual wrong. Personal property hinders individualism at every step.' It is to be noted that Jesus never says that impoverished people are necessarily good, or wealthy people necessarily bad. That would not have been true. Wealthy people are, as a class, better than impoverished people, more moral, more intellectual, more well behaved. There is only one class in the community that thinks more about money than the rich, and that is the poor. The poor can think of nothing else. That is the misery of being poor. What Jesus does say is that man reaches his perfection, not through what he has, not even through what he does, but entirely through what he is. And so the wealthy young man who comes to Jesus is represented as a thoroughly good citizen, who has broken none of the laws of his state, none of the commandments of his religion. He is quite respectable in the ordinary sense of that extraordinary word. Jesus says to him, 'You should give up private property. It hinders you from realising your perfection. It is a drag upon you. It is a burden. Your personality does not need it. It is within you, and not outside of you, that you will find what you really are, and what you really want.' To his own friends he says the same thing. He tells them to be themselves, and not to be always worrying about other things. What do other things matter? Man is complete in himself. When they go into the world, the world will disagree with them. That is inevitable. The world hates individualism. But that is not to trouble them. They are to be calm and self-centred. If a man takes their cloak, they are to give him their coat, just to show that material things are of no importance. If people abuse them, they are not to answer back. What does it signify? The things people say of a man do not alter a man. He is what he is. Public opinion is of no value whatsoever. Even if people employ actual violence, they are not to be violent in turn. That would be to fall to the same low level. After all, even in prison, a man can be quite free. His soul can be free. His personality can be untroubled. He can be at peace. And, above all things, they are not to interfere with other people or judge them in any way. Personality is a very mysterious thing. A man cannot always be estimated by what he does. He may keep the law, and yet be worthless. He may break the law, and yet be fine. He may be bad, without ever doing anything bad. He may commit a sin against society, and yet realise through that sin his true perfection.

There was a woman who was taken in adultery. We are not told the history of her love, but that love must have been very great; for Jesus said that her sins were forgiven her, not because she repented, but because her love was so intense and wonderful. Later on, a short time before his death, as he sat at a feast, the woman came in and poured costly perfumes on his hair. His friends tried to interfere with her, and said that it was extravagance, and that the money that the perfume cost should have been expended on charitable relief of people in want, or something of that kind. Jesus did not accept that view. He pointed out that the material needs of man were great and very permanent, but that the spiritual needs of man were greater still, and that in one divine moment, and by selecting its own mode of expression, a personality might make itself perfect. The world worships the woman, even now, as a saint.

Yet there are suggestive things in individualism. Socialism annihilates family life, for instance. With the abolition of private property, marriage in its present form must disappear. This is part of the programme. Individualism accepts this and makes it fine. It converts the abolition of legal restraint into a form of freedom that will help the full development of personality, and make the love of man and woman more wonderful, more beautiful, and more ennobling. Jesus knew this. He rejected the claims of family life, although they existed in his day and community in a very marked form. 'Who is my mother? Who are my brothers?' he said, when he was told that they wished to speak to him. When one of his followers asked leave to go and bury his father, 'Let the dead bury the dead,' was his terrible answer. He would allow no claim whatsoever to be made on personality.

And so he who would lead a Christ-like life is he who is perfectly and absolutely himself. He may be a great poet, or a great man of science, or a young student at a university, or one who watches sheep upon a moor; or a maker of dramas, like Shakespeare, or a thinker about God, like Spinoza; or a child who plays in a garden, or a fisherman who throws his net into the sea. It does not matter what he is as long as he realises the perfection of the soul that is within him. All imitation in morals and in life is wrong. Through the streets of Jerusalem at the present day crawls one who is mad and carries a wooden cross on his shoulders. He is a symbol of the lives that are marred by imitation. Father Damien was Christ-like when he went out to live with the lepers, because in such service he realised fully what was best in him. But he was not more Christ-like than Wagner when he realised his soul in music; or than Shelley, when he realised his soul in song. There is no one type for man. There are as many perfections as there are imperfect men. And while to the claims of charity a man may yield and yet be free, to the claims of conformity no man may yield and remain free at all.

Individualism, then, is what through Socialism we are to attain. As a natural result the state must give up all idea of government. It must give it up because, as a wise man once said many centuries before Christ, there is such a thing as leaving mankind alone; there is no such thing as governing mankind. All modes of government are failures. Despotism is unjust to everybody, including the despot, who was probably made for better things. Oligarchies are unjust to the many, and ochlocracies are unjust to the few. High hopes were once formed of democracy; but democracy means simply the bludgeoning of the people by the people for the people. It has been found out. I must say that it was high time, for all authority is quite degrading. It degrades those who exercise it, and degrades those over whom it is exercised. When it is violently, grossly and cruelly used it produces a good effect by creating, or at any rate bringing out, the spirit of revolt and individualism that is to kill it. When it is used with a certain amount of kindness, and accompanied by prizes and rewards, it is dreadfully demoralising. People, in that case are less conscious of the horrible pressure that is being put on them, and so go through their lives in a sort of coarse comfort, like petted animals, without ever realising that they are probably thinking other people's thoughts, living by other people's standards, wearing practically what one may call other people's second-hand clothes, and never being themselves for a single moment. 'He who would be free,' says a fine thinker, 'must not conform.' And authority, by bribing people to conform, produces a very gross kind of overfed barbarism amongst us.

With authority, punishment will pass away. This will be a great gain – a gain, in fact, of incalculable value. As one reads history, not in the expurgated editions written for schoolboys and passmen, but in the original authorities of each time, one is absolutely sickened, not by the crimes that the wicked have committed, but by the punishments that the good have inflicted; and a community is infinitely more brutalised by the habitual employment of punishment than it is by the occasional occurrence of crime. It obviously follows that the more punishment is inflicted the more crime is produced, and most modern legislation has clearly recognised this, and has made it its task to diminish punishment as far as it thinks it can. Wherever it has really diminished it, the results have always been extremely good. The less punishment, the less crime. When there is no punishment at all, crime will either cease to exist, or, if it occurs, will be treated by physicians as a very distressing form of dementia to be cured by care and kindness. For what are called criminals nowadays are not criminals at all. Starvation, and not sin, is the parent of modern crime. That indeed is the reason why our criminals are, as a class, so absolutely uninteresting from any psychological point of view. They are not marvellous Macbeths and terrible Vautrins. They are merely what ordinary, respectable, commonplace people would be if they had not got enough to eat. When private property is abolished there will be no necessity for crime, no demand for it, it will cease to exist. Of course, all crimes are not crimes against property, though such are the crimes that the English law, valuing what a man has more than what a man is, punishes with the harshest and most horrible severity (if we except the crime of murder, and regard death as worse than penal servitude, a point on which our criminals, I believe, disagree). But though a crime may not be against property, it may spring from the misery and rage and depression produced by our wrong system of property-holding, and so, when that system is abolished, will disappear. When each member of the community has sufficient for his wants, and is not interfered with by his neighbour, it will not be an object of any interest to him to interfere with anyone else. Jealousy, which is an extraordinary source of crime in modern life, is an emotion closely bound up with our conceptions of property, and under Socialism and individualism will die out. It is remarkable that in communistic tribes jealousy is entirely unknown.

Now as the state is not to govern, it may be asked what the state is to do. The state is to be a voluntary association that will organise labour, and be the manufacturer and distributor of necessary commodities. The state is to make what is useful. The individual is to make what is beautiful. And as I have mentioned the word labour, I cannot help saying that a great deal of nonsense is being written and talked nowadays about the dignity of manual labour. There is nothing necessarily dignified about manual labour at all, and most of it is absolutely degrading. It is mentally and morally injurious to man to do anything in which he does not find pleasure, and many forms of labour are quite pleasureless activities, and should be regarded as such. To sweep a slushy crossing for eight hours on a day when the east wind is blowing is a disgusting occupation. To sweep it with mental, moral or physical dignity seems to me to be impossible. To sweep it with joy would be appalling. Man is made for something better than disturbing dirt. All work of that kind should be done by a machine.

And I have no doubt that it will be so. Up to the present, man has been, to a certain extent, the slave of machinery, and there is something tragic in the fact that as soon as man had invented a machine to do his work he began to starve. This, however, is, of course, the result of our property system and our system of competition. One man owns a machine which does the work of five hundred men. Five hundred men are, in consequence, thrown out of employment, and, having no work to do, become hungry and take to thieving. The one man secures the produce of the machine and keeps it, and has five hundred times as much as he should have, and probably, which is of much more importance, a great deal more than he really wants. Were that machine the property of all, everybody would benefit by it. It would be an immense advantage to the community. All unintellectual labour, all monotonous, dull labour, all labour that deals with dreadful things and involves unpleasant conditions, must be done by machinery. Machinery must work for us in coal mines, and do all sanitary services, and be the stoker of steamers, and clean the streets, and run messages on wet days, and do anything that is tedious or distressing. At present machinery competes against man. Under proper conditions machinery will serve man. There is no doubt at all that this is the future of machinery; and just as trees grow while the country gentleman is asleep, so while humanity will be amusing itself, or enjoying cultivated leisure – which, and not labour, is the aim of man – or making beautiful things, or reading beautiful things, or simply contemplating the world with admiration and delight, machinery will be doing all the necessary and unpleasant work. The fact is that civilisation requires slaves. The Greeks were quite right there. Unless there are slaves to do the ugly, horrible, uninteresting work, culture and contemplation become almost impossible. Human slavery is wrong, insecure and demoralising. On mechanical slavery, on the slavery of the machine, the future of the world depends. And when scientific men are no longer called upon to go down to a depressing East End and distribute bad cocoa and worse blankets to starving people, they will have delightful leisure in which to devise wonderful and marvellous things for their own joy and the joy of everyone else. There will be great storages of force for every city, and for every house if required, and this force man will convert into heat, light or motion, according to his needs. Is this Utopian? A map of the world that does not include Utopia is not worth even glancing at, for it leaves out the one country at which humanity is always landing. And when humanity lands there, it looks out, and, seeing a better country, sets sail. Progress is the realisation of Utopias.

Now, I have said that the community by means of organisation of machinery will supply the useful thing, and that the beautiful things will be made by the individual. This is not merely necessary, but it is the only possible way by which we can get either the one or the other. An individual who has to make things for the use of others, and with reference to their wants and their wishes, does not work with interest, and consequently cannot put into his work what is best in him. Upon the other hand, whenever a community or a powerful section of a community, or a government of any kind, attempts to dictate to the artist what he is to do, art either entirely vanishes, or becomes stereotyped, or degenerates into a low and ignoble form of craft. A work of art is the unique result of a unique temperament. Its beauty comes from the fact that the author is what he is. It has nothing to do with the fact that other people want what they want. Indeed, the moment that an artist takes notice of what other people want, and tries to supply the demand, he ceases to be an artist, and becomes a dull or an amusing craftsman, an honest or a dishonest tradesman. He has no further claim to be considered as an artist. Art is the most intense mood of individualism that the world has known. I am inclined to say that it is the only real mode of individualism that the world has known. Crime, which, under certain conditions, may seem to have created individualism, must take cognisance of other people and interfere with them. It belongs to the sphere of action. But alone, without any reference to his neighbours, without any interference, the artist can fashion a beautiful thing; and if he does not do it solely for his own pleasure, he is not an artist at all.

And it is to be noted that it is the fact that art is this intense form of individualism that makes the public try to exercise over it an authority that is as immoral as it is ridiculous, and as corrupting as it is contemptible. It is not quite their fault. The public has always, and in every age, been badly brought up. They are continually asking art to be popular, to please their want of taste, to flatter their absurd vanity, to tell them what they have been told before, to show them what they ought to be tired of seeing, to amuse them when they feel heavy after eating too much, and to distract their thoughts when they are wearied of their own stupidity. Now art should never try to be popular. The public should try to make itself artistic. There is a very wide difference. If a man of science were told that the results of his experiments, and the conclusions that he arrived at, should be of such a character that they would not upset the received popular notions on the subject, or disturb popular prejudice, or hurt the sensibilities of people who knew nothing about science, if a philosopher were told that he had a perfect right to speculate in the highest spheres of thought, provided that he arrived at the same conclusions as were held by those who had never thought in any sphere at all – well, nowadays the man of science and the philosopher would be considerably amused. Yet it is really a very few years since both philosophy and science were subjected to brutal popular control, to authority in fact – the authority of either the general ignorance of the community, or the terror and greed for power of an ecclesiastical or governmental class. Of course we have to a very great extent got rid of any attempt on the part of the community, or the church, or the government, to interfere with the individualism of speculative thought, but the attempt to interfere with the individualism of imaginative art still lingers. In fact, it does more than linger; it is aggressive, offensive and brutalising.

In England, the arts that have escaped best are the arts in which the public take no interest. Poetry is an instance of what I mean. We have been able to have fine poetry in England because the public do not read it, and consequently do not influence it. The public like to insult poets because they are individual, but once they have insulted them, they leave them alone. In the case of the novel and the drama, arts in which the public do take an interest, the result of the exercise of popular authority has been absolutely ridiculous. No country produces such badly written fiction, such tedious, common work in the novel form, such silly, vulgar plays as England. It must necessarily be so. The popular standard is of such a character that no artist can get to it. It is at once too easy and too difficult to be a popular novelist. It is too easy, because the requirements of the public as far as plot, style, psychology, treatment of life and treatment of literature are concerned are within the reach of the very meanest capacity and the most uncultivated mind. It is too difficult, because to meet such requirements the artist would have to do violence to his temperament, would have to write not for the artistic joy of writing, but for the amusement of half-educated people, and so would have to suppress his individualism, forget his culture, annihilate his style, and surrender everything that is valuable in him. In the case of the drama, things are a little better: the theatre-going public like the obvious, it is true, but they do not like the tedious; and burlesque and farcical comedy, the two most popular forms, are distinct forms of art. Delightful work may be produced under burlesque and farcical conditions, and in work of this kind the artist in England is allowed very great freedom. It is when one comes to the higher forms of the drama that the result of popular control is seen. The one thing that the public dislike is novelty. Any attempt to extend the subject-matter of art is extremely distasteful to the public; and yet the vitality and progress of art depend in a large measure on the continual extension of subject-matter. The public dislike novelty because they are afraid of it. It represents to them a mode of individualism, an assertion on the part of the artist that he selects his own subject, and treats it as he chooses. The public are quite right in their attitude. Art is individualism and individualism is a disturbing and disintegrating force. Therein lies its immense value. For what it seeks to disturb is monotony of type, slavery of custom, tyranny of habit, and the reduction of man to the level of a machine. In art, the public accept what has been, because they cannot alter it, not because they appreciate it. They swallow their classics whole, and never taste them. They endure them as the inevitable, and as they cannot mar them, they mouth about them. Strangely enough, or not strangely, according to one's own views, this acceptance of the classics does a great deal of harm. The uncritical admiration of the Bible and Shakespeare in England is an instance of what I mean. With regard to the Bible, considerations of ecclesiastical authority enter into the matter, so that I need not dwell upon the point.

But in the case of Shakespeare it is quite obvious that the public really see neither the beauties nor the defects of his plays. If they saw the beauties, they would not object to the development of the drama; and if they saw the defects, they would not object to the development of the drama either. The fact is the public make use of the classics of a country as a means of checking the progress of art. They degrade the classics into authorities. They use them as bludgeons for preventing the free expression of beauty in new forms. They are always asking a writer why he does not write like somebody else, or a painter why he does not paint like somebody else, quite oblivious of the fact that if either of them did anything of the kind he would cease to be an artist. A fresh mode of beauty is absolutely distasteful to them and whenever it appears they get so angry and bewildered that they always use two stupid expressions – one is that the work of art is grossly unintelligible; the other, that the work of art is grossly immoral. What they mean by these words seems to me to be this. When they say a work is grossly unintelligible, they mean that the artist has said or made a beautiful thing that is new; when they describe a work as grossly immoral, they mean that the artist has said or made a beautiful thing that is true. The former expression has reference to style, the latter to subject-matter. But they probably use the words very vaguely, as an ordinary mob will use ready-made paving-stones. There is not a single real poet or prose-writer of this century, for instance, on whom the British public have not solemnly conferred diplomas of immorality, and these diplomas practically take the place, with us, of what in France is the formal recognition of an Academy of Letters, and fortunately make the establishment of such an institution quite unnecessary in England. Of course, the public are very reckless in their use of the word. That they should have called Wordsworth an immoral poet, was only to be expected. Wordsworth was a poet. But that they should have called Charles Kingsley an immoral novelist is extra-ordinary. Kingsley's prose was not of a very fine quality. Still there is the word, and they use it as best they can. An artist is, of course, not disturbed by it. The true artist is a man who believes absolutely in himself, because he is absolutely himself. But I can fancy that if an artist produced a work of art in England that immediately on its appearance was recognised by the public, through their medium, which is the public press, as a work that was quite intelligible and highly moral, he would begin seriously to question whether in its creation he had really been himself at all, and consequently whether the work was not quite unworthy of him, and either of a thoroughly second-rate order, or of no artistic value whatsoever.

Perhaps, however, I have wronged the public in limiting them to such words as 'immoral', 'unintelligible', 'exotic', and 'unhealthy'. There is one other word that they use. That word is 'morbid'. They do not use it often. The meaning of the word is so simple that they are afraid of using it. Still, they use it sometimes, and, now and then, one comes across it in popular newspapers. It is, of course, a ridiculous word to apply to a work of art. For what is morbidity but a mood of emotion or a mode of thought that one cannot express? The public are all morbid, because the public can never find expression for anything. The artist is never morbid. He expresses everything. He stands outside his subject, and through its medium produces incomparable and artistic effects. To call an artist morbid because he deals with morbidity as his subject-matter is as silly as if one called Shakespeare mad because he wrote *King Lear*.

On the whole, an artist in England gains something by being attacked. His individuality is intensified. He becomes more completely himself. Of course, the attacks are very gross, very impertinent, and very contemptible. But then no artist expects grace from the vulgar mind, or style from the suburban intellect. Vulgarity and stupidity are two very vivid facts in modern life. One regrets them, naturally. But there they are. They are subjects for study, like everything else. And it is only fair to state, with regard to modern journalists, that they always apologise to one in private for what they have written against one in public.

Within the last few years two other adjectives, it may be mentioned, have been added to the very limited vocabulary of art-abuse that is at the disposal of the public. One is the word 'unhealthy', the other is the word 'exotic'. The latter merely expresses the rage of the momentary mushroom against the immortal, entrancing and exquisitely lovely orchid. It is a tribute, but a tribute of no importance. The word 'unhealthy', however, admits of analysis. It is a rather interesting word. In fact, it is so interesting that the people who use it do not know what it means.

What does it mean? What is a healthy or an unhealthy work of art? All terms that one applies to a work of art, provided that one applies them rationally, have reference to either its style or its subject, or to both together. From the point of view of style, a healthy work of art is one whose style recognises the beauty of the material it employs, be that material one of words or of bronze, of colour or of ivory, and uses that beauty as a factor in producing the aesthetic effect. From the point of view of subject, a healthy work of art is one the choice of whose subject is conditioned by the temperament of the artist, and comes directly out of it. In fine, a healthy work of art is one that has both perfection and personality. Of course, form and substance cannot be separated in a work of art; they are always one. But for purposes of analysis, and setting the wholeness of aesthetic impression aside for a moment, we can intellectually so separate them. An unhealthy work of art, on the other hand, is a work whose style is obvious, old-fashioned and common, and whose subject is deliberately chosen, not because the artist has any pleasure in it, but because he thinks that the public will pay him for it. In fact, the popular novel that the public call healthy is always a thoroughly unhealthy production, and what the public call an unhealthy novel is always a beautiful and healthy work of art.

I need hardly say that I am not, for a single moment, complaining that the public and the public press misuse these words. I do not see how, with their lack of comprehension of what art is, they could possibly use them in the proper sense. I am merely pointing out the misuse; and as for the origin of the misuse and the meaning that lies behind it all, the explanation is very simple. It comes from the barbarous conception of authority. It comes from the natural inability of a community corrupted by authority to understand or appreciate individualism. In a word it comes from that monstrous and ignorant thing that is called public opinion, which, bad and well meaning as it is when it tries to control action, is infamous and evil meaning when it tries to control thought or art.

Indeed, there is much more to be said in favour of the physical force of the public than there is in favour of the public's opinion. The former may be fine. The latter must be foolish. It is often said that force is no argument. That, however, entirely depends on what one wants to prove. Many of the most important problems of the last few centuries, such as the continuance of personal government in England, or of feudalism in France, have been solved entirely by means of physical force. The very violence of a revolution may make the public grand and splendid for a moment. It was a fatal day when the public discovered that the pen is mightier than the paving-stone, and can be made as offensive as the brickbat. They at once sought for the journalist, found him, developed him, and made him their industrious and well-paid servant. It is greatly to be regretted, for both their sakes. Behind the barricade there may be much that is noble and heroic. But what is there behind the leading-article but prejudice, stupidity, cant and twaddle? And when these four are joined together they make a terrible force, and constitute the new authority.

In the old days men had the rack. Now they have the press. That is an improvement certainly. But still it is very bad, and wrong, and demoralising. Somebody – was it Burke? – called journalism the fourth estate. That was true at the time, no doubt. But at the present moment it really is the only estate. It has eaten up the other three. The Lords Temporal say nothing, the Lords Spiritual have nothing to say, and the House of Commons has nothing to say and says it. We are dominated by journalism. In America, the president reigns for four years, and journalism governs for ever and ever. Fortunately, in America, journalism has carried its authority to the grossest and most brutal extreme. As a natural consequence it has begun to create a spirit of revolt. People are amused by it, or disgusted by it, according to their temperaments. But it is no longer the real force it was. It is not seriously treated. In England, journalism, except in a few well-known instances, not having been carried to such excesses of brutality, is still a great factor, a really remarkable power. The tyranny that it proposes to exercise over people's private lives seems to me to be quite extraordinary. The fact is that the public have an insatiable curiosity to know everything, except what is worth knowing. Journalism, conscious of this, and having trades-man-like habits, supplies their demands. In centuries before ours the public nailed the ears of journalists to the pump. That was quite hideous. In this century journalists have nailed their own ears to the keyhole. That is much worse. And what aggravates the mischief is that the journalists who are most to blame are not the amusing journalists who write for what are called society papers. The harm is done by the serious, thoughtful, earnest journalists, who solemnly, as they are doing at present, will drag before the eyes of the public some incident in the private life of a great statesman, of a man who is a leader of political thought as he is a creator of political force, and invite the public to discuss the incident, to exercise authority in the matter, to give their views, and not merely to give their views, but to carry them into action, to dictate to the man upon all other points, to dictate to his party, to dictate to his country; in fact, to make themselves ridiculous, offensive and harmful. The private lives of men and women should not be told to the public. The public have nothing to do with them at all.

In France they manage these things better. There they do not allow the details of the trials that take place in the divorce courts to be published for the amusement or criticism of the public. All that the public are allowed to know is that the divorce has taken place and was granted on petition of one or other or both of the married parties concerned. In France, in fact, they limit the journalist, and allow the artist almost perfect freedom. Here we allow absolute freedom to the journalist and entirely limit the artist. English public opinion, that is to say, tries to constrain and impede and warp the man who makes things that are beautiful in effect, and compels the journalist to retail things that are ugly, or disgusting, or revolting in fact, so that we have the most serious journalists in the world and the most indecent newspapers. It is no exaggeration to talk of compulsion. There are possibly some journalists who take a real pleasure in publishing horrible things, or who, being poor, look to scandals as forming a sort of permanent basis for an income. But there are other journalists, I feel certain, men of education and cultivation, who really dislike publishing these things, who know that it is wrong to do so, and only do it because the unhealthy conditions under which their occupation is carried on oblige them to supply the public with what the public wants, and to compete with other journalists in making that supply as full and satisfying to the gross popular appetite as possible. It is a very degrading position for any body of educated men to be placed in, and I have no doubt that most of them feel it acutely.

However, let us leave what is really a very sordid side of the subject, and return to the question of popular control in the matter of art, by which I mean public opinion dictating to the artist the form which he is to use, the mode in which he is to use it, and the materials with which he is to work. I have pointed out that the arts which had escaped best in England are the arts in which the public have not been interested. They are, however, interested in the drama, and as a certain advance has been made in the drama within the last ten or fifteen years, it is important to point out that this advance is entirely due to a few individual artists refusing to accept the popular want of taste as their standard, and refusing to regard art as a mere matter of demand and supply. With his marvellous and vivid personality, with a style that has really a true colour-element in it, with his extraordinary power, not over mere mimicry but over imaginative and intellectual creation, Mr Irving, had his sole object been to give the public what they wanted, could have produced the commonest plays in the commonest manner, and made as much success and money as a man could possibly desire. But his object was not that. His object was to realise his own perfection as an artist, under certain conditions and in certain forms of art. At first he appealed to the few: now he has educated the many. He has created in the public both taste and temperament. The public appreciate his artistic success immensely. I often wonder, however, whether the public understand that that success is entirely due to the fact that he did not accept their standard, but realised his own. With their standard the Lyceum would have been a sort of second-rate booth, as some of the popular theatres in London are at present. Whether they understand it or not, the fact however remains, that taste and temperament have, to a certain extent, been created in the public, and that the public is capable of developing these qualities. The problem then is, why do not the public become more civilised? They have the capacity. What stops them?

The thing that stops them, it must be said again, is their desire to exercise authority over the artists and over works of art. To certain theatres, such as the Lyceum and the Haymarket, the public seem to come in a proper mood. In both of these theatres there have been individual artists who have succeeded in creating in their audiences – and every theatre in London has its own audience – the temperament to which art appeals. And what is that temperament? It is the temperament of receptivity. That is all.

If a man approaches a work of art with any desire to exercise authority over it and the artist, he approaches it in such a spirit that he cannot receive any artistic impression from it at all. The work of art is to dominate the spectator: the spectator is not to dominate the work of art. The spectator is to be receptive. He is to be the violin on which the master is to play. And the more completely he can suppress his own silly views, his own foolish prejudices, his own absurd ideas of what art should be, or should not be, the more likely he is to understand and appreciate the work of art in question. This is, of course, quite obvious in the case of the vulgar theatre-going public of English men and women. But it is equally true of what are called educated people. For an educated person's ideas of art are drawn naturally from what art has been, whereas the new work of art is beautiful by being what art has never been; and to measure it by the standard of the past is to measure it by a standard on the rejection of which its real perfection depends. A temperament capable of receiving, through an imaginative medium, and under imaginative conditions, new and beautiful impressions, is the only temperament that can appreciate a work of art. And true as this is in a case of the appreciation of sculpture and painting, it is still more true of the appreciation of such arts as the drama. For a picture and a statue are not at war with time. They take no account of its succession. In one moment their unity may be apprehended. In the case of literature it is different. Time must be traversed before the unity of effect is realised. And so, in the drama, there may occur in the first act of the play something whose real artistic value may not be evident to the spectator till the third or fourth act is reached. Is the silly fellow to get angry and call out, and disturb the play, and annoy the artists? No. The honest man is to sit quietly and know the delightful emotions of wonder, curiosity and suspense. He is not to go to the play to lose a vulgar temper. He is to go to the play to realise an artistic temperament. He is to go to the play to gain an artistic temperament. He is not the arbiter of the work of art. He is one who is admitted to contemplate the work of art, and, if the work be fine, to forget in its contemplation all the egotism that mars him – the egotism of his ignorance, or the egotism of his information. The point about the drama is hardly, I think, sufficiently recognised. I can quite understand that were *Macbeth* produced for the first time before a modern London audience, many of the people present would strongly and vigorously object to the introduction of the witches in the first act, with their grotesque phrases and their ridiculous words. But when the play is over one realises that the laughter of the witches in *Macbeth* is as terrible as the laughter of madness in *Lear*, more terrible than the laughter of Iago in the tragedy of the Moor. No spectator of art needs a more perfect mood of receptivity than the spectator of a play. The moment he seeks to exercise authority he becomes the avowed enemy of art, and of himself. Art does not mind. It is he who suffers.

With the novel it is the same thing. Popular authority and the recognition of popular authority are fatal. Thackeray's *Esmond* is a beautiful work of art because he wrote it to please himself. In his other novels, in *Pendennis*, in *Philip*, in *Vanity Fair* even, at times, he is too conscious of the public, and spoils his work by appealing directly to the sympathies of the public, or by directly mocking at them. A true artist takes no notice whatever of the public. The public are to him non-existent. He has no poppied or honeyed cakes through which to give the monster sleep or sustenance. He leaves that to the popular novelist. One incomparable novelist we have now in England, Mr George Meredith. There are better artists in France, but France has no one whose view of life is so large, so varied, so imaginatively true. There are tellers of stories in Russia who have a more vivid sense of what pain in fiction may be. But to him belongs philosophy in fiction. His people not merely live, but they live in thought. One can see them from myriad points of view. They are suggestive. There is soul in them and around them. They are interpretative and symbolic. And he who made them, those wonderful, quickly moving figures, made them for his own pleasure, and has never asked the public what they wanted, has never cared to know what they wanted, has never allowed the public to dictate to him or influence him in any way, but has gone on intensifying his own personality, and producing his own individual work. At first none came to him. That did not matter. Then the few came to him. That did not change him. The many have come now. He is still the same. He is an incomparable novelist.

With the decorative arts it is not different. The public clung with really pathetic tenacity to what I believe were the direct traditions of the Great Exhibition of international vulgarity, traditions that were so appalling that the houses in which people lived were only fit for blind people to live in. Beautiful things began to be made, beautiful colours came from the dyer's hand, beautiful patterns from the artist's brain, and the use of beautiful things and their value and importance were set forth. The public were really very indignant. They lost their temper. They said silly things. No one minded. No one was a whit the worse. No one accepted the authority of public opinion. And now it is almost impossible to enter any modern house without seeing some recognition of good taste, some recognition of the value of lovely surroundings, some sign of appreciation of beauty. In fact, people's houses are, as a rule, quite charming nowadays. People have been to a very great extent civilised. It is only fair to state, however, that the extraordinary success of the revolution in house-decoration and furniture and the like has not really been due to the majority of the public developing a very fine taste in such matters. It has been chiefly due to the fact that the craftsmen of things so appreciated the pleasure of making what was beautiful, and woke to such a vivid consciousness of the hideousness and vulgarity of what the public had previously wanted, that they simply starved the public out. It would be quite impossible at the present moment to furnish a room as rooms were furnished a few years ago, without going for everything to an auction of second-hand furniture from some third-rate lodging-house. The things are no longer made. However they may object to it, people must nowadays have something charming in their surroundings. Fortunately for them, their assumption of authority in these art-matters came to entire grief.

It is evident, then, that all authority in such things is bad. People sometimes enquire what form of government is most suitable for an artist to live under. To this question there is only one answer. The form of government that is most suitable to the artist is no government at all. Authority over him and his art is ridiculous. It has been stated that under despotism artists have produced lovely work. This is not quite so. Artists have visited despots, not as subjects to be tyrannised over, but as wandering wonder-makers, as fascinating vagrant personalities, to be entertained and charmed and suffered to be at peace, and allowed to create. There is this to be said in favour of the despot, that he, being an individual, may have culture, while the mob, being a monster, has none. One who is an emperor and king may stoop down to pick up a brush for a painter, but when the democracy stoops down it is merely to throw mud. And yet the democracy have not so far to stoop as the emperor. In fact, when they want to throw mud they have not to stoop at all. But there is no necessity to separate the monarch from the mob; all authority is equally bad.

There are three kinds of despot. There is the despot who tyrannises over the body. There is the despot who tyrannises over the soul. There is the despot who tyrannises over the soul and body alike. The first is called the prince. The second is called the pope. The third is called the people. The prince may be cultivated. Many princes have been. Yet in the prince there is danger. One thinks of Dante at the bitter feast in Verona, of Tasso in Ferrara's madman's cell. It is better for the artist not to live with princes. The pope may be cultivated. Many popes have been; the bad popes have been. The bad popes loved beauty, almost as passionately, nay, with as much passion, as the good popes hated thought. To the wickedness of the papacy humanity owes much. The goodness of the papacy owes a terrible debt to humanity. Yet, though the Vatican has kept the rhetoric of its thunder, and lost the rod of its lightning, it is better for the artist not to live with popes. It was a pope who said of Cellini to a conclave of cardinals that common laws and common authority were not made for men such as he; but it was a pope who thrust Cellini into prison, and kept him there till he sickened with rage, and created unreal visions for himself, and saw the gilded sun enter his room, and grew so enamoured of it that he sought to escape, and crept out from tower to tower and, falling through dizzy air at dawn, maimed himself, and was by a vine-dresser covered with vine leaves, and carried in a cart to one who, loving beautiful things, had care of him. There is danger in popes. And as for the people, what of them and their authority? Perhaps of them and their authority one has spoken enough. Their authority is a thing blind, deaf, hideous, grotesque, tragic, amusing, serious and obscene. It is impossible for the artist to live with the people. All despots bribe. The people bribe and brutalise. Who told them to exercise authority. They were made to live, to listen and to love. Someone has done them a great wrong. They have marred themselves by imitation of their superiors. They have taken the sceptre of the prince. How should they use it? They have taken the triple tiara of the pope. How should they carry its burden? They are as a clown whose heart is broken. They are as a priest whose soul is not yet born. Let all who love beauty pity them. Though they themselves love not beauty, yet let them pity themselves. Who taught them the trick of tyranny?

There are many other things that one might point out. One might point out how the Renaissance was great, because it sought to solve no social problem, and busied itself not about such things, but suffered the individual to develop freely, beautifully and naturally, and so had great and individual artists and great and individual men. One might point out how Louis XIV, by creating the modern state, destroyed the individualism of the artist, and made things monstrous in their monotony of repetition, and contemptible in their conformity to rule, and destroyed through-out all France all those fine freedoms of expression that had made tradition new in beauty, and new modes one with antique form. But the past is of no importance. The present is of no importance. It is with the future that we have to deal. For the past is what man should not have been. The present is what man ought not to be. The future is what artists are.

It will, of course, be said that such a scheme as is set forth here is quite unpractical, and goes against human nature. This is perfectly true. It is unpractical, and it goes against human nature. This is why it is worth carrying out, and that is why one proposes it. For what is a practical scheme? A practical scheme is either a scheme that is already in existence, or a scheme that could be carried out under existing conditions. But it is exactly the existing conditions that one objects to; and any scheme that could accept these conditions is wrong and foolish. The conditions will be done away with, and human nature will change. The only thing that one really knows about human nature is that it changes. Change is the one quality we can predicate of it. The systems that fail are those that rely on the permanency of human nature, and not on its growth and development. The error of Louis XIV was that he thought human nature would always be the same. The result of his error was the French Revolution. It was an admirable result. All the results of the mistakes of governments are quite admirable.

It is to be noted that individualism does not come to the man with any sickly cant about duty, which merely means doing what other people want because they want it, or any hideous cant about self-sacrifice, which is merely a survival of savage mutilation. In fact, it does not come to a man with any claims upon him at all. It comes naturally and inevitably out of man. It is the point to which all development tends. It is the differentiation to which all organisms grow. It is the perfection that is inherent in every mode of life, and towards which every mode of life quickens. And so individualism exercises no compulsion over man. On the contrary, it says to man that he should suffer no compulsion to be exercised over him. It does not try to force people to be good. It knows that people are good when they are let alone. Man will develop individualism out of himself. Man is now so developing individualism. To ask whether individualism is practical is like asking whether evolution is practical. Evolution is the law of life, and there is no evolution except towards individualism. Where this tendency is not expressed, it is a case of artificially arrested growth, or of disease, or of death.

Individualism will also be unselfish and unaffected. It has been pointed out that one of the results of the extraordinary tyranny of authority is that words are absolutely distorted from their proper and simple meaning, and are used to express the obverse of their right signification. What is true about art is true about life. A man is called affected, nowadays, if he dresses as he likes to dress. But in doing that he is acting in a perfectly natural manner. Affectation, in such matters, consists in dressing according to the views of one's neighbour, whose views, as they are the views of the majority, will probably be extremely stupid. Or a man is called selfish if he lives in the manner that seems to him most suitable for the full realisation of his own personality, if, in fact, the primary aim of his life is self-development. But this is the way in which everyone should live. Selfishness is not living as one wishes to live, it is asking others to live as one wishes to live. And unselfishness is letting other people's lives alone, not interfering with them. Selfishness always aims at creating around it an absolute uniformity of type. Unselfishness recognises infinite variety of type as a delightful thing, accepts it, acquiesces in it, enjoys it. It is not selfish to think for oneself. A man who does not think for himself does not think at all. It is grossly selfish to require of one's neighbour that he should think in the same way, and hold the same opinions. Why should he? If he can think, he will probably think differently. If he cannot think, it is monstrous to require thought of any kind from him. A red rose is not selfish because it wants to be a red rose. It would be horribly selfish if it wanted all the other flowers in the garden to be both red and roses. Under individualism people will be quite natural and absolutely unselfish, and will know the meanings of the words, and realise them in their free, beautiful lives. Nor will men be egotistic as they are now. For the egotist is he who makes claims upon others, and the individualist will not desire to do that. It will not give him pleasure. When man has realised individualism, he will also realise sympathy and exercise it freely and spontaneously. Up to the present, man has hardly cultivated sympathy at all. He has merely sympathy with pain, and sympathy with pain is not the highest form of sympathy. All sympathy is fine, but sympathy with suffering is the least fine mode. It is tainted with egotism. It is apt to become morbid. There is in it a certain element of terror for our own safety. We become afraid that we ourselves might be as the leper or as the blind, and that no man would have care of us. It is curiously limiting, too. One should sympathise with the entirety of life, not with life's sores and maladies merely, but with life's joy and beauty and energy and health and freedom. The wider sympathy is, of course, the more difficult. It requires more unselfishness. Anybody can sympathise with the sufferings of a friend, but it requires a very fine nature – it requires, in fact, that nature of a true individualist – to sympathise with a friend's success.

In the modern stress of competition and struggle for place, such sympathy is naturally rare, and is also very much stifled by the immoral ideal of uniformity of type and conformity to rule which is so prevalent everywhere, and is perhaps most obnoxious in England.

Sympathy with pain there will, of course, always be. It is one of the first instincts of man. The animals which are individual, the higher animals, that is to say, share it with us. But it must be remembered that while sympathy with joy intensifies the sum of joy in the world, sympathy with pain does not really diminish the amount of pain. It may make man better able to endure evil, but the evil remains. Sympathy with consumption does not cure consumption; that is what science does. And when Socialism has solved the problem of poverty, and science has solved the problem of disease, the area of the sentimentalists will be lessened, and the sympathy of man will be large, healthy and spontaneous. Man will have joy in the contemplation of the joyous life of others.

For it is through joy that the individualism of the future will develop itself. Christ made no attempt to reconstruct society, and consequently the individualism that he preached to man could be realised only through pain or in solitude. The ideals that we owe to Christ are the ideals of the man who abandons society entirely, or of the man who resists society absolutely. But man is naturally social. Even the Thebaid became peopled at last. And though the coenobite realises his personality, it is often an impoverished personality that he so realises. Upon the other hand, the terrible truth that pain is a mode through which man may realise himself exercises a wonderful fascination over the world. Shallow speakers and shallow thinkers in pulpits and on platforms often talk about the world's worship of pleasure and whine against it. But it is rarely in the world's history that its ideal has been one of joy and beauty. The worship of pain has far more often dominated the world. Mediaevalism, with its saints and martyrs, its love of self-torture, its wild passion for wounding itself, its gashing with knives, and its whipping with rods – mediaevalism is real Christianity and the mediaeval Christ is the real Christ. When the Renaissance dawned upon the world, and brought with it the new ideals of the beauty of life and the joy of living, men could not understand Christ. Even art shows us that. The painters of the Renaissance drew Christ as a little boy playing with another boy in a palace or a garden, or lying back in his mother's arms, smiling at her, or at a flower, or at a bright bird; or as a noble, stately figure moving nobly through the world; or as a wonderful figure rising in a sort of ecstasy from death to life. Even when they drew him crucified they drew him as a beautiful God on whom evil men had inflicted suffering. But he did not preoccupy them much. What delighted them was to paint the men and women whom they admired, and to show the loveliness of this lovely earth. They painted many religious pictures – in fact they painted far too many, and the monotony of type and motive is wearisome, and was bad for art. It was the result of the authority of the public in art-matters, and is to be deplored. But their soul was not in the subject. Raphael was a great artist when he painted his portrait of the pope. When he painted his Madonnas and infant Christs, he was not a great artist at all. Christ had no message for the Renaissance, which was wonderful because it brought an ideal at variance with his, and to find the presentation of the real Christ we must go to mediaeval art. There he is one maimed and marred, one who is not comely to look on, because beauty is a joy; one who is not in fair raiment, because that may be a joy also: he is a beggar who has a marvellous soul; he is a leper whose soul is divine, he needs neither property nor health; he is a God realising his perfection through pain.

The evolution of man is slow. The injustice of men is great. It was necessary that pain should be put forward as a mode of self-realisation. Even now, in some places in the world, the message of Christ is necessary. No one who lived in modern Russia could possibly realise his perfection except by pain. A few Russian artists have realised themselves in art; in a fiction that is mediaeval in character, because its dominant note is the realisation of men through suffering. But for those who are not artists, and to whom there is no mode of life but the actual life of fact, pain is the only door to perfection. A Russian who lives happily under the present system of government in Russia must either believe that man has no soul, or that, if he has, it is not worth developing. A Nihilist who rejects all authority because he knows authority to be evil, and welcomes all pain, because through that he realises his personality, is a real Christian. To him the Christian ideal is a true thing.

And yet, Christ did not revolt against authority. He accepted the imperial authority of the Roman Empire and paid tribute. He endured the ecclesiastical authority of the Jewish Church, and would not repel its violence by any violence of his own. He had, as I said before, no scheme for the reconstruction of society. But the modern world has schemes. It proposes to do away with poverty, and the suffering that it entails. It desires to get rid of pain, and the suffering that pain entails. It trusts to Socialism and to science as its methods. What it aims at is an individualism expressing itself through joy. This individualism will be larger, fuller, lovelier than any individualism has ever been. Pain is not the ultimate mode of perfection. It is merely provisional and a protest. It has reference to wrong, unhealthy, unjust surroundings. When the wrong, and the disease, and the injustice are removed, it will have no further place. It was a great work, but it is almost over. Its sphere lessens every day.

Nor will man miss it. For what man has sought for is, indeed, neither pain nor pleasure, but simply life. Man has sought to live intensely, fully, perfectly. When he can do so without exercising restraint on others, or suffering it ever, and his activities are all pleasurable to him, he will be saner, healthier, more civilised, more himself. Pleasure is nature's test, her sign of approval. When man is happy, he is in harmony with himself and his environment. The new individualism, for whose service Socialism, whether it wills it or not, is working, will be perfect harmony. It will be what the Greeks sought for, but could not, except in thought, realise completely because they had slaves, and fed them; it will be what the Renaissance sought for, but could not realise completely except in art, because they had slaves, and starved them. It will be complete, and through it each man will attain to his perfection. The new individualism is the new Hellenism.

WORDSWORTH CLASSICS

GENERAL EDITORS *Marcus Clapham & Clive Reynard*

WORDSWORTH CLASSICS

WORDSWORTH CLASSICS

WILLIAM SHAKESPEARE
All's Well that Ends Well
Antony and Cleopatra
As You Like It
The Comedy of Errors
Coriolanus
Hamlet
Henry IV Part 1
Henry IV Part 2
Henry V
Julius Caesar
King John
King Lear
Love's Labours Lost
Macbeth
Measure for Measure
The Merchant of Venice
The Merry Wives of Windsor
A Midsummer Night's Dream
Much Ado About Nothing
Othello
Pericles
Richard II
Richard III
Romeo and Juliet
The Taming of the Shrew
The Tempest
Titus Andronicus
Troilus and Cressida
Twelfth Night
Two Gentlemen of Verona
A Winter's Tale

MARY SHELLEY
Frankenstein
The Last Man

TOBIAS SMOLLETT
Humphry Clinker

LAURENCE STERNE
A Sentimental Journey
Tristram Shandy

ROBERT LOUIS STEVENSON
Dr Jekyll and Mr Hyde

The Master of Ballantrae & Weir of Hermiston

BRAM STOKER
Dracula

HARRIET BEECHER STOWE
Uncle Tom's Cabin

R. S. SURTEES
Mr Sponge's Sporting Tour

JONATHAN SWIFT
Gulliver's Travels

W. M. THACKERAY
Vanity Fair

LEO TOLSTOY
Anna Karenina
War and Peace

ANTHONY TROLLOPE
Barchester Towers
Can You Forgive Her?
Dr Thorne
The Eustace Diamonds
Framley Parsonage
The Last Chronicle of Barset
Phineas Finn
The Small House at Allington
The Warden
The Way We Live Now

IVAN SERGEYEVICH TURGENEV
Fathers and Sons

MARK TWAIN
Tom Sawyer & Huckleberry Finn

JULES VERNE
Around the World in Eighty Days & Five Weeks in a Balloon
Journey to the Centre of the Earth
Twenty Thousand Leagues Under the Sea

VIRGIL
The Aeneid

VOLTAIRE
Candide

LEW WALLACE
Ben Hur

ISAAC WALTON
The Compleat Angler

EDITH WHARTON
The Age of Innocence

GILBERT WHITE
The Natural History of Selborne

OSCAR WILDE
De Profundis, The Ballad of Reading Gaol and Other Writings
Lord Arthur Savile's Crime & Other Stories
The Picture of Dorian Gray
The Plays
IN TWO VOLUMES

VIRGINIA WOOLF
Mrs Dalloway
Orlando
To the Lighthouse

P. C. WREN
Beau Geste

CHARLOTTE M. YONGE
The Heir of Redclyffe

TRANSLATED BY VRINDA NABAR & SHANTA TUMKUR
Bhagavadgita

EDITED BY CHRISTINE BAKER
The Book of Classic Horror Stories

SELECTED BY REX COLLINGS
Classic Victorian and Edwardian Ghost Stories

EDITED BY DAVID STUART DAVIES
Shadows of Sherlock Holmes
Tales of Unease

Distribution

AUSTRALIA & PAPUA NEW GUINEA
Peribo Pty Ltd
58 Beaumont Road, Mount Kuring-Gai
NSW 2080, Australia
Tel: (02) 457 0011 Fax: (02) 457 0022

CZECH REPUBLIC
Bohemian Ventures s r. o.,
Delnicka 13, 170 00 Prague 7
Tel: 042 2 877837 Fax: 042 2 801498

FRANCE
Copernicus Diffusion
81 Rue des Entrepreneurs, Paris 75015
Tel: 01 53 95 38 00 Fax: 01 53 95 38 01

GERMANY & AUSTRIA
Taschenbuch-Vertrieb
Ingeborg Blank GmbH
Lager und Buro Rohrmooser Str 1
85256 Vierkirchen/Pasenbach
Tel: 08139-8130/8184 Fax: 08139-8140

Tradis Verlag und Vertrieb GmbH (Bookshops)
Postfach 90 03 69, D-51113 Köln
Tel: 022 03 31059 Fax: 022 03 39340

GREAT BRITAIN
Wordsworth Editions Ltd
Cumberland House, Crib Street
Ware, Hertfordshire SG12 9ET
Tel: 01920 465167 Fax: 01920 462267

INDIA
Om Books
1690 First Floor, Nai Sarak,
Delhi – 110006
Tel: 3279823/3274303 Fax: 3278091

IRELAND
Easons & Son Limited
Furry Park Industrial Estate
Santry 9, Eire
Tel: 003531 8733811 Fax: 003531 8733945

ISRAEL
Sole Agent —**Timmy Marketing Limited**
Israel Ben Zeev 12, Ramont Gimmel, Jerusalem
Tel: 972-2-5865266 Fax: 972-2-5860035
Sole Distributor – Sefer ve Sefel Ltd
Tel & Fax: 972-2-6248237

ITALY
Logos — Edizioni e distribuzione libri
Via Curtatona 5/J
41100 Modena, Italy
Tel: 059-418820/418821 Fax: 059-418786

NEW ZEALAND & FIJI
Allphy Book Distributors Ltd
4-6 Charles Street,
Eden Terrace,
Auckland,
Tel: (09) 3773096 Fax: (09) 3022770

MALAYSIA & BRUNEI
Vintrade SDN BHD
5 & 7 Lorong Datuk Sulaiman 7
Taman Tun Dr Ismail
60000 Kuala Lumpur,
Malaysia
Tel: (603) 717 3333 Fax: (603) 719 2942

MALTA & GOZO
Agius & Agius Ltd
42A South Street, Valletta VLT 11
Tel: 234038 - 220347 Fax: 241175

PHILIPPINES
I J Sagun Enterprises
P O Box 4322 CPO Manila
2 Topaz Road, Greenheights Village,
Taytay, Rizal
Tel: 631 80 61 TO 66

SOUTH AFRICA
Chapter Book Agencies
Postnet Private bag X10016
Edenvale, 1610 Gauteng
South Africa
Tel: (++27) 11 425 5990
Fax: (++27) 11 425 5997

SLOVAK REPUBLIC
Slovak Ventures s r. o.,
Stefanikova 128, 949 01 Nitra
Tel/Fax: 042 87 525105/6/7

SPAIN
Ribera Libros, S.L.
Poligono Martiartu, Calle 1 - no 6
48480 Arrigorriaga, Vizcaya
Tel: 34 4 6713607 (Almacen)
      34 4 4418787 (Libreria)
Fax: 34 4 6713608 (Almacen)
      34 4 4418029 (Libreria)

UNITED STATES OF AMERICA
NTC/Contemporary Publishing Company
4225 West Touhy Avenue
Lincolnwood (Chicago)
Illinois 60646-4622
USA
Tel: (847) 679 5500 Fax: (847) 679 2494

DIRECT MAIL
Bibliophile Books
5 Thomas Road, London E14 7BN,
Tel: 0171-515 9222 Fax: 0171-538 4115
Order hotline 24 hours Tel: 0171-515 9555
Cash with order + £2.50 p&p (UK)